A Summer with the Earl

A REGENCY AND RIVALRY STORY

MAUDE WINTERS

EDITED BY
DANIEL FLASPOHLER

Copyright © 2023 by Maude Winters

All rights reserved.

This novel is entirely a work of fiction. The names, characters and incidents portrayed in it are the work of the author's imagination. Any resemblance to actual persons, living or dead, events or localities is entirely coincidental.

Designations used by companies to distinguish their products are often claimed as trademarks. All brand names and product names used in this book and on its cover are trade names, service marks, trademarks and registered trademarks of their respective owners. The publishers and the book are not associated with any product or vendor mentioned in this book. None of the companies referenced within the book have endorsed the book.

ISBN: 979-8-9892609-2-8

To my husband, for reading my spiciest book yet and never batting an eye.

Author's Note

I love this book because it brought me to the spiciest place yet, but readers should note a few things.

One, this is a prequel to Regency and Rivalry that takes place about 27 years before *London Season* but you do not need to read London Season to enjoy it! However, if you do enjoy it, *London Season* will be there for you after your read.

Two, Sabine is a complicated character who has experienced a lot of loss. She is also very beloved in Regency and Rivalry. However, one should note that her origin story is complicated. She was adopted by her birth mother's brother after she passed away, so a theme of parental loss flows throughout.

SPOILERS BELOW

Malcolm's father has heart problems and his health underpins some of the story.

Sabine experiences a surprise pregnancy as well, so if this is not a trope you enjoy, this may not be for you.

CHAPTER 1
Becoming Royal

SABINE

"Come back to bed," I pleaded.

My boyfriend Geoff sucked down some water in front of the open mini fridge in my Ottawa dorm room.

"You are relentless. I have practice in the morning," he groaned.

I giggled, kicking my legs behind me. "But you never turn me down."

He sighed. "I just played a full game with OT."

"And I just gave you a rousing bit of head before I let you fuck me properly."

Geoff shook his head. Yes, I had gone down on him.

"If your accent wasn't so charming, I'd tell you no."

Geoff was a sucker for a British girl. He was a tall, buff forward on our hockey team. We'd gone at it off and on for a couple months. The only thing required of me was to show up in his jersey and cheer him on. This evening, my sister Margaux and I attended his game and done just that. He'd won. We drank with the team a bit before retiring to our suite across campus. Or, rather, Geoff slung me over his shoulder and delivered me here.

Geoff sat the cup down on my desk and dove back into bed. To my utter delight, he went straight for my pussy, burying his head in between my legs. A flash of sheer pleasure rolled over me. I sputtered and gripped his hair as he sucked on my clit. He may not have been the sharpest tack or even the best player on the ice, but he was delightful in bed.

He stopped, looking at me.

"I want to fuck you," he said. "Really fuck you."

"Sure," I said, all-too-happy to oblige him.

I lay there as he found a condom in the already-open filing cabinet where I kept them. Margaux and I had bought a massive box of condoms, hopeful the year would be a fruitful one. To date, I was its only patron.

Geoff crawled back to bed once more, pulling me towards him. He slid into me. I was very wet, having cum a couple of times during our last round. I didn't know if he could get me off again, but I was game to try. He thrusted, tickling a spot inside me that always did the most to bring me close to climax.

"More," I moaned.

"More?" he looked down on me, surprised.

"Harder," I said, in French now. "Fuck me harder."

He picked up the pace a bit. No matter what I told boys, they never *quite* got the memo. I wanted it hard, fast, and relentless. It was just as he'd said.

There was a knock. We assumed it was someone on the floor telling us to keep it down. So, we ignored it, continuing. I was so close to climax, about to come when a man announced he was with the RCMP.

Mounties? What the fuck? I panicked, confused. Geoff, feeling somehow chivalrous, hopped up. He answered the door in nothing but boxer-briefs.

He called. "Yo, Sabine! Man at the door!"

I stole Geoff's t-shirt and wandered to the door. The fluorescent light hit me hard. I saw the outline of a suit. It was strange. I became nervous.

The man in a suit bowed. I pulled a face, squinting. He looked confused about my appearance, if not a bit embarrassed. It was the Governor General of Canada, my aunt's representative on the ground.

"Your Royal Highness, may I speak with Princess Margaux?"

"I'm sorry," I shook my head. "She's... not here."

She wasn't. She retreated to her boyfriend's suite after the party. I wasn't about to barge over there and interrupt my sister's only attempt to lose her virginity after months of pining.

"Where is she ma'am? We need to find her immediately."

"She's across campus," I replied.

He looked confused.

I said, "She was with a... friend."

He didn't get it. "We need to speak with her, ma'am. The Princess of Wales was pronounced dead an hour ago in Manchester. We must speak to her immediately. These orders are coming imminently from Her Majesty."

My stomach turned. I knew what this meant. The impossible happened. Margaux's entire life was about to change.

"Let me put on trousers," I said.

I shouted at Geoff in French to pack his shit. I knew we'd be leaving for home and may never return. My heart didn't break because I was leaving Geoff. It broke because Cecilia had shone bright as the sun and was *gone*. How did the world lose a seventeen-year-old, the centre of her mother's universe like this? It was senseless. My heart broke for Maggie. It broke for everything we'd lost. It broke because, like it or not, my shy, reserved, and sweet sister's entire life altered course.

The thought either of us could be queen never occurred to me. I was not born British, let alone royal. My origin story began in a working-class neighbourhood in Montreal, where I was born to my mother—named Margaux also— who loved me to the moon and back from the instant I was born. That changed when

3

A drink-driver crossed a median and rammed my mother's car. She was driving late, trying to settle a fussy baby. Suddenly, I was alone. My father died before my birth and my mother faded fast. My mother's dying wish was for me to go to her brother, Simon, since she didn't trust my Canadian grandparents.

At eight weeks old, I returned to the UK with my new guardians—Simon Bouchard and his wife, Beth. Beth wasn't just any girl, though. She was the daughter of King Alfred. The main complication upon my new arrival to the family was my mother was already pregnant with my sister, Margaux. Or, as the rest of us call her, Maggie. She was named after my birth mother.

With only ten months between us, Maggie and I were known as "virtual twins" and raised as if we were. No matter how different I was, my sister Maggie and I were never far apart. She was the blonder, shorter, cleverer sidekick wherever we went. I was the live wire who made friends with the wall. Maggie was the shy, anxious one, but loved me dearly. We had each other's backs no matter where we went or what we did. When I elected to go to uni in Canada to get away from the press, Maggie joined me the next year.

We could get away with it. While our mum was Duchess of Kent, she was the second child of the King. Our Aunt Margaret was the heir. She had one hard-won baby, Princess Cecilia. When Aunt Greta took over, our beloved cousin Cecilia became the second Princess of Wales in her own name, after her mother.

Cecilia was a bright light of a girl, but she had a genetic disorder that brought about seizures. While the man did not mention that her death was a result of such a seizure, my gut told me something awful happened as a result. She hadn't had them in years, but we all worried a seizure would happen at the worst time and when we least expected.

I dressed in jeans and a coat before leading the Governor General and a dozen Mounties across campus in the snow. The wind howled miserably.

"When I get there," I said. "I will speak with her first. You can do the official bit, but I want to do this. She's my sister. She doesn't want to hear this from you. Mum would want it that way."

He looked surprised my directness but nodded. We reached Jake's door. I knocked. His roommate, Ben, appeared. A cloud of cannabis smoke permeated from the room. Ben was a notable stoner. He and Jake didn't get on well. Jake was a square, like Maggie.

"Is Maggie around?" I asked.

"I dunno." Ben peered out and chuckled nervously at the Mounties. They would turn a blind eye, I suspected. There were much bigger matters at hand.

"She's supposed to be here. I need to speak with her," I insisted. "Now."

"Jake! Maggie! Sabine is here with... some dudes."

Maggie and Jake appeared within a second, fully-clothed. If the two got up to anything, it was ages ago. I took that as a sign that nothing happened. Poor Maggie. I wondered if she would *ever* get laid. She was beautiful, but now a princess in a tower. The worst part? She had no idea.

"Maggie, I need to speak with you alone," I spoke in French.

"Sabine, what is going on?" She was confused. "Sir, why are you here?"

"Speak with the Princess, Your Royal Highness." The Governor General held the line.

"Margaux, Cecilia is gone. Something happened. We need to return home, I suspect," I said.

Maggie's eyes darted from me to the Governor General. Her mouth gaped and tears welled. She then beat it down until emotion was gone.

"The Princess fell from a horse in competition. Ma'am we will have time to pack, but you both are requested back in London as soon as possible. Transportation is being arranged as we speak. We have a transport coming from Thunder Bay."

"Brilliant," I remarked.

"Okay," Margaux said.

So, in a flash, Mum became Aunt Greta's heir. And, by default, Maggie was now a future queen. It was never supposed to happen. I was leapfrogged, forced out by my origin story. It wasn't that I minded. I didn't want to be queen, either. None of us did. Cecilia would have made a brilliant queen. Now, she was gone too soon. Maggie faced an uphill battle. Mum would put on the bravest, most dutiful face. She had always been Greta's henchwoman, after all. And maybe I would be Maggie's. She needed me more than ever.

This night changed my life—and Maggie's—forever but, for me, my biggest moment had yet to arrive. That story began several years later during a hot summer in London's social season. I met an earl with poor intentions and my entire life changed.

CHAPTER 2
The Earl

MALCOLM

I was raised the son of a Duke. My father, Niall Ferguson, was born to the Duke of Lauderdale and his wife, Princess Rikhild of Norway. Farmor, we called her, was born to the widowed former queen. She married my grandfather and was the centre of his universe until the day she died. She was a lightning bolt until she died in my teenage years. To that point, my life was easy. I was Master Malcolm and nothing more. Suddenly, I was the Earl of Lauderdale, and it was all new. All different.

When you gain a title, it is expected you will gain responsibility. Suddenly, I differed greatly from my sister Kiersten. She was only two years my junior, but a world away. The world's expectations for her and I were laid clear. The disparity could not have been starker. While we'd both be raised in the quiet Scottish Borders, our adulthood would differ.

Kiersten's sole responsibility was to be properly turned out like a fancy show horse. She would land the right sort of man and run off into the sunset with prince charming. She was pretty, would marry well, and live a life of luxury and lunching. My dear sister went to university to study art history and fuck off otherwise. I was jealous.

I had no such hope. My life focused on taking over the estate. Father wanted me to stay near home and learn the family businesses—property and horse racing. He was a racing baron, as was his father. My grandmother was an equestrian in her own right. The entire family revolved around horses, something I cared little for. My other goal was to marry a suitable woman who would give me babies.

I went to the best schools, gained the poshest accent so I could fit in with my English peers, and participated in sport I cared nothing about. I ticked all the boxes. By the time university rolled around, I attended Oxford for law. This pleased my father. I didn't want to do it, but decided I would embrace the independence and make it work. It turned out that law more than suited me. I loved being an attorney. I loved it so much that I got an LLM. I didn't study estate law like my father wished. I studied intellectual property law.

I landed in London at a big firm, a new barrister with excellent credentials. I thought I was tough shit but had no idea what I was doing. I soon integrated and became partner by thirty. My father wanted me to return home all this time, but knew I loved my work. He wanted to see us happy. He hoped my staying in London would lead to me finding a suitable mate. And as I was still busy on partner track, I wasn't pressured to settle down.

So, I took full advantage. By the time I was thirty, I had burned through an impressive list of models and it-girls. As a future duke and heir to one of the largest estates in the UK, I was a hot commodity. Still, I loathed society darlings and the daughters of aristocrats. "Suitable" girls were a bore. I preferred leggy blondes who laughed at my jokes and took a booty call without batting an eyelash.

The daughters of aristocrats were a bore. But, as I turned thirty, I was running out of excuses. The fact of the matter was if I did not have children, the line ended. I wasn't getting any younger and my women weren't getting older. My mother and father became impatient. A list of women was floated to me. Yes, an actual *list*.

It was laden with every eligible heiress and daughter of a noble. And to my surprise, at the top of the list was Princess Margaux, the future queen. Well, I ruled that out completely. She was too young for me, one. Two, she seemed sweet and innocent. I'd never be satisfied with a woman like that.

So there I was—thirty-three, with few prospects, and a desire to get my parents off my back. It wasn't uncommon for society unions to be marriages of convenience. I didn't see myself as a man who chased romantic love, even if I loved the thrill of the chase. I resigned myself to the idea through the first part of the year. I would spend London Season trying to find a woman.

That was how I found myself on a date with Jessica Bowden, daughter of an Earl of some such random place. My mother told me all about her, almost producing a fact sheet. She was tall, pretty, and affable. She was a dedicated supporter of children's charities, and at twenty-nine probably wanted to fill our family estate with babies. So, keen to get on with it. Her family wasn't flush with cash due to her father's poor business investments and her mother's conspicuous consumption, but they kept up with appearances.

I took her to a posh London spot called Story. It was the pretentious sort of place where one was served twelve courses of bite-sized, odd things. You were required to ooh and ahh over it, but it wasn't necessarily satiating. I'd want a kebab after this. I just knew it. I booked the reservation to impress my date, not enjoy the meal. It amazed her. Getting a table was difficult unless, like me, you made such reservations regularly to impress women. I tried, at least. I didn't say I was honourable.

"The food is just... so flavourful," Jessica said.

We were served some sort of deconstructed fish foam. It was pleasing to the palate but not the eye. I wasn't too over the moon about it, but I nodded.

"So, you're a barrister? That's... sexy."

"Not sure if it is *sexy*," I said. "But yes."

"And how is that?"

"I like it. It agrees with me."

"What about it?"

"Litigation. Argument," I replied. "I like taking cases that go to a hearing."

"Don't you all do that?"

"Many solicitors and barristers don't end up there often and many also loathe being in court," I replied. "It's not for everyone, but I think oral argument is a high."

She nodded as our plates were cleared. Some sort of risotto arrived.

"What fills your days, Jessica?"

Note that I did *not* ask what she did for a living. Like my sister, the answer was nothing for pay.

"I serve on the Children's Cancer Trust board," Jessica said.

"Oh, that's good."

I knew that, of course. Mum was good for that.

"I love working with charities. Don't you?"

I couldn't say I did.

"I don't have time," I answered. "I work a lot."

"Oh, that's dreadful." She pulled a face.

She had expected I was mainly focused on the estate, as was my father. He worked, too. But he was home and schmoozing half the time. Schmoozing was work, but it was painful. I wasn't an introvert by any stretch but kissing the arses of the wealthy while wheeling and dealing dreadful horses held little appeal.

"Well, it suits me."

"Everyone is different," she said.

We had *nothing* in common. She hadn't gotten any of my political humour. She was fit. I fancied her on a physical level. It wouldn't hold my attention. She ticked every box on paper but did nothing more. There was no real sexual chemistry. If this were a normal night out, I would have asked her back to mine, but it wasn't worth it. She was a *nice* girl. I wasn't going to give her ideas or drag her through the mud. She was the type of girl who cared about her reputation. I was a rake if I took her home and never called again.

So, at the end of the night, I gave her a kiss on the cheek and sent her on her way in my car. I walked home to my apartment, having a nightcap on my own as I reviewed case notes from my associates. It was another long, boring evening. More tomorrow. I wanted to hit the club and pull a girl, but that was a non-starter. Onto more heiresses—all summer. My hope was to get to the end of the list and call it a day. Or, alternatively, I'd get lucky and be able to call it a win.

CHAPTER 3
Stranded

SABINE

"What is it?" Maggie grumbled. "What *possibly* went wrong here? This place... this garage... it's an ice box."

"It's a hangar," I said.

We sat in an airplane hangar in Greenland during a rare spring storm. We were freezing, unable to go into the terminal for whatever reason. Maggie picked me up in Ottawa. We'd attended two events before boarding a plane. My entire life was in its cargo hold. I had just graduated with my bachelor's in politics. Maggie was the only one to attend. Both my parents wanted to, but Aunt Greta fell ill. They had to replace her at a summit in Jordan. So, they were in the heat. We were in the freezing cold. I was fine. I'd lived in Canada.

My sister forgot what actual winter looked like. Maggie sat, teeth chattering in a skirt suit. She refused to change on the plane. She wanted to look just as formal when we arrived. While the girl I loved was still in there, Maggie changed unimaginably in the three years I'd been away at school. She was rigid, formal, and organised to a fault. That was fine in some ways. The world needed more badass queens with their shit together, but I missed the Maggie who laughed things off.

I felt some guilt. I had three years to make friends, attend classes, go to parties, and sleep with fit men with impunity. She, on the other hand, took up the reins as our aunt's apprentice. Maggie eased Aunt Greta's grief a bit. I'd be lying if I didn't believe I was nervous to live at the palace with Maggie and Aunt Greta. That was the plan. They felt it best for me to "learn the ropes" this summer. I was slated to take a master's course in autumn but would be a working royal when not at class.

Maggie worked full-time. This was her life. Always on. Always controlled. I didn't like it—for her or me. The court jester within me died to get under her skin for a laugh or cause chaos. I knew some of this was due to the plane. A landing for a "technical problem" would give anyone a fright, right? Maggie was terrified of flight. She loathed it. For spending most of her life traveling, she was the world's most nervous flyer. Now she was not permitted to fly with Aunt Greta or Mum, worsening her anxiety. I hoped my presence might centre her a bit.

"Are you freezing, Maggie?" Marilyn, my sister's private secretary, approached.

"I am," Maggie admitted. "It's bloody miserable in here and I am so knackered."

That was when the day's most pleasant surprise appeared. Cue sexy pilot. Or, at least, I assumed he was the pilot. Either way, he was delivered to us in a delicious package. All of us salivated immediately. With ruddy brown hair, shoulders that could carry about anything, and a jaw that cut like glass, he was altogether too pretty for the RAF. He had a lumberjack look. Yet, he was all business.

He bowed. "Your Royal Highnesses. Shouldn't be but maybe an hour more. We had a minor issue with one engine. They are repairing it now."

"Brilliant, thank you," I said.

Maggie was silent. Was she mesmerised by Captain Sexy? That was *so* unlike her. It was precious if so.

He sensed Maggie was living her own hell, freezing here. "Do you all need anything? How can I help?"

"She's freezing. Sorry, what's your name, sir?" I chimed in.

"I'm Flight Lieutenant McDonough," he answered. "I'm the pilot. My first officer is dealing with the rest of the crew and maintenance lads."

"What do people *call* you?" I followed up.

"Keir, ma'am."

Maggie glared. "Nice to meet you, Lieutenant."

"I'm going to see what I can do for you ladies. You cannot go to the terminal?"

"Security risk," Marilyn said.

"Okay, well, I can," Keir said. "Give me just a moment. Let me see what I can do."

He left.

"He's bloody gorgeous," Marilyn noted.

"He's so hot," I said. "Smoking hot."

"Let's not be overly-familiar or objectify him," Maggie protested. "He's here to do his job, as we are here to do ours."

"Oh, for fuck's sake, Maggie! Live a little, darling!"

The sexy pilot returned with a little reflective piece of plastic and a to-go cups of something for us. He didn't struggle to contain them. The man was massive—like a wall. He was tall *and* broad. He had a lovely smile. I noted that Maggie was enraptured and giddy at his presence. She struggled to find the words. Maggie did not mince words. She was blunt and to-the-point. And while she was often shy, she didn't struggle with conversation. She just didn't say more than she needed to. That was more my thing. I didn't know what parsimony meant.

"I brought you an emergency blanket—best I could do. And some coffee, ma'am. That's all they had. No tea, I'm afraid, but it's warm."

God, I figured out what it was that just made him over-the-top sexy and probably set Maggie on fire. His Highland lilt was something out of a historical romance movie. Maggie tripped over herself.

"Oh, th-thank you, Lieutenant McDonough. I... appreciate it," Maggie stammered.

She was altogether formal.

"That's so kind, Keir," I remarked.

"Of course, ma'am. Anything else I can do?"

"No," I replied. "Don't think so. This is lovely."

He turned and I called. "Actually, Keir?"

"Yes, ma'am?" he turned, as if at attention.

"Will you be our pilot *leaving* Aberdeen later this week?"

"Can't say, ma'am, but if I am assigned to it, I will be. I'm about to rush home for a couple days of leave."

"Where is home?" Maggie chirped.

"Inverness, ma'am."

"Lovely place." Maggie struggled with eye contact. She was flustered. It was adorable.

Keir nodded and left.

I stared at Maggie in disbelief, switching to French. "You realise I know you're crushing on him, right?"

"I am not!"

"Nonsense."

She glared. "I cannot be. It would be *unprofessional*, and I am supposed to be paraded around like a horse at auction tomorrow, so I will focus on that."

She referred to the party our parents hosted for charity on Balmoral's grounds. They hoped to do so under less chaotic circumstances, but every aristocratic family in Scotland sent its best and brightest. This was my sister's first official season on offer. And, by that, I mean she was at an age considered "eligible" for marriage. She was a sweet twenty-one and on parade. Any man of a good family background vied for her if he were under thirty-five. Or, rather, his mother would hope that Maggie and our parents took a shine to her son.

"You're a dead woman walking." I switched to English.

"Yes. Well, it's my duty and all that. I am trying to... keep an open mind. Why aren't you excited? You're the boy crazy one."

I snickered, "I have no interest in landing a husband. Now or probably ever. And the idea of boring society men is lost on me. I don't gravitate to those types. You know that."

"But that is what is *expected* of us, Sab. That is what we are supposed to do."

"That is what you must do, darling. I can be wild."

"Mummy will discourage it. You bloody well know it."

It was annoyingly true. And I hated it. I would have to *try*. I was, thankfully, less desirable as the non-royal-bred, tempestuous sister. My reputation as the one who shagged hockey players and had recently—to my mother's absolute dismay—done a charity shoot for *Tatler* where I flashed too much cleavage. I regretted nothing. However, I got an earful for it.

Marilyn announced proudly, "Well, we will have Keir on the way back and every time we fly for as long as he is available for transport. I am putting in the request."

"I'm sorry, but... what?" Maggie went white as a sheet.

"Consider it done, Maggie."

"Yes! Oh my God! Yes!" I clapped.

"No, no, no. He will think I am *into* him. That I *fancy* him. That looks desperate! Make it stop."

"Maggie, calm the fuck down, it is *fine*," I said. "Besides, I benefit from the eye candy. I won't argue if Mr. Sexy Pilot flies us for the rest of eternity."

She shot me daggers, but deep down I knew she wanted this. She was smitten. Maybe she'd get up the courage to *tell* him. I certainly hoped. I was now invested in making this happen. This was far more entertaining than her ending up with Lord Whatshisface of Whitestown.

CHAPTER 4
The Parade

MALCOLM

"Mum, back off," I grumbled, standing in a guest room at Balmoral Castle.

My mother fussed with my bowtie for approximately the tenth time this evening. My darling sister, Kiersten snickered. She enjoyed my discomfort.

My gruff father looked up from his newspaper. "He's a grown man, Carolyn. Leave the boy!"

We stayed at Balmoral, invited guests of the Duchess and Duke of Kent. My father and mother were friends of theirs, but that wasn't why we were invited to stay and attend their charity ball. No. I was to be paraded in front of Princess Margaux as a potential suitor. My job was to impress her. I had no idea why I was chosen for this honour, but it seemed like a dreadful idea. However, if I did *not* comply, my father was apt to stop paying for several expenses I held dear. I gave it an honest try from the outset. I would be charming as ever and *nice*, but she was a child. I wasn't about to make a move.

"She's a girl, Mum."

"She's a full-grown woman and very pretty. I hear she is quite clever. Per her mother, the girls are both very clever," Mum said.

Clever *did* appeal to me much more than daft. However, clever didn't get on with me generally because I was mostly interested in sleeping with girls I dated rather than meeting their parents and carrying on like we were playing house. Daft girls put up with that bit. Clever girls didn't tolerate it.

"Just... try," Mum pleaded. "Try to be charming. Bethany and Simon would prefer she end up with someone clever."

"I have no desire to be a prince, mother. I don't even *like* society girls. I have no interest in producing children like it's quite literally my job. I am not one of dad's stud horses. It's altogether ridiculous."

"Just *try*. We were invited because Beth thinks well of your legal career. She is impressed by intellect. I suspect your *very* outspoken political leanings do not phase Simon who is much like you."

"Yes, but is the Duke allowed to even *have* political opinions, Mum?"

"Well, in private," she answered.

I rolled my eyes. "Bully for him. Poor Canadian bastard can't even have opinions about the colonial power that terrorised his entire province."

"What?" Kiersten asked.

"He's French-Canadian. Did you never take a history class? We weren't exactly kind colonial overlords."

"Let's not speak like that!" Our mother cringed. "Dreadful talk."

"You're such a breath of fresh air, darling brother," Kiersten laughed. "Now, can we bloody well get on with this? I am desperate to see Mariah. She's come up mainly for me. Scott doesn't even want to be here."

Kiersten wanted to be seen but had no desire to marry, either. We were both a constant disappointment to our poor parents. The older she got; the more Mum clutched her pearls. I was allowed to be indecisive. I was the man. Kiersten, as a woman, had already defied convention by making it to thirty with no sense of urgency to marry. She was a society maven who preferred to spend her time sleeping with men in the south of France at our family's riviera house. I was often jealous of her for that. Not that I wanted to sleep with men, of course, but I would have been happy to have a few fun, easy hook-ups with French women. Unfortunately, I was a workaholic and had little time for such escape. Hell, I had briefs to work on now instead of this mess!

We filed onto the lawn where the girls ran to one another, screeching excitedly. Everyone mingled. I spotted the Duke and Duchess and was soon introduced. I bowed like a good boy and took my place near a bar, scoping both the women and the competition. As for that, there wasn't much I thought that Princess Margaux *should* entertain. Most of them were boring. At least I wasn't that. Few were anything to write home about. There were some pretty women, but no one I was particularly drawn to. That was until I looked over to see the backside of a ginger in a teal dress. She had a *spectacular* arse.

I continued staring probably for too long before she moved aside, and I spotted the companion she spoke to. Her little friend was Princess Margaux. As the ginger turned, I realised the woman I was thirsting for was Princess Sabine. Well, that all went out the window. But *damn* if she wasn't downright perfect. If she were anyone else, I would have chatted her up. She had these beautiful blue eyes, skin the colour of milk, and full lips that just *begged* for more.

Margaux seemed in a daze, talking through something, but Princess Sabine's gaze met mine. We locked eyes. She took a sip of her drink, tilted her head, and gave me a cheeky grin before turning back to her sister.

Fuck. The girl was beautiful. Too young for me, but damn. I could make it work if only she weren't Maggie's sister. She was tall, though, and made the impression she was a bit wild. While her sister seemed ready for a business meeting, Princess Sabine was here for the people watching and the party. Damn. I tried to pull myself together and *not* envision myself with her in an uncompromising position, but it was hard. Rarely did I see a woman and find her *this* charming without at least speaking to her. Sabine's glance said it all. She fancied me.

We made our way into the banqueting tent. I found my place card and took a seat. That was foolish, as within a minute, Princess Margaux of Kent appeared, leaving everyone in a fifty-metre radius bobbing in her wake. I did the same as she stopped, opposite me and took her seat delicately.

"Hello, Your Royal Highness." I looked across the table politely.

She smiled, kindly enough, little round face staring back at me. She, too, was pretty, but in an almost angelic sort of way. Untouchable, really. Not the sort that interested me.

"And you are?"

"I'm Malcolm Ferguson. My father is—"

"The Duke of Lauderdale. You're the Earl of Lauderdale."

I nodded.

"Lovely to meet you. My mother says you are an excellent solicitor."

"Barrister, ma'am," I corrected.

I probably shouldn't have. I should have let it go.

"Oh." She was a good sport. "Apologies. Yes, barrister. I get the two confused, but barristers are... more advanced, right?"

"I litigate, yes," I said. "But solicitors are crucial for any firm. For barristers, litigation is bread and butter."

She nodded kindly enough. "Do you enjoy a break from Edinburgh then?"

"Uh, I'm primarily in London. This is a bit of a city break for me. I came to join my parents and my sister, Kiersten. She's somewhere around here."

"Oh, you live in London? Well, that's interesting."

"I arrived and never left. My father would like me to leave, I suppose."

"Ah, yes, familial duty and all that."

She groaned. Then, realising she was on display, pulled herself back together.

The Princess was like a trained dog. She knew what to say and how to say it. She was sufficiently prepped for her mission with proper responses. However, she seemed unsure of herself and struggled with authenticity.

I chuckled, trying to put the girl at ease.

She seemed nice enough. "You know how it is. But you're so young, ma'am, you do not need to—"

"Oh, please, call me Maggie," she insisted. "And yes. It all feels stuffy. I am struggling with this."

"You don't like parties?"

"No, no. I... I do. I mean, I don't know. I have never even attended a state banquet. I have done formal engagements, but it was thought I wasn't quite *old* enough until I turned twenty-one and we've not hosted one since then."

"You're... twenty-one... I coughed."

"Apologies. I'll be twenty-two in October."

She was younger than I even knew. I thought she was at least twenty-three. Somehow that two-year difference made a big one. A girl of twenty-two was still a *girl*. Once a postgrad or working person of twenty-three, you were a real woman. I didn't generally date women under the age of twenty-five. And, as I got longer in the tooth, that seemed less and less appealing. My career meant I worked long hours. Younger women had no patience for that. They didn't understand it. This was going *nowhere*. I silently cursed my Mum for this awkward and unfortunate attempt to marry me off.

"You don't have to..." I searched for words.

Maggie looked up and cocked her head like an adorable spaniel. "What?"

"You don't... don't let them force you into anything. You seem like a nice girl, Maggie. A clever one. You're young. You should have a bit of fun."

She looked down, as if I admonished her.

"Oh, I didn't mean to make you feel badly," I insisted.

"No, no," she finally looked up. "God, it's mental. Sabine says it is, too. She is... she's the lively one. Either way, she refuses to be tied down. I wish I felt I could push back a bit more confidently."

I smiled sympathetically.

"I shouldn't say that, Lord Ferguson. I should... well, I should try. You do seem like a nice person."

It was the first time I had heard that in a while.

"I'm not," I joked. "I am honest, but I am not *nice* per-se. You do seem genuine, though."

"Thanks. No, honest is good. People do not tell me things in an honest, straightforward manner. That is what I most appreciate. I am a bit blunt, believe it or not. And you... You seem to understand that."

I nodded. "I do. I'm rubbish at it because of my profession. You needn't worry about offending me, Maggie. I am not. This was all arranged by our parents. And really—"

"There is zero chemistry."

I snickered. "Apologies. You seem lovely, but I agree. Friends?"

"Friends," she agreed.

CHAPTER 5
The Rake

SABINE

I found myself looking for the strange man who had met my gaze earlier. Damn if he wasn't fit as hell. A little wiry, but fit. I finally spotted him again. His blonde hair caught my eye. At least, the way he swooped it back. He looked *suave*. That probably sounds cheesy, but he did. He wore a perfectly-tailored with flash wingtips. He was seated with my sister at dinner. She'd been whisked away by Mum, so I couldn't ask for a proper introduction. I would have to do it myself.

As I approached the bar, I spotted a very nice Longines timepiece and wondered who the hell this guy was. He had swagger. I was intrigued.

"Whisky, please," I said. "Neat."

The bartender complied. I looked over at the man and he stared back.

"Who are you?" I asked.

"Malcolm Ferguson," he replied.

"And you're—"

"The son of the Duke of Lauderdale," he explained flatly.

"Sorry, I was asking what you were drinking," I clarified.

His drink popped up along with mine. "Same as you."

"Brilliant," I agreed as we stepped from the bar.

"You're Maggie's sister?"

"Guilty as charged. She was swept off, then?"

"I let her go. Seemed unfair to hog all her time. Nice girl."

"She's a doll."

"We had a laugh over the ridiculousness of us being seated across from one another. We aren't a match, it turns out."

I smiled. "Yes, I could tell. There were *zero* sparks when I saw you two at dinner. Maggie is a nice girl, but sweet..."

I took a slow sip.

"She's... innocent." He blushed.

Oh, he liked me. I had him flustered. *Yes, please.* The uneasy look on his phase eventually eased into a slight smile. He had a lovely one. He also had dimples. God, I loved dimples.

"Uh, I gathered, yes. You girls are—"

"Do not cast me in the same light, sir. We are not cut from the same cloth there."

"Oh?" Malcolm raised an eyebrow.

"I'm her older sister, so I must be fiercely protective of her. I do not have an older sister to do the same for me. Nor do I need one, Lord Ferguson."

He shifted on his feet and took a swig. He wanted me. I wondered if I would be able to take him back to the house without getting caught. It was a couple of weeks since I'd gotten into trouble. It was at least a year since I had done it on British soil. I was due.

"I sense you aren't aware that I am too old—"

"I like older men," I looked up at him slightly.

He was tall, another bonus. In heels like this, I was almost six feet.

"Well, I think—"

"Do you think I am some sort of lovesick little girl? I am not. I can handle you. If that is your concern—"

"I... I..."

"You look at me like I am a divine steak." I bit my lip flirtatiously. "You don't want me?"

He gaped.

"Oh, well, I tried," I turned to walk off.

He reached for my hand and pulled me back.

"You are not supposed to touch me," I pulled my arm away. "You know that right?"

"You want me to touch you," he said.

We now stood only inches away from one another. His mouth was so close to mine that I could have leaned in and kissed him. I could feel his breath as he whispered.

"You are a naughty girl."

"Yes," I replied.

Fuck. I flushed.

"You should be punished. I should ignore you," Malcolm said. "But damn if I don't want you. I shouldn't. I am supposed to avoid anyone of notable background tonight."

"Well, I'm the black sheep who does things like pose suggestively in society magazines and date hockey players, so, you have the right sister, I think."

"Oh, really?"

"Yes. What of it?"

"Would you like that... for me to punish you?" he asked me.

Oh, fuck. What was this? Who was this man? I was wet just *thinking* about it.

I whispered, "For speaking to me that way, I should punish *you*. You're a rake, aren't you?"

"Guilty as charged if you say it." He shrugged. His voice grew low, "You could sit on my face. Might be punishment."

Oh, fuck! Well sign me up! I wanted that very badly. Any man who didn't even know me but presumptuously talked dirty to me deserved it. Also, he *knew* who I was and was *still* unintimidated by it. I was going to have a bit of fun.

"Meet me at the house in five," I told him. "Meet me near the front staircase."

He nodded. "Okay, Princess."

I left, trying to appear normal. Overall, I did not care about the party. I wished to leave. It wasn't that I hated parties, it was that I hated parties where I was on parade. And, whether anyone knew it, I was viewed as less than my sister. If we were both at auction, the short, cute, royal-born blonde was going to outclass her leggy, flighty, ginger sister. I didn't need this emphasised to me when I had a man willing to properly fuck me. Or so I hoped.

We met up by the front stairs. The place was dead. With everyone down at the party for probably another hour, I fled upstairs with Malcolm. Together we found my room and ducked in. There, I practically jumped on him, throwing myself into his arms and pressing my lips against his tight. Like a train flying down the track, he pinned me against the door, both hands on my face. It was this sort of animal attraction I had never experienced before.

Yes, I had hooked up with a guy at a party. I had done so frequently, in fact. However, like this? Never. Never had I had a five-minute conversation with someone and wanted to jump in bed with them. I had also never had a man talk dirty to me like this. I wanted to see him naked and let him do everything to me.

He soon kissed my neck. It sent tingles through my body. I gasped, unable to hold back. It was like I might float away if he wasn't pinning me to the wall with some force.

He backed up and stared at me. "You alright, Princess?"

"Don't call me Princess," I growled, feigning annoyance.

"That *is* your title, correct?"

"What should I call you? Future Duke? Man Du Jour?"

He smiled slyly and brushed my lips playfully with his thumb. "I'm technically an earl but if you call me that, I won't fuck you. If you behave—"

"Fuck me then," I pleaded. "Please."

"You're going to behave?"

"Yes."

He ran his hand down to my breasts and shook his head. "They are absolutely spectacular."

I was surprised by that. I had nice tits. They were not the massive tits the rest of the women on my mother's side were blessed with. I would take the compliment.

"Do you want to see me naked?" I asked.

"Yes. If you—"

"Yes, I do," I replied. "I want you. Let's just clarify that now."

It seemed like our little play would go off the rails if he checked in at every moment.

Malcolm helped me unzip my dress, kissing my neck as he did. It felt so good. I imagined if he just pinned me to the bed like this and went for it how it might feel. I bet it would be lovely.

I dropped my dress to the floor, now completely naked.

"You don't have knickers on?" he asked.

"It's tight through the hips. Lines," I said. "Your turn."

"You can wait," he told me.

Oof. I loved that he was demanding!

Malcolm took his jacket and tie off before pushing me back on the bed. He towered over me for a minute, kissing me as his fingers found their way to my clit, then inside of me. I took in a sharp breath and moaned, completely overwhelmed.

"You are dripping," Malcolm said.

"Well, most of the time, men don't talk to me the way you do."

"Clearly, they should do it more often. Are you love-starved, Sabine?"

"Not quite, but few are so demanding. Most fear me."

He shook his head, said nothing, and proceeded to kiss down my body. His head landed between my thighs, his tongue barely tickling my clit at first before homing in on it like a missile. He used his fingers at the same time, finding my g-spot to send me into orbit. I grasped his full head of hair pushing him more forcefully into my pussy than I probably had ever done before. I came so hard and so fast that I didn't even have time to speak, merely screeching before my legs fell to either side of his face.

Fingers still inside me, stroking my g-spot, he looked up.

Malcolm said, "Good girl."

I could have died. *Good girl?* The audacity he had to pass judgement! And yet, I wanted to do it all over again.

CHAPTER 6
Not the Worst Idea

MALCOLM

Sabine came like a hurricane. She was dripping. I was quite proud of myself. She seemed rather surprised. I didn't know if that was unusual for her, but I was going to build on it. We shuffled around, finding a condom. I finally disrobed, having been glad to torture her a bit. She lay on the bed, breathing heavily, and looking like any man's version of perfection. I didn't deserve her, but I wasn't going to stop, either.

I climbed on the bed and kissed her some more. To my surprise, she wrapped herself around me tightly. I wanted to torture her some more, so I pushed her legs back down.

"You don't get to rush me," I said, sternly.

"Oh, you think you can tell me what to do?"

"Yes, Princess."

She deliberately disobeyed, grabbing my cock. It was playful enough, but it also felt good. She ran her thumb across the head and stared at me.

"It's nice. Rather impressive. At least for what weight you throw around, it doesn't come as part of a small man complex," she said.

"Get on your hands and knees, then," I said.

I decided if she wanted to toy with me and act unimpressed, I would be an asshole.

"Why should I?"

"Because you want to fuck me." I pinched her left nipple.

She moaned, sighed deeply, and complied.

Her soft, supple little arse felt lovely in my hands. I gave it a good smack.

"Good girl," I said.

I started slowly. She was very wet, so it wasn't difficult. But again, I wanted to continue to hold her back. I wanted to torture her.

"Fuck me, please," she pleaded as I slowly pumped away.

"You want me to be rough?" I said, trying not to kill the mood with too much concern.

I got the feeling men could be gingerly with her due to her station. I realised that the real Sabine liked getting roughed up. Maybe she didn't know that before me, but she knew it now.

"Yes," Sabine said.

Her voice was a low growl.

I forced her head into the pillow and increased the speed of my thrusts. She was so wet. I'd at least done a good job at getting her off so far, but I wanted to hear her cum again. I wanted to feel her cum with me inside her. She was close, her breathing picking up again. She started to moan more. I reached around and rubbing my fingers over her clit until she squeaked out a "please" from the pillow.

It was sexy beyond measure to hear her beg. I was riding a high. I continued until she came. I could tell because she was now running down me.

More impressive was the line she uttered after. "Oh, fuck, Malcolm! Fuck me harder!"

I loved it. I grabbed onto her arse with both hands again and railed her with abandon. She came a third time, so wrapped up that she looked for anything to hold onto. She grabbed her own hair. That was a new one. I decided to pull her hair now. Much had fallen from the bun that had previously wrapped it in a tidy form along with the half-dozen diamond encrusted ornaments.

I didn't make it longer. The sound of her panting and little moans into the pillow, coupled with the jiggling of her perfect arse, was too much to overcome. The feel of her at the end was exceptional. It was rare a woman got *this* wet.

"Fuck. Sorry." I rolled off to the side and stared as she did the same.

"Why are you apologising. I usually fuck athletes and they don't pound me as hard as you just did. Well done."

Her accent was so exacting, prim, and proper like something out of a production of the Royal Shakespeare Company, that I burst out laughing.

"What?" she asked.

I ducked out of bed to deal with the prophylactic. I loathed it but damn if this wasn't worth it.

"You're just so... so very naughty one minute and then praising me for being a good boy the next," I said.

"I have been told I am incorrigible and should mind myself."

"Well, add me to the list of people that applies to." I returned to her, laying sideways. She looked up at the canopy of the bed. Yes, of *course* she had a canopy fit for a damn princess.

Sabine looked over. "You didn't mind."

"No. You are fabulous," I said. "You get so... wet."

"I squirted," she was matter of fact. "Never did it with someone taking me from behind but it was mesmerising when it happened. You touching my clit did it. That was amazing. Hopefully, that wasn't like... weird."

"Weird?"

"An ex sort of freaked out."

I wondered if the boy knew what he'd *done* in that case, but not wanting to call attention to the elephant-in-the-room and make myself feel even more like a pervert who had just fucked a woman far too young for him, I let it go.

"I was not concerned. It was hot."

"You know we'll never hear the end of this, right? We must get dressed and go back down there, but you've destroyed my hair," she pouted.

"I'll get an earful. My mother and father *so* wanted me to end up wooing your sister. It's not that they would necessarily mind you. I am sure they would think you were lovely. You are... lovely, Sabine. They will only be disappointed that after thirsting for you through cocktail hour, dinner, and a few minutes by the bar, I bedded you. That is despicable of me, and you deserved better."

She bit her lip. "I had a dreadful time, obviously."

I wanted to do it all again. She made the fear of being lit on fire worth it. She was magnetic. I wanted so badly to fuck her, this time in missionary so I could watch her lose all control. Maybe with her feet on my shoulders? I wondered if she was lithe enough to pin down? That would be a treat!

"Look, maybe we could use it to get out of the rigamarole. I mean if you don't mind me. We've been caught red-handed with our mitts in the biscuit tin, right?" Sabine asked.

She ran her finger around my collarbone absentmindedly as she said it.

"Yes, me more than you, darling."

"Well, you and I both fit into the same world where everyone *wants* people like us to end up together. It will be an endless nightmare of boring men who don't fuck me properly if I don't have someone to do it right. Who cares what *I* think, Malcolm?"

I smiled. "Yes, lots of heiresses. They aren't my type. Present company exempted."

She bit her lip again. "Well, if you want to keep me company for a bit, I'd let you do that a few times. Hell, I'd be willing to suffer the terrible indignity of sitting on your face a dozen times or such to avoid my mother trying to pair me with some son of a Duke... present company exempted."

"You are something else," I shook my head. "Are you suggesting—"

"We lie. We join forces and combine to throw them off our scent. I do not expect you to be stuck with me. I ask you would be discrete if you fuck someone else. I'm not asking you to settle down or be my boyfriend, but tongues will already wag, and this gives us a fairy-tale love story rather than the real underlining truth that this is unbridled, animalistic lust."

"You're domineering. I like it," I said.

"Keep fucking me like that and I can rest easy and have a fun summer in peace. I'm not waiting around either, mind you."

"If one of us falls for another person, we break it off," I agreed.

"Exactly. But we can avoid unpleasant needling in the meantime."

I smiled at her and nodded. "We have a deal, Sabine."

"Good. Fake boyfriend, welcome to my ridiculous royal web. Keep going down on me like that and we'll be fine."

I thought to myself if she kept on playing the obedient little good girl she was, I would lose my mind but thoroughly enjoy my summer as well. She was beautiful. I didn't need convincing to be seen with her. She was fun in bed. We could make this work. And, as she suggested, it took us both off the market.

CHAPTER 7
The Hoax

SABINE

Malcolm and I pretended *nothing* happened for the first five minutes together at Sunday's breakfast. We behaved ourselves, having put together a perfectly choreographed approach the night before. We'd act as if nothing was going on, make eyes at one another, and then people would start asking questions, we'd *try* to stay mum, but eventually, I would spill the beans and that would be the end. Boom! Instant fake relationship.

It happened a little sooner than I expected. Malcolm was gorgeous. I was infatuated. He knew what he was doing. He wasn't afraid to rough me up. Everything about him was *impeccable*. He had this whole sexy boss thing going. To date, no one made me cum so hard quite so fast—or at all, really. I wanted every ounce of him again and *quickly*.

Thankfully, I was about to arrive back in London for summer and would have easy access to his cock—or so I hoped. I wasn't about to settle into anything serious. I was allowing myself to be a girl-about-town this year. I wanted a taster of everything first. Without a distraction, Mum and

Aunt Greta would never accept my wild summer. I needed a diversion.

With Saint Maggie of London running around to save us all, anything even remotely outside of the normal, heteronormative love-marriage-baby way of going was bound to get me into deep shit. I would be called the whore by the press, shamed by my family, and told to calm down. I needed excuses *and* someone who made me scream his name.

My preference was to give Malcolm the summer *he* wanted with great cover. I knew men like him chased girls like me on the regular, but sensed I was far cleverer than the average woman he slept with. I captured his attention. I hoped I had, anyway. God, it was hot, though. He certainly had all *my* attention.

"Why are you staring at him like that?" Maggie whispered.

"What?" I feigned surprised.

"You are *staring* at the Earl."

"Which earl? There are about fourteen."

My sister rolled her eyes. "Don't be daft. The Earl of Lauder."

I shrugged.

"No, you don't get to make eyes at him, have him basically drooling at you from the bloody buffet, and act like all is normal. It's not."

I tossed my hair. "I may have a crush on him."

"A crush?"

"Or, rather, he may have a crush on me."

"He looks... it's indecent. I thought he was just a bit misunderstood but—"

"He's not indecent. I may have fucked him last night... a couple of times. Don't act like you have no knowledge of the morning after energy. Oof. I didn't want to get out of bed."

Malcolm approached. I felt Maggie melting down. I wondered why my sister was being *so* prudish. She looked at him as if he had done something awful to me.

"Be nice," I warned.

"I am *always* nice," Maggie said.

Malcolm bowed in greeting. "May I sit here, Your Royal Highnesses?"

Maggie glared. "Depends. Are you here to *behave* yourself?"

"Maggie, it's time to call off the Welsh guards, alright?" I asked, annoyed. "Jesus! Yes, Malcolm, sit, please."

Malcolm fought a laugh. "I did warn you, Princess Margaux, that I had a tendency to get myself into massive trouble and could be... misguided."

"My sister is a nice, respectable girl," Maggie protested. "I'll have you know—"

I cut her off, in French. "Maggie, calm down! Two consenting adults are allowed to do as they please. Two consenting adults! Calm down!"

Maggie glared, cross and in grave disagreement. She would have let me have it if she didn't know it was unbecoming. She could not break character. God, this new version of her was so *boring*. She couldn't be found giggling or doing anything out-of-bounds. I already resented her. I loved my sister. She was my best friend but weren't we beyond pearl-clutching over such things?

Malcolm smoothed things over well. "She is a very nice, clever, quite respectable sort of girl. Far too good for me. And yet, I find her utterly charming. I do apologise for staring or for monopolising her last night, Your Highness. She's just... irresistible."

The way that he stared at me made my palms sweat. He sold it well. My heart fluttered girlishly. I wanted that level of adoration. It may have been put on, but it made me feel he was treating me as the most delicious thing he'd ever seen. I wanted more. No one who spoke in more than two-syllable words gave me this treatment. I was hanging on Malcolm's every word. I *blushed*.

Margaux crossed her arms looking so very much like our Mum. "So, you recognise she should be treated with care then, Malcolm?"

"I do, of course. Your sister is no delicate flower. She can handle herself, but I would never do anything willingly to harm her. She's deserving of nothing but respect."

And yet, the man could do anything he wanted to me, including degrade me a bit, and I would be putty in his hands. I said nothing, just smiled like an idiot. I felt like a lovesick schoolgirl with a massive crush on her hot, young teacher. Yes, I knew there was a *bit* of an age gap. It wouldn't be completely taboo. Wealthy, powerful men married women my age without much fanfare.

The irony of this was if he took a shine to Maggie, it would have been smoothed over. No one would call out the age gap. Everyone was fine with her entering an economically and politically advantageous marriage. I didn't quite understand it until Malcolm pointed it out. As I lay on his chest last night, he said such a union would be beneficial to Maggie and thus, my family. Malcolm's father was active in the Lords—one of its most active members—and quite close to other political movers and shakers. Mum and Auntie had a few pet projects they wanted funded. Nothing sinister, but key. An alliance could prove fruitful.

On the other hand, I think my father wanted me to have more opportunities. Dad and I were closer than I was to Mum. Dad, despite having very clear socialist leanings, stayed the hell out of politics for Mum's sake. He wasn't British by birth, but he had many opinions on all things. As the vestiges of colonialism fell, he sat there quietly satisfied about these turns of events. Dad wanted me to have the world. He wanted me to live my life as a normie.

Dad was the reason we was raised so normally in the first place. They met while Mum finished her doctoral work in Canada. Mum was allowed to study whatever she wanted. She, like myself, studied politics. Daddy was a painter teaching classes at the university. They met at a cafe overlooking the Rideau Canal. I used to study there whenever I was homesick. It made me feel more connected to my family across the ocean. We were never supposed to live a royal life. And, until everything changed for Maggie, we lived like any other wealthy family.

After she became the second-in-line, I returned to Canada. Dad basically forced me to go. He knew Maggie would have a different life and, as much as I wanted, I couldn't spare her. He knew it would be harder for us to each find ourselves living in London together. It was why we'd been separated growing up into different clubs and groups. It was easier to keep us apart so we could each learn and thrive in our own ways.

Maggie nodded at Malcolm, agreeing to calm it down. "I trust as long as you understand you will take care not to damage her reputation or break her heart, Lord Ferguson."

"No, ma'am," Malcolm said. "I would never do such a thing."

Maggie looked dubious but left it.

"Malcolm, will you be attending the charity benefit at the flower show?" Malcolm's father asked.

Malcolm looked concerned. He shook his head.

"The Chelsea Flower Show," Maggie presumed, and then threw a mulligan. "Because Sabine is slated to deliver some awards. I am going to be held up, travelling with Aunt Greta. She was so kind to have volunteered for it."

"Oh, yes, I do plan to go… for charity's sake," Malcolm said. "I might… see you there, Sabine."

"Yes, what a lovely thing to do for charity." Maggie tried to help.

There was my twin sister. There she was. Somewhere, she realised I liked him. I did like him, but not in a *serious* way. She didn't know that yet. No one needed to. We could keep this up for a bit longer and really sell it. Now, Maggie was a supporter. She'd help me.

I smiled at Maggie. "Yes, it really is."

CHAPTER 8
A Bit Thorny

MALCOLM

I had no time to play with a charity flower show, but I couldn't give up the ruse. Sabine and I managed to make having awful, naughty sex somehow acceptable. Anything could be allowable in the pursuit of securing one's estate's success for dozens more years. And while I told Sabine, the political alliance was a main draw, there was more ridiculousness there. My father told me he wanted this to work because her mother and aunt had the only breeding string of racehorses in true competition with ours in all Britain and Ireland. He wanted desperately to align us.

It was the most idiotic reason to marry me to a child. Poor Maggie. She was clever, I'd grant her, but seemed downright puritanical. Or, at least, too inexperienced to have an honest conversation about anything more than *slightly* cheeky. It would never have worked, and it would have been unfair to us both—but mostly her. Queens aren't known for being able to run off to have an affair. In contrast, nobles and princes are *encouraged* to do so.

Sabine was different. Per research, they were less than a year apart in age, but Sabine was worldly. She was wilder and wiser.

She oversaw herself, while Maggie was awkward and still figuring life out. I found Sabine's security in herself sexy. Yes, she was this gorgeous, nubile nymph of a thing, but within forty-eight hours of making her acquaintance, I found her to be a great laugh with a dark sense of humour. That was rare in a woman.

It meant that even though I cared not for flowers, I would show up somewhere in a jacket to spend a bit of time with the hot young thing. We had to sell it. We must keep people off our backs. The added benefit was that as Ascot, Goodwood, and Cowes approached, our shacking up would be morally endorsed. Well, we were *in love*, so it was expected. People had high hopes. My darling parents all but forced the issue.

My assistant buzzed. "Malcolm, the Private Secretary to Princess Margaux is on the line for you. Should I patch her through?"

I was confused. "Yes?"

That was odd.

"Hello?"

"Hello, Lord Ferguson. My name is Marilyn Louis. I am Private Secretary to Princess Margaux and Princess Sabine."

"Yes. How may I help you?"

"Princess Sabine will be attending the Chelsea Flower Show tonight. She will host a cocktail reception from 19:00 to 21:00 hours, presenting three awards for outstanding displays. She wonders if you plan to attend?"

"Could she not ring me?" I asked.

"Sir, that is not how this works," Marilyn said, voice flat. "I manage her diary."

"Alright. Yes, I had planned to attend."

"Brilliant. She will be glad to see you. Would you like me to forward her diary for the day to you? I can do so via fax or if you have electronic mail—"

"That won't be necessary," I insisted. "I will be there for the reception at seven. Thanks."

"She will be happy to see you."

The call ended. I went back to my brief, wondering what in the hell that was about. Why did I need the Princess's schedule? Why would I care about that? It was so odd. This was why I did not attach myself to women of this social strata. Still, the possibility of taking her from behind and listening to her scream my name made the nonsense abate from memory.

I finished up around 17:30 and continued reading through my files on the ride home. I changed, quickly, debated getting rid of my five-o-clock shadow and decided against it. I had little time to shave. I changed into another suit and dashed to the old NHS hospital that held the show. Mountains of flowers greeted me from all angles. It was beautiful as could be.

I saw a friend, Jason, standing around with his wife, Belinda. It wasn't surprising to see them. They were known to attend such events. Jason was an MP who loved the high life, born to industrialists who made their money while he was a baby. They owned an impressive yacht and he never wanted for anything but, of course, power. Belinda was young—not much older than Sabine—and his favourite trophy to trot out. I attended their wedding a year ago. Belinda, like any good society wife, fell pregnant soon after. Their nanny must have been working late.

"Malcolm, you cheeky bastard! What are you doing here?" Jason called.

I shook his hand. "Mum and Dad couldn't make it. Sent me. You look lovely, Belinda. How are you? How is the baby?"

"Oh, Rhys is a delight," Belinda crowed happily. "As ever. We're well."

"Well, cheers again. Glad the little man is well."

I had no idea what to say. I was not a baby person. I knew I would someday produce children. That was the fun bit. The *having* them bit was the miserable part. They were so demanding. And everyone I knew who had children complained that it turned their wives into madwomen. It did not appeal to me.

"He's fine, yes, thanks," Jason said. "You go out on weeknights now, Malcolm? Since when, mate?"

I shrugged. "Sometimes. It has been busy."

"We're hosting a party next weekend," Belinda said. "Before everything gets all mad with Ascot and all that. You should come."

"I might be spoken for already," I said, seeing the seas parting down the line.

Yes. I hoped that was a sign the Princess arrived. I loathed parties where I was the lone unmarried man, thrown some sort of ill-chosen woman as a sweetener for being there. No thank you.

Sabine arrived, saving me from explanation. Her eyes met mine and the same magnetic attraction I felt the first time hit me once more. She couldn't have been sexier if she tried. She was in some sort of pink dress, her hair pulled back in a fabulous row of diamonds on one side of her head. Again, the impulse to kiss her neck overwhelmed me.

"I didn't know who we would get. It said Princess Margaux would be here, but then they said there was a change of plans," Belinda said.

I nodded. "I knew. I spoke with Princess Sabine last weekend. I was up in Scotland with my family at Balmoral. Princess Maggie had to be somewhere with the Queen. Sabine agreed to help."

"You're on a first-name basis now, old boy?" Jason joked.

"Yes, I suppose."

Sabine stepped closer, only two groups from us. She made her rounds, but I was desperate for her to stop and chat with us. With me, rather. I listened to Belinda drone on about a friend of hers who would be "perfect" for me. Meanwhile, I could think of nothing more than Sabine naked in my bed and how much I wanted that to be a reality.

Sabine approached, making eyes at me. Damn. We bowed and exchanged pleasantries.

"Malcolm, I am delighted you listened to your mum and venture out," Sabine said.

"Yes, ma'am. I do sometimes follow directions," I joked.

She smiled cheekily and shook her head. "And how are you finding the flowers?"

"Very like... flowers."

She snickered. "That is the best you can do, darling?"

"I do my best, Your Royal Highness."

"And how do you all know one another?" Sabine asked.

"Malcom and I used to work at the same firm out of uni. Before I left to enter political life," Jason said.

"Dreadful politics." Belinda pulled a face. "Not that you have to worry about that, Your Royal Highness."

"Oh, I rather love discussing them in private. But my official line is, yes, dreadful."

I smiled at her through the corners of my mouth. I couldn't even control it. It was the way her perfume smelled, the way her hips bounced as she walked, and the way she never dropped her glance when she saw me. It was this degree of confidence. That, coupled with political shit talking, was a dynamite combination. If I could have built an ideal woman, she would have come close to Sabine. She'd also be slightly older and would have no title. No dice.

"Intriguing," Jason said.

"Malcolm, might I have you join me for a but a moment? I have a legal question that needs answering and... I figured I might pick your brain," Sabine said.

"Of course. Excuse me." I followed her.

She looked up at me slightly. In the heels she was wearing, she didn't struggle to meet my gaze. I wasn't short, but she was statuesque in comparison to her miniature sister.

"I do not seek legal advice, Mal," Sabine insisted. "I only wanted to get you to myself for one moment. One, to make tongues wag—"

I looked around, every eye in the place trained on us. "I think you can call that mission a success, Princess."

She smiled slightly and shook her head. "Well, you asked for it. Anyway, if you want to see me, it's rather complicated. However, after I leave here, you can, too. I live at the palace. If you decide you'd like a nightcap, pop round to Clarence House and we shall see what we can do."

"What?"

"If you want a nightcap, just do as I say. The service entrance will ring me. Got it?"

I stared, confused. "Of course. A nightcap sounds... good?"

"Brilliant. Then, they will ring me."

I had no idea what I was doing. At the same time, I was not about to tell Sabine no.

"Until then," she left.

Watching her hips sway pained me. She was gone for now. That was all I got. Or, rather, that was all she gave. She had an entire room to talk to. I shared her with everyone. I hated it.

CHAPTER 9
The Murder Dungeon

SABINE

I returned to my quarters at Buckingham Palace, trying not to seem *too* desperate for the Clarence House gate to ring me. The truth was, as much as I wanted to sleep with Malcolm, I hated being alone. I didn't like living in the palace walls. I missed Mum, Dad, and my idiot baby brothers. They were all over at KP. If Maggie didn't insist on living with Aunt Greta like an emotional support animal, we could have a house of our own on KP's grounds.

I needed Maggie to cut the apron strings. I also needed better plans about how to make this all work. Marilyn helped me *this* time, but she wouldn't always go to bat for me. Maggie would have big feelings about Malcolm ever coming back to my rooms. And if my aunt found out, I worried she would lose her mind and give me hell. I probably should not have organised this, but I had needs.

Around eleven, the guards rang. I proceeded over to collect Malcolm. He waited, confused and a bit annoyed. I didn't know what he could possibly be cross with me for. He knew he was getting laid.

"What is all this?" Malcolm gestured.

I rolled my eyes and shook my head.

"Ma'am." The service door attendant bowed deeply as I approached.

"Good evening," I said. "Malcolm, don't be cross with me."

"Ma'am, do we need to make any sort of arrangements or—"

"He will leave through the service entrance of the palace," I clarified.

I took Malcolm's hand and pulled him down the hall.

"Tell your driver to come round to the other side when he comes to collect you. This way, no one is the wiser."

"What?"

"It's a thing. A tried-and-true work around. Mum used to do it."

Malcolm snickered.

"What? She had a life, too. Our personal secretary swears it will work. I may have had to coerce her into that tip, but it is palace lore."

"So, am I not staying?" Malcolm asked.

I laughed. "No, darling."

Malcolm stopped.

"Oh, Malcolm, don't look put out. Did you think we were going to make love and then bask in the glow of one another's eyes?"

He answered as we entered the service lift—our first stop on this journey. "I had no such hope."

There was an awkward silence.

"You can kiss me, you know?" I asked. "I don't bite."

"With everyone around—"

"It's not as if they are allowed to care," I laughed. "I don't recall you being shy."

"Nor you, Your Royal Highness."

The way he said it made me wish he would kiss me. The way he looked at me made me want him to fuck him.

The doors to the lift opened. As we stepped out, Malcolm burst into laughter.

"What?" I followed him into the corridor.

"Is this your murder dungeon? Did you lure me here with promises of sex and then take me here to black widow me in poor lighting."

"I would have to fuck you first," I strode ahead. "This tunnel is a secret. It was created after the second world war primarily to connect households and store things we might not want people to find."

"This runs under the tube?"

"Uh-huh."

"Bloody hell. It's terrifying."

"Are you afraid of the dark?"

"No, no."

"Women with dark intentions?"

"Certainly not. I prefer them."

I felt a tingle in my spine. It wasn't only what Malcolm said. It was the way he said it.

"You know, I loathe following you around," Malcolm said.

"I thought you rather liked observing me from behind, darling."

He chuckled. "Touché. Your arse is—as always—spectacular. But I don't fancy following you about like an errand boy."

"What would you rather do?" I asked.

"Fuck you, obviously. Have you come to me."

"Well, it's not that easy, Malcolm. However, you *will* be seeing me at Ascot. Might you stay with us?"

We reached the second lift—the one that would take us back to the land of the living.

"I am terribly busy with work, Sabine."

"Do you want me or do you not? That's the question."

We boarded the lift.

"I want you. That is *not* the issue. I have work."

I bit my lip, toying with him. He hadn't so much as kissed me. It was killing me to watch him do this.

"You want to fuck me?" Malcolm shook his head.

"Yes, of course I do. Or, rather, I want a reprisal of you fucking me."

He kissed me, finally. It was slow and tempting. Then, it took off. I let him push me against the wall of the lift. I was already wet, wondering if we could just shag here. Then, Malcolm pulled away. He left me gasping for breath, feeling a mess. And he was *enjoying* it. He wanted to watch me squirm.

We proceeded towards the apartment I shared with my sister. Everything was still, quiet, and undisturbed.

"It is eerie," Malcolm said. "And no one minds me being here?"

I snickered. "No one knows. And that is another reason for the bloody smoke and mirrors."

"The treachery only makes it better."

We landed at my door. "And this is me. Well, and Margaux, but my room..."

I opened the door and pointed. "Right there. And we're very much alone."

"It is... smaller than I anticipated."

"You are judging our palace?" I scoffed.

"You haven't seen my parents' house on Regent's Crescent, Sabine," Malcolm said. "It is grand."

"Grander than this?"

"Well, the bedrooms are. It's impeccably cared for."

"I will grant you that it could use a bit of a freshening up," I admitted.

"Yes. Well, that is why your mother would put up with me visiting you during Ascot. Her hope is that I have some sort of magical effect on the men in the Lords. And that I will get her and your aunt what the so desperately want."

"Which is?"

"Funds to renovate this massive money pit."

"As sexy as politics are," I sighed. "I need you to unzip me."

"Politics aren't sexy enough for you, Princess?"

"No. I could talk for hours about political parties and partisanship. But I prefer to discuss federal systems. The unitary system is quite boring. Add a Westminster bent in and I'm totally falling asleep."

Malcolm chuckled. I stepped out of my dress and turned to see him remove his clothes.

"You are such an interesting, unusual girl, Sabine."

"I am no girl, Malcolm. We've been over this. I'm a woman. Full stop, darling."

Malcolm looked up from his shirt, his gaze gravitating down my body and up again. He took me in while unbuttoning his shirt.

"No, you're right. You aren't." He was off in another world.

Part of me hated that I was most powerful like this, standing in front of a man mostly naked, only in my knickers. I had his full attention. However, if I started spurting off about neoconservatives, would he care in the least? I worried not. I was more than a pretty face. I wasn't intimidated by my own looks. Some women refused to be defined by them. My sister hated when people pointed out she was pretty, insisting her intellect alone was *enough*. No, I took pride in being pretty and feminine. It was part of my persona. I wasn't *afraid* of it or admitting that like this, hair all done up and makeup perfectly placed, I was beyond enticing. Malcolm's face said all of that. But it was true. As a society girl, my power wasn't in my knowledge of world politics or social policy. In this moment I captivated the male gaze. That was where I thrived.

Malcolm kissed me again, our mostly naked bodies entangling impressively. My body shivered and vibrated as he ran his hand across my back and to my arse. He snapped the side of my knickers and pulled back.

"Take those off. No need for them."

"You take them off," I said.

"I make the rules, not you. Get on the bed." He was forceful.

Oof. I loved being ordered around. I didn't know it before, but I now lived for it.

I climbed onto the bed, propped on my elbows. "Do you want me this way or on my knees?"

"I want to fuck you on your back. I want to see you cum and watch you lose yourself."

He whipped my knickers off and forcefully pulled me towards him by my thighs. It was *efficient*. Malcolm was on a mission. He wanted me to think it was about *him*, but I knew better. That was what made this delicious. I held all the cards. He could boss me around and take every bit of the breath from my lungs, but I could send him away at any point. It was a delightful, delirious fantasy.

I gasped a bit as Malcolm slid inside me. The man was hung. I wasn't sure if he was the best endowed man I'd been with, but he was close if not. It felt delightful. I'd been so keyed up all night, wishing for this. I arched my back, my head pushing back onto the bed. Then, as if I were a ragdoll, he pulled my legs up from around his waist to his shoulders.

"What are you doing?" I panted as he continued to fuck me with abandon.

"You've never done this?"

"No," I replied. "But don't stop."

He bent forward. "It's a shame. You're glorious."

My legs ended up near *my* ears. I was folded in half. Damn, it felt good. I dug my fingers into his back and held on for dear life as I came *hard*. I gasped his name. He backed off, a satisfied expression on his face as he pulled away, my ankles by his ears.

"Is it good?" I gasped.

"It's amazing. Your tits are... perfect."

"You're trying not to cum?" I asked.

"Shh!" he shook his head. "I want to get you off again, but only if you behave yourself, Sabine."

"Are you saying I am being naughty?"

"When you scream my name that loudly, you certainly are. You're no lady right now."

I bit my lip. He moved faster and faster, playing with my clit as he did. My ankles remained around his neck, my legs pressing into his shoulders for dear life. I gripped the headboard and came, shouting a line of obscenities. It felt so good. It was his utter lust for me, but also his satisfaction watching me cum which took me over the edge. By the time he came, I was a hot, sweaty mess. It was bliss. It was perfect. It was surprisingly convincing. Both our needs met, we fell to our respective sides of the bed, satisfied.

CHAPTER 10
Her Majesty's Invitation

MALCOLM

Watching Sabine unravel was the sweetest end to a frustrating day. I loathed attending charity events. I despised donning a tuxedo for no reason. I almost resented this sort of arrangement—this clandestine hook-up where I felt more like a teenage boy sneaking into his girlfriend's house while her parents were out. Watching her come undone made it worthwhile.

She let me play with her, but she knew that it was her situation to control. That was why I hated that I had to come to *her* and sneak in here. I loathed that, but damn if she wasn't completely tempting. Everything about her felt decadent. She was the type of woman you knew deserved to be spoiled, but she was more than that. Sabine was quick-witted. She matched my sarcasm and bitterness in an unexpected way. We were becoming *friends*. I liked that. If I had to spend the summer being a good boy and following her, I would at least enjoy her company in all ways.

"You should go," Sabine advised. "Not that I don't enjoy our post-coital talks. However, at some point, you'll get found out. Best to ring your driver and leave under cover of darkness."

"How do you know I have a driver?" I asked, feigning surprise.

"Darling, there is *no* way you attend events without a driver. I know your family can afford one—probably even more easily than mine can."

She said it so flippantly.

"You make assumptions, Princess."

"Because my assumptions are founded, they aren't assumptions. I am stating the obvious."

I shrugged. I had a driver. It was one of the perks of being me. Yes, I had a car and could drive myself sometimes, but I relished working in gridlock more than driving myself everywhere. Or, God forbid, battling the everyman on the tube. I didn't say that. It was implicit. I suspected Sabine had never seen an Underground station.

"What now?" I changed the subject.

"Well, I think we show up at Ascot together and sell it. Tonight will make the gossip columns suspicious, but we should really lay it on thick for Ascot."

"It's complicated for me. Your mother and my father both have horses running."

"Yes, darling, I know. Even more reason to hype it up. I will ride in to open things. I expect you to be there waiting for me to make a scene in the Royal Enclosure. Again, do not deny you have a box. I know you do."

"We do, yes."

"Do you want this to be convincing or would you like to leave doubt on the table so our mothers can shuffle us about to prospects?"

She was right. While my parents were convinced I was interested in Sabine, they were cross I refused to say we dated. I wasn't about to admit to something so ridiculous after meeting her *one* time. I expected someone to find out we were shagging, but only her sister seemed aware of that finer point. My parents just thought I found her attractive and wanted to pursue her. My mother accepted this, but she wanted a confirmation. Again, Sabine was a hot commodity. I wasn't the only one in the running for her affections. She and Margaux were prime real estate.

"Fine," I agreed.

"Oh, come on, don't act abused, Mal. I don't hurt your image, do I? If anything, I raise it. You get the beautiful young thing on your arm. You get the questions to stop. I raise your credibility. I am utterly charming, Malcolm."

"You think highly of yourself, Princess."

Sabine crossed her arms and glared. She tossed on a t-shirt, no bra. We were at this point, I supposed. She was correct. She was utterly charming and all wrong for me. On paper, if I were a good boy, she'd be perfect. Unfortunately, I was no good boy.

"I am grateful for the arrangement," I allowed. "But just to be clear—"

"Neither one of us is beholden to the other apart from in public? Yes. The good news with me is that I cannot and will not either confirm or deny the existence of a relationship. We don't do that. You're safe."

I smiled. "Perfect."

"But it goes both ways. You can sleep around, but so can I. If I see something I want, I'm going to have it. And you'll just have to watch me take it."

Oof. That was the part I loathed. I did not like to share. It was fair, of course. We agreed to this, but I did not like to think about another man railing her. I could only hope he'd be no comparison to me and what I did. I had to work hard to stay number one in that category. She was a lovely distraction from work, but I wasn't without other distractions, too. It was only fair.

We proceeded to the palace service entrance but got no further than the first turn before running into two people I least wanted to see on my covert walk of shame. Princess Margaux and the Queen chatted in the corridor.

Margaux spotted us first, gaping at the mere sight. It was clear what we were up to. Here I was with a barely-put-together tux. Sabine was dress down in a t-shirt and barely-there shorts. We looked like a ridiculous pair. It looked *bad*. The Queen turned, surprised.

"Lord Ferguson," she said. "To what do we owe the honour?"

I stared at Sabine, finding words. I had forgotten to bow.

I bowed to both before choking on my words. "Well, just visiting. On my way."

"I invited him back for a nightcap, Auntie," Sabine said, calmly. "Don't worry, no one saw him. He's on his way out."

"Well, aren't you just the Hostess with the Mostess?" Margaux said, flatly.

The look she shot her sister was disapproving.

"I try to be kind," Sabine said.

"Well, have a good evening," the Queen said. "Lord Ferguson, will be you be joining us in Windsor for Ascot? I assumed Bethy might invite your parents. Given that you and Sabine have... hit it off?"

"Oh, I am quite busy with my cases—"

"Can you not put it off a few days? We'd very much like you to join," Her Majesty said. "Obviously, Sabine would be pleased to see you, sir."

"Oh, well, ma'am—"

"I insist," the Queen said, cheerfully.

Sabine looked at me, knowing full well that I must agree now.

"I will see what I can do," I winced. "I will do my best and speak with my mother."

"Splendid!"

"Yes, splendid," Margaux said in a tone that convinced me she didn't agree with her aunt.

"Well, cheers, Your Highness and Your Majesty. I'm going to head home," I said.

We left. Sabine took my hand.

"Don't say it," I said.

"Why are being so grumpy? You get a break. You get to have unfettered access to every inch of me. And there will be *no* doubt that we're up to something."

"True, but now I must mostly behave myself for the better part of a week. I also have work, Sabine. I *do* work."

"I know, which you blame everything on. Malcolm, you needn't behave too much. I don't *want* you to be a good boy. Don't you see that?"

I didn't.

"And you will be—"

"A wonderfully good girl," Sabine promised. "Unimpeachable as ever. I will be an adoring, charming girlfriend. I can pull it off."

"I know you can," I agreed. "So, are we going all in on this farce now?"

"We are fake girlfriend and fake boyfriend with benefits. Brilliant benefits." Sabine smiled.

CHAPTER 11
Flirting with Benefits

SABINE

"How did the tour of air station go?"

Our mother and Aunt Greta hosted Margaux and I for tea. We did this once a week. I missed seeing my Mum. I was only a mile away, but rarely saw her. Margaux was fine with this, but I was homesick. Multiple times, I asked to move home and was told I needed to live "independently" and had. I lived across an ocean for four years. Now, I was back. Why could I not move home? I hated this "independent" shit. Margaux was on her own. It suited her to live on an island where she ran her own show and kept her diary close. Everything was on the diary.

"It was fine," I said.

Margaux rolled her eyes. "Well, apart from you flirting with every man."

"You should talk!"

"I never did. I was very well-behaved. Mum, I swore she threw herself at every man. Any of the photos could suggest it. The tape of her sitting in a plane was indicative of how she was all day."

I let out a groan. "They were terribly fit. Let me have my fun. You may have been born fifty. I was not. I will only be this pretty once in my life. I will only be this fit for so long. I'm going to enjoy life while I'm young and beautiful."

"You have so many years left. Shush!" Aunt Greta laughed. "It's fine. Your mother would have done the same at your age."

"What? I would not—"

"You were the wild one. I recall a particular officer—"

"No! Margaret, I swear—"

"Your mother was wild," Greta giggled. "Ignore her protests."

Margaux and I snickered.

"It's fine. Let her play. Although, I must question this given that Lord Ferguson was here for a nightcap earlier this week."

"What?" my mother asked. "Why?"

"He was just dropping by. We got to chatting at the flower show and I invited him round. It's not a big deal," I answered. "Margaux acted like we committed a cardinal sin."

"I do not! But I suspect you were up to something—"

"I am not fifty! Stop being so worried and prudish, sister!"

"What is going on with him then?" Margaux asked point blank.

"I am dating him, obviously," I said.

"Uh-huh," Margaux looked suspicious.

"I invited him to Windsor. His mother sent her acceptance and thanks. So, he's signed on now. This just confirms he is enamoured with you," Greta said. "Oh, darling, this is good."

"Well, we shall see." I shrugged.

"I don't know," Mum sighed. "He is quite a bit older and seems to... well, I get the feeling he chases you for all the wrong reasons."

"I can have a bit of fun, mother." I rolled my eyes. "We're not getting married or settling down. Calm yourself. Everyone acts like it is this big thing and we're in some rush."

"That is because he is in his mid-thirties and should have children by now," mother said.

"He seems in no hurry," Margaux said. "He's charming, I'll grant you, sister. Still, there is something about him I do not trust."

"Well, I like him. He makes me laugh. We like to discuss politics and all manner of things. He doesn't treat me like a baby. People can stop getting worked up over our age difference. It is stupid to worry."

"Uh-huh," Margaux was displeased.

There was a knock.

"Come!" Greta called.

A footman appeared with a wrapped box.

"Your Majesty, a gift has arrived for Princess Sabine."

"What? How?" I asked.

"Via courier. Appears to come from Cartier, ma'am."

My mother waved him over. "Bring it here, then."

He handed me the box, bowed, and left.

I unwrapped the card, sealed within a beautiful gold envelope.

SABINE,
A BIT OF A REMINDER SO YOU CAN THINK ABOUT ME THE NEXT TIME YOU ARE FLIRTING WITH AN ENTIRE SQUADRON OF AIRMEN.
—M

I said nothing, setting the card down to unwrap the box. Inside was a smaller gold velvet box. I peeled it back to reveal a beautiful bangle in white gold, encrusted in diamonds. It was delicate but made a statement.

"Who sent you that?" Mum asked.

Margaux held the note. "Who do you think?"

I snatched it. "None of your business!"

"I can think of only one admirer who could bankroll that," Mum said.

"It's just a bracelet," I protested.

"And it's only about eight grand worth of diamonds!" Mum scoffed.

"It's beautiful," Aunt Greta mooned. "Well, he has good taste. You can wear that out. It's rather practical, I suppose."

"That was the point," I put it on my wrist.

Margaux was mum. She knew if she said something rude, I'd call her on it. She was the world's biggest sceptic.

I looked at the spoils of whatever my flirtation wrought. Malcolm showered me with gifts. He *must* be jealous. We finished tea, me constantly staring down at my benefit of his admiration. I left, deciding to ring him. I closed and locked my door, to Margaux's dismay.

"You are about as opaque as water, Sab!"

I flipped her off through the door, "Love you, darling!"

I dialled his office number, knowing he'd be there. Sadly, I got his assistant. He was in court and would be back in the afternoon. When I was getting a manicure with Margaux, he rang back. The switchboard transferred the call at my behest.

I popped over to our couch and answered. "Yes?"

"I was told you wanted to speak with me, Sabine? Or were you just fucking with me?"

"Oh, yes." I smiled at his charm. "You know what you did."

"I thought I was being generous."

"It was a lovely gift, yes."

"Well, good. Wear it to Ascot."

"Are you trying to mark your territory?" I asked.

I could hear Margaux groan out of secondary embarrassment.

"I would prefer to do even more to mark my territory. This is just a *kind* reminder."

"Do you get jealous?"

"Do you take pleasure in torturing me by flirting with other men?"

"Of course," I answered. "I like to wind you up."

"I could do the same."

"I won't care. I'm not the jealous type, Mal."

He seemed frustrated by that. I *had* wound him up. He *was* jealous. It was hot. I loved hitting a nerve.

"I will see you at Ascot," Malcolm said. "With my parents. The whole thing. I deserve a thank you—a proper one."

"I will comply, of course. I'm nothing if not a well-behaved girl."

"I'd disagree. You're devilish."

"You crave it. Don't deny it."

"I do, yes," Malcolm said. "Be good. And wear it."

"I will if it tickles my fancy."

"I plan to mark my territory again by week's end."

"You realise you don't own me, Malcolm?"

"I do," Malcolm agreed. "But I like to toy with the idea. Doesn't it make you want me more? To be owned?"

I bit my lip. My pulse raced. "It does. But down boy. Be good. I will see you next week."

"Maybe before?"

"In your dreams, darling!"

"I can be very convincing."

"I'd like to see you try. I must go. Busy," I said.

We hung up and I went to sit back down for my pedicure.

"The two of you make me want to be sick," Margaux groaned.

"I could say the same about you and the sexy pilot. You are flirting with him all the time now."

"He is a nice person. That is all. He's too old for me, I'm sure of it. A lesson you'd be wise—"

"Oh, get off your high horse, Margaux. Malcolm is fun. I enjoy him. He spoils me. Should I turn him away? Let yourself luxuriate in being adored. Lean into it. Seriously! We are young. Let yourself fall for someone."

"Are you falling for Malcolm?"

I shrugged. "Probably not like that. But I am enjoying a summer. I am loving this summer."

CHAPTER 12
Rendezvous

MALCOLM

If I struggled to distract myself from thinking about Sabine in the throes of climax before I saw her cum with her toes curled around my ears, it was near-impossible *after* the event. I was loathed returning to the palace for fear of running into her family. Her aunt was no problem. Or, well, less a problem. It was her damn sister. Margaux was either a nun or jealous that Sabine had someone around. I couldn't tell which. Maybe it was both?

So, I was thinking about Sabine's breasts flopping around as I pounded her instead of whatever one of the solicitors told me. It was late. My brain was shot. I didn't give a flying fuck about some sort of proprietary material a company had ripped off a small inventor. They were goliath. I wasn't invested.

"Let's pick it up in the morning." I shut down my PC.

"Really?"

"Yes." I packed my briefcase. "Go home, Sharon. It's late."

"You practically live here, Malcolm! You have plans?"

"Not particularly," I answered. "But I'm going to try to rest.

Maybe read a book or watch telly. My mind is garbled. Can't work like this."

"Fair enough. Have a good evening."

"Thanks."

She left and I shook my head. I picked up dinner on the way home. I rode the elevator to my penthouse—a generous gift from my father. It was technically part of the estate. I loved it. The views were impeccable. I sat on my sofa, gas fireplace lit, looking at Westminster. It was getting late, and the sun was setting. People who had lives were going out to clubs and shows. Me, I had this.

I was bored. I could have gone out but, as of late, I was too exhausted to bother. That was another reason I found Sabine so tempting. She was there when I wanted her and not when I didn't. She never bothered me. We weren't beholden.

It began again, this desire to see her. Really, to *have* her. It was so frustrating. I was like a desperate teenage boy with a school crush. She was too good to ignore. So, rather than do what I should be, which was sleeping, I rang her. Unfortunately, the wrong sister answered.

"Yes?"

"Hello, it's... Malcolm," I said. "Is Sabine around?"

"Who is it?" Sabine asked loudly in the background.

I heard music on television.

"It's your boyfriend," Margaux said flatly.

I could have burst out laughing at the sheer underwhelm in the girl's voice.

Sabine excitedly picked up. "Yes, Malcolm? What is it?"

"What are you doing?"

"Doing or wearing?"

"Both," I chuckled.

"Nothing. And nothing impressive. What about you?"

"Shorts and a t-shirt. Drinking whisky and watching the sun go down on London."

"Oh, posh."

"You should talk, Sab."

She giggled, "Yes, and you should be reminded of your place, Malcolm. You sent me a gift earlier. Now you are ringing me. Are you desperately missing me?"

I was desperately missing the way she screamed my name and the face she made upon climax. It was ridiculous and raw. She was so fabulous.

"No. But I am bored."

"Oh, you'd rather treat me like a plaything then?"

I thought for certain that was a yes, but I could not *say* that.

"No. I just thought maybe you could... come round."

"You realise it doesn't work like that, darling, right?"

"We could make it work that way," I said.

"No. It's risky and—"

"Would you like me to fuck you up against the glass of my apartment?"

"Uh... what now?" That got her attention.

She was so predictable. The woman was more sex-crazed than most.

"I'd fuck you against the glass. Pin you against it and take you from behind. Sound good?"

"Sounds... lovely," she sounded spacey while visualizing it.

"So, you'll come?"

She groaned. "Yes, Malcolm."

"Good girl."

"Damn it. You get me in trouble. I must square this, but I will get there somehow."

"You have my address?"

"No," she said. "Give it to me."

I almost made a joke, but I let it go. I gave my address. She marvelled at my postcode. I hoped that in about twenty-five minutes, barring traffic, she would appear. If she stood me up, I'd be cross.

Sabine arrived as promised about twenty minutes later. She didn't have far to go. Her hair was wild, and she was *not* dressed up for this excursion, but damn if she wasn't sexy as hell. I got hard the minute she tossed her trousers and shirt aside.

Then, in her bra and knickers, she demanded. "Give me a tour of this place. I must see it."

"Fine. Not much to see. Three bedrooms, four bathrooms."

"Well, go on!"

I obliged. The house was impressive in aesthetic, but not size. While Sabine's current residence was extravagant in its space, the place needed work. This was a new build, and everything was top-of-the-line.

"It's nice," Sabine said.

"Nice? Just nice?" I scoffed. "This is 10 million in real estate—and you haven't even seen the roof deck."

"Well, that's lovely, Malcolm, but it's not my taste."

"And what is your taste?"

"Grander. More... formal."

"Uh-huh."

"Uh-huh what?" Sabine's hand was on her hip.

I struggled. She stood practically naked in the middle of my apartment and told me why she didn't like my house.

"Just that it's..."

Sabine dropped down to her knees before I could finish.

She looked up at me. "It's what, Mal? Cat got your tongue?"

I shook my head no as she pulled my shorts and pants down, freeing the very swollen cock. Now *this* was a nice evening in, I thought to myself. All my hubris about my beautifully simple apartment faded to black as she took me in her mouth. How in the world was this just *happening*? Who *was* she?

"Oh, fuck, Sab. That feels so good," I almost whimpered.

It felt impossibly good—nearly too good.

She pulled back, slowly, sucking on the head of my cock before letting it go. Her eyes looked up at me, but her hands remained on my shaft, working away. "See, I told you I would be a good girl."

"A very good girl," I said.

I played with her hair. It felt good.

"My hair is a mess because—"

"No, I like it like this," I cut her off. "It's lovely."

She shrugged and got back to work. If she kept going, I was going to cum. So, instead I said the one thing I wished I could avoid but needed to say.

"Sab, I'm gonna blow if you don't stop."

Sabine looked up again.

She wiped her mouth. "Yes?"

"I want to fuck you. I want to be inside you when I cum."

"Alright," Sabine hopped up. "Where do you want to fuck me? Still game for the window?"

I couldn't believe she took me seriously. That was pillow talk—a fantasy—but if she was game, so was I.

"Yeah, sure."

She looked around and pointed. "Here."

I obliged her, unable to do much else apart from smash her body up against the glass. She stood awkwardly until I was inside her. It was a challenging angle, but she was game and wet, and I wanted her. I made it work. I kissed her neck as we started. She moaned; hands pressed against the glass. I held one, interlacing our fingers as I fucked her there. She came, her face smashed against the glass with a big scream.

"Oh, Malcolm! Oh, fuck! God! Yes!"

The sheer excitement of it, coupled with her blowing me within an inch of me cumming in her mouth, led me to come fast and hard. We held onto one another, pressed against the glass for a moment as we caught our breaths.

"That was... glorious," she panted.

I kissed her neck, still inside and not wanting to leave. "It was amazing, yes. You are fabulous. A very good girl."

CHAPTER 13
Getting to Know You

SABINE

Malcolm wandered to the kitchen and tossed me a kitchen towel. We were downright reckless at this point. I should have policed us and suggested he put on a bloody rubber, but I was in a hurry and wanted him to fuck me against the glass. It was a total thrill. I'd never complain. However, unprotected sex was a mess. I didn't understand how married women did it.

Malcolm saw my horrified reaction as I did damage control. "Sorry. I didn't have a wank this morning. No time. So—"

"My knickers are a mess, Malcolm!"

He smiled, self-satisfied.

"Get that bloody smirk off your face."

"Sorry. Can I get you anything?"

"A pair of pants would be the *nice* thing to do," I insisted.

Malcolm fetched pants from his bedroom. By now, I'd given up doing anything. I got him back in the exchange, handing him the disgusting hand towel as I took the pants.

He grumbled but kept his opinion on the matter to himself.

"What got into you?" Malcolm asked.

"I thought it sounded fun."

"You were... wow. Who the fuck taught you to give head like that?"

"Ex-boyfriend," I answered. "He was a dick, but he also taught me a lot of fun things. So, not a total wash. It's a little different with you, but same idea."

"Same idea? What? I'm bigger."

"Oh, that's cute." I laughed. "Yes. You are. I was more referring to the fact that you are uncut."

He cocked his head.

"He was Canadian. Canadians and Americans are often circumcised," I said. "You're not."

"Oh, shit. Really?"

"Yes," I said. "I have seen more that were than weren't."

"What!? How!? You're British? Didn't you have a boyfriend here? Or were you a late bloomer?"

I flopped on the couch and stole his glass. Malcolm brought another glass and bottle over. He topped me up and I decided to spill the beans for the sake of unabated honesty. I knew he wouldn't judge me. We were both depraved, cut from the same cloth.

"I was not a late bloomer. I lost my virginity at fifteen."

"Oh, you definitely weren't."

"You?"

"Seventeen, actually." Malcolm blushed.

"Nothing to be ashamed of."

"Who was he? Someone in our social strata? A prince from far away?"

"He was a she."

Malcolm gaped.

"Don't look so bloody surprised. It was an... experiment of sorts. I don't dislike women. She got me off. An older girl. One of our friends. I haven't been with many women. Most don't particularly appeal to me. I am not quite sure what to read into it. This is not public knowledge—"

"No, I could imagine not. Does your family—"

"Maggie does, but I am sure she assumed it was a phase. She never freaked out, mostly felt like she'd never get laid."

"She's a bit uptight."

"Give her a break, okay? Life as the heir is hard. Neither of us wanted this. Maggie isn't naturally suited to being the centre of attention, Malcolm. It runs her batteries."

He backed off. "So, when was the first time with a guy?"

"Uh... a few months down the line. I was sixteen. It was *lousy*. I worried all men were totally shit in bed and couldn't find my clit."

Malcolm snickered. "A woman spoiled you?"

"She knew what she was doing. I dunno. We were girls. You know how boarding school is."

"Um, I never got up to that. Yes, I will admit the idea of boys-only housing is a bit queer, but..."

"Well, it's fine. No need to freak out. Like I said, I rarely find myself *that* attracted to other women. I don't think I would settle down with one. Anyhow, I couldn't. Now, I've told you my secrets. You tell me yours."

"I had sex in a supply closet in Westminster when I was interning for a cabinet minister," Malcolm said. "Sex with an older woman. Only a year, but still. It counts. I wasn't in uni yet."

I giggled. "Older as in she was in uni already?"

"Correct."

"Oh, Malcolm, that's silly. But, lovely. I mean, I just made you fuck me right there so you could do it to me right in *front* of the Great Palace of Westminster. There was something depraved about it. Thrilling, in fact."

"You cheeky little minx!"

"I can be, yes." I sat cross-legged to face him. "Strangest place you ever did it?"

"Other than the supply closet?"

"Yes."

"A plane."

"That's not strange!"
"Hospital."
"I don't believe you! Do not say you shagged a nurse!"
"Nah. I wish. That could have been hot."
I rolled my eyes.
"No. I fell down the stairs," Malcolm said. "Drunken shenanigans. I was trying to impress a girl at this party and fell down the stairs. Ended up with a pin in my arm. I had to stay in the hospital because I had surgery. She stayed with me and then blew me."
"Oh, wow! And you didn't marry her?" I scoffed. "Did she dump you?"
"First of all, you could teach her a thing or two, I'll say. Second, she was dumb as a brick. Beautiful, but boring. She was the type of girl I probably should marry but won't."
I tilted my head. "What are you actually looking for, Malcolm?"
"What is it with you and the questions. It's like a bloody deposition!"
"Aren't you supposed to be good at that, darling?"
"I *am* good at it. I'm a bloody ace, Sabine!"
"Uh-huh." I bit my lip.
I knew it drove him mad.
"Oh, stop it. I'm spent for at least another thirty minutes," he sighed. "You are so tempting. I hate it."
I gave a cheeky smile.
"You have a gorgeous smile."
"So do you, darling. But you aren't answering my question."
"Fine. Fair question, but only if you will do the same."
I nodded.
"I want someone who can hold my attention. She must be pretty, yes. I'd prefer that. I'm quite vain. I will cop to it. More than that, she must be clever. I want someone who can make me laugh and who will get my stupid political jokes. I need someone who can keep up with me. Unfortunately, none of that qualifies them to be my wife."

"What? Why? Are your parents planning on you settling down with a hideous brick of a woman who lacks a sense of humour?"

"It's not that, Sabine. No. A duke requires a wife who can be lady of the house, manage the children and the household, and who is willing to live on a country estate in the Scottish Borders. It would be a bonus if she were good with horses."

"Well, I don't know if I am suited to run a household. I don't much want children at this moment. I do love Scotland and I adore horses. I know far more about racing stock than you, I'd bet."

"It doesn't take much. No, you are ideal in many ways," Malcolm said.

"It would never work. I'm... I'm entering a law program this fall. And, anyway, you think I am a baby."

"Nah. I think you are beautiful and far too good for me. Now, the question, my dear. What do you want?"

"Uh... someone who can get me off, make me laugh, and spoil me mercilessly," I admitted.

"Spoil you?"

"Do not look so surprised, sir. I have expensive taste. And I have a style of living I have become accustomed, too. Even better if he is devilishly handsome."

"You're as bad as me. I won't judge you. You should be spoiled. You are altogether giving when you get a small gesture."

"The bracelet was no small gesture," I said. "I blew you because I wanted to. It wasn't transactional. I do like to be spoiled but the two are unrelated."

His gaze made me tingle. The way Malcolm looked at me made me weak. I told myself it was nothing, but it felt like the whole world was right there in his blue eyes. They were beautiful. I couldn't look away. He put my drink on the coffee table, leaned in to kiss me, and pushed me back on the couch. We were about to do it all over again.

CHAPTER 14
Ascot

MALCOLM

I arrived at Windsor, dressed for a barbecue, along with my dear parents. They fought all the way whether the gift I brought was appropriate or whether I would get them on a restricted list.

The whiskey I was gifting the Queen and her fair sister was not from our home country. It was received from a friend who sold racing stock to my father and owned a family distillery in Kentucky. He was one of the few racing people I entertained. We met on a plane years ago. I introduced him to my father. The rest was history. And now, every time Ralph came through London or stopped to visit up north, he brought us a rare case of the stuff. It defied all customs law, but when you flew private, you could do that.

We were brought into a courtyard. I heard two boys fighting over something and the Duchess bellow.

"Hugo and Lars! Stop fighting."

"Stop being dicks! You almost took me out!" Margaux shouted at her brothers.

Sabine approached, looking semi-nervous. Everyone was tense. This was off to a *brilliant* start.

"Mum, Dad, Malcolm and his parents are here," she called.

I approached, unsure if I should kiss her. What were the rules of engagement?

Instead, I was altogether chaste. I did nothing but say hello. Sabine's parents arrived along with her aunt and Uncle.

"We brought you a little something," I said. "Something different."

"Oh, really?" Princess Beth opened the gift bag.

She was the grabby one. Queen Margaret handed the bag to the Duke of Cambridge and slowly unwrapped it.

"Oh, bourbon. You must like us," Beth said. "Well, well, Greta."

"How kind of you. I like different," Margaret said.

The woman was a sweetheart. She was a treasure.

Sabine's father took the bottle. "Nice. Hey, Gary, let's have some. You want some, folks?"

He was asking us.

"Sure, of course," I replied.

My parents nodded, surprised the royals were unoffended. They were *chuffed*.

So, the night started with drinks. I tried not to think about my caseload or how much work I would come back to when I returned to London on Sunday. I told myself that it was best we sold the thing. And, anyway, I was having fun with Sabine. It was a bit awkward. I liked her more than I thought I would.

Adding to it, I'd decided to go out drinking last night with friends and had gone home with a woman. It was not my finest hour. She was attractive, no doubt, but I felt this pang of guilt upon seeing Sabine. We'd been getting on so well. I knew there was an *arrangement*. And I was smart to not invite the woman round to mine just in case. Still, I wondered if she would think poorly of me. I had an urge to *tell* her, but why? What good did it do? No one knew about it but me. I wasn't cheating on her. There was no such expectation.

As Sabine's father doled out drinks, a boy approached. Based on Sabine's mother's admonishment, I assumed this was either Hugo or Lars. He was tall, lanky, and in that awkward teenage phase. It was laughable Sabine could have siblings so young. She seemed so much more mature than even Maggie, let alone these babies.

The kid pointed at me. "So, who is he?"

Sabine set her jaw, annoyed. "Malcolm, this is my brother. Hugo, Malcolm."

The other boy rushed over as Sabine's father finally handed us drinks. The contrast between standing only a few metres away from Her Majesty and this plastic cup was laughable.

The boys asked in unnerving unison, "Can I have some?"

"No," their father was quick to say.

They pouted.

Sabine rolled her eyes. "And Malcolm, this is Lars. Lars, Malcolm."

"You're the old bloke, right?" Lars asked.

Well, that was a kick in the teeth.

Sabine slapped his arm and corrected him in a language, sounding like French.

"What? He's old."

"He's not old. Hush!"

"I'm the old bloke, yes." I relented.

He was just a kid trying to get under Sabine's skin like a typical younger sibling.

"You're Sabine's boyfriend?" Hugo asked.

I looked at her, not sure how to answer.

"Oh, that's a no!" Lars snickered.

"No, no. I am. We just... it's not a big deal," Sabine said.

I nodded like an idiot. Well, I almost got us into a bit of a pickle.

"Meh," Hugo said.

"If there's no booze, I'm leaving," Lars concurred.

The two stalked off. I survived.

"You need to be better at this," Sabine said. "You are my boyfriend, remember? Or are you getting cold feet?"

"I am sorry, Sab. I fucking froze."

"You could certainly show me some interest, as well. You didn't so much as hug me when you got here."

"I was trying to behave around your family."

"Everyone knows we're shagging. You can relax."

I flushed.

"Oh, stop it. It's nothing. Margaux will eventually adjust, and Mum and Aunt Greta found it entertaining."

"What of your father?"

"He's a bloody painter. He's bohemian. He could give a flying fuck."

I laughed. Well, that was a relief.

"I will do better," I promise.

"You'd better or you're getting none of me later."

"Oh, you're calling the shots now?"

"My turf."

"Uh-huh," I said. "We'll see about that later."

Our foreplay was cut short by the arrival of two more. One I knew as the Queen's youngest brother, Prince Jamie. He was more than a decade her junior. He had less than a decade on me, in fact. There was a beautiful brunette on his arm who I didn't recognise.

"Uncle Jamie, hello," Sabine said. "Back from the States?"

He nodded. "Back, finally. Your mother is giving me grief."

"Join the club. I should introduce you to my new boyfriend, Malcolm Ferguson. Malcolm, this is my Uncle Jamie."

I bowed slightly. "Your Royal Highness."

"Jamie, please." He shook his head. "Pleasure to meet you."

"Uncle, who is this delightful creature?"

"This would be my girlfriend, Jessica."

Jessica smiled broadly and extended her hand first. A no-no.

Sabine looked at her hand and was a good sport. The girl was American by the sounds of it. She didn't know better. Of course, Jamie should have taught her how to handle things.

"Nice to meet you," Sabine said. "And will you be staying on?"

"We will be travelling for a few weeks," Jessica answered. "I have found London very dreary to date, but Jamie is insistent these races will cheer me up."

"I plan to bring her up to Balmoral as well later in the season."

"Will you bring her to Goodwood?" Sabine asked. "You certainly *must*."

"I don't think so. Maybe Cowes. Malcolm, do you sail?"

"I do. We go to Cowes most years," I answered. "My parents spend more time down there than I do. We have a sailing yacht and a house."

Sabine looked at me, surprised.

"What? You didn't know?"

"Well, no, I did not. See, Uncle Jamie, you have a friend now!" Sabine laughed.

"So, obviously, you will join us for Cowes, then," Jamie said to his niece.

"We'll see. I prefer to lay out on yachts rather than watch races."

"Same here," Jessica said in an overly-familiar tone.

The girl was out horsed. She needed some work.

"Well, it was nice meeting you, Malcolm. We're going to keep making the rounds."

The two left.

"She's doomed," I said.

"She's out of her element. She seems nice. She's pretty. Jamie was the perpetual child. I swear he's only just grown up. It's nice he has a girlfriend. Mummy babies him to no end. He's not much older than you, of course. People forget that. Aunt Chloe and you are very close in age."

Chloe was the product of the late King Fred's second

marriage. After losing a wife in childbirth and being widowed, he became king and remarried now-Dowager Queen Georgina, a delightful woman I had yet to meet. Their child, Chloe was, indeed *quite* close in age to me.

"Do you enjoy pointing this out?" I asked.

"I relish it," Sabine replied, swirling the liquor in her glass flirtatiously.

"You're treading on thin ice, Princess."

"I know. You love it."

"I have half a mind to take you inside and—"

"What?" She cut me off. "Fuck me?"

I was surprised. I was intrigued. I wanted to follow through even if it was a dreadful idea.

"I thought we were trying to behave?"

"I thought we were madly in love?"

Madly in lust, more like it. Why did she make me want her *so* badly? Never in my life had someone broken me like this. She was irresistible. I could blame it on the fact that she gave head like a sex goddess or that her body was a fifteen out of ten. I could even blame it on the way she let me rough her up a bit, but it wasn't true. It was something else. There was some sort of addictive quality to Sabine I couldn't quite shake. Perhaps I never would.

"I'll make you wait," I told her. "Be good. And stop propositioning me or it will be worse for you."

She bit her lip. "Yes, Lord Ferguson."

CHAPTER 15
Sleeping with the Enemy

SABINE

The most important day of Royal Ascot for socialites was Ladies Day. This was when everyone paraded in their best outfits and finest hats. Dress code was taken to ridiculous standards. The entry to the impossible-to-access Royal Enclosure was a runway. All eyes were on Margaux and me as we made our way with our parents to open it. Our brothers were still too young to either care or attend. This was for the best. They wouldn't annoy us.

I chose a white, perfectly tailored summer dress along with a green and white hat. I looked like a million bucks. I wanted to win all the awards the press would grant. I wasn't *trying* to upstage my more conservative sister. Instead, I tried to take heat off her. She loathed this sort of thing. She lived for the horses and the race, much like our mother, but didn't care much for the parade. I relished it.

We'd been here for two days now. Malcolm spent little time in our box, building up the anticipation for the big relationship ruse. I planned on visiting the Ferguson box *first* and making an appearance on the balcony. It was supposed to look casual, but also prove that, yes, we were some sort of item, even if we'd never confirm it. Given that the Ferguson string was in direct competition with our own, it felt a little like sleeping with the enemy.

Malcolm met me at the box's entrance, escorting me. It was terribly posh. Not all in the enclosure were. Ours was, of course. I had seen the boxes of friends which paled in comparison to this. Malcolm's family had more money than God, having made what amounted to billions in railroad fortunes. Like any good old money family, they never spoke of it. And while they would have been new money a hundred years ago, they were now cemented. It had taken an heiress to marry in to make his family's estate better. And now, so long as no one fucked with the finances, they'd forever be on easy street. The box solidified it.

"You look divine." Malcolm gave me a quick kiss at the door.

He worked on being less robotic.

I found it so odd. The two of us were dynamite in bed together. We could talk for hours about *nothing*. I considered him a good friend. However, in public, he froze up and got so nervous. It dawned on me that Malcolm did not know how to be a boyfriend. He was so noncommittal that he had limited experience—even less than I. In one way, I found it frustrating. In another, I found it adorable. That was mostly because I liked upstaging him socially and didn't mind carrying a conversation. He rather seemed to approve.

"Thank you," I agreed. "As do you."

"I am ridiculous."

"No, you are handsome."

He was. He always was in a way that made me want him all the time. We was having sex everywhere the last two days. It was ill-advised and I was frightened we might get caught. Still, we'd gotten it on any time we had a moment to slip away. Combined, we were like horny teenagers. I knew that would end at some point, but for now, I rode the wave—and him—quite happily.

"You know you outperform Maggie all the time, right?"

"Trust me. She appreciates it. I am the clown. She is the steady-eddy. This has always been our dynamic, darling."

"I'd loathe Kiersten if she did that."

"Kiersten is gorgeous. She already does that," I said.

He gave me *the look*. The one that told me I was making him cross but not really. The way he playfully set his jaw made me want to kiss him. So, rather than wait, I did.

"Don't worry. I still adore you." I pulled away.

"What was that for?"

"To be convincing. You looked upset, as well."

"Do you think that makes it better?"

"I think it should."

"I cannot be around you without wanting you, so it's the inverse," Malcolm whispered. "But, really, I'm being rude. I should get you a drink."

I smiled. "Yes, well, you should. I'm your beloved, right? And I think the sun rises and sets with you?"

He snickered. "Well, you were saying my name in a *very* convincing manner this morning."

I blushed.

He shook his head. "Oh, don't be a Maggie."

Malcolm left, staring at a girl who *glared* at me. Oh, that *had* to be an ex. I didn't care if she fancied Malcolm or had longing feelings, but I did rather like provoking people. So, when he returned, a Pimm's Cup in hand, I kissed him with abandon in front of everyone in the box. I surprised Malcolm most.

He chuckled nervously as I pulled away. "You alright?"

"The girl over there... the blonde with your sister. Is she your ex?"

He looked at me, surprised.

"We shagged on and off during uni. She's one of Kiersten's mates now. Like a posse of petty women."

I chortled. "Malcolm, that's dreadful."

"You don't know them. Why? You jealous?"

"Hardly. She was glaring at me. I read into it. But I don't care. Fuck her if you like."

His face dropped. I wondered what about that he didn't like? Then, with no warning, his tone changed.

"No, no. She's... well, compared to my current girlfriend, she's nothing to write home about."

Malcolm's father approached. That must have been it.

"Your Royal Highness, you joined us?"

"Yes, Your Grace. I came over to the dark side. My loyalties are divided today between Rare Coin and Mercury Trace today," I replied.

"Well, you should be assured that good old Mercury will pull through. Have you placed your wager?"

"Not yet. I thought Malcolm might take me down. I must collect Maggie, though. She wants to come down with me. We've done this together the last few years."

I could tell Malcolm was lukewarm at best on that idea.

"Can we persuade you, then?"

I debated whether I should tell him what I *actually* thought of his chances after reading the racing form and thinking about the line breeding involved. *What the hell? You only live once!*

"I will say this. I think Rare Coin is probably my mother's best homebred. And I do not say this lightly. The paring was a match made in heaven. Copper Built, the mare, is long in the back but was a fabulous distance horse. Scarce Commodity does well at a sprint and has a nice short back. He's compact. Toby is a beautiful horse—one of the most beautiful you could ever see—and he has many gears."

"You'd say Mercury isn't in it then?" Niall asked.

I shrugged. "I am not a fortune teller, but I feel that you have sank yourself a bit with the linebreeding. Zenith was good stock, but he struggles to throw anything that can compete in less than a mile and a half. And Mercury has it on all sides. I'm not saying Toby is a perfect colt. He's not, but he has the capacity to be even faster on the break. Yes, Mercury can hold the line over a longer distance, I'd bet, but if you look at their workout times with breezing, I don't know he could keep up in a shorter race. You need more sprinters in your broodmare herd."

Malcolm stared at me, then his father, to see the reaction. His father appraised me for a bit before breaking into a grin and patting Malcolm's back.

"She's a keeper, Malcolm," he said with a hearty laugh. "This one is a keeper. Feisty. Opinionated. And she knows her bloodlines. Don't anger her."

"I do not intend to, father," Malcolm said, annoyed.

Niall soon dispersed, unbothered by my opinionated rant.

"You're miraculous," Malcolm said. "We'll be married by the end of the weekend at this point."

"You should only be so lucky," I joked.

"I could do a lot worse. You, on the other hand, could do much better."

I looked at Malcolm, shaking my hand. "I told your father his breeding program needs work. Why on *Earth* would he want me to join in on the family fun?"

"For exactly that reason," Malcolm replied.

CHAPTER 16
An Open Invitation

MALCOLM

We lost the Gold Cup, but somehow I managed to win. Or, at least, that was the line everyone floated. Sabine surprised me when she returned to our box to watch the race. It ended up being a bit of press heaven when she and Maggie playfully taunted one another up and down the row—their balcony catty-corner from ours. It was humorous. But it ended when the horse they called Toby raced forward, leaving ours in the dust. He won by ten lengths. Sabine was right.

Sabine's excitement was infectious. Yes, we'd lost, but here she was, bouncing off the walls excitedly. I couldn't help but kiss and congratulate her. She was just so fun and exuberant. Who the fuck was I these days? The press got exactly what they wanted out of us. Everyone was *convinced* we were together. And, in a way, I found myself wishing it were true in some sense. She was undoubtedly so much better than any other woman on offer. She was also a princess, that life sounded daunting, and I wasn't sure if I had it in me to keep that up. Plus, she'd even said she didn't care if I fucked someone else.

At that, my heart should have leapt. I should have been relieved. Instead, it felt bad. Or, at least, I had no desire to seek out anyone in the vicinity. She was heads and tails better than the rest. I could write it off on the animal attraction I had for her. That was, until that evening.

We were having dinner with her family at Windsor. We were seated near her uncle and his new girlfriend, Jessica. I had a bad feeling about that woman. She was pretty, but always seemed to know better than the rest of us. She was so out of place here yet did not want to learn any social norms.

"So, how have you found Ascot?" Sabine asked cheerfully.

"Well, it's fine," Jessica said. "I do love the fashion. The horses are adorable. But it's a bit... restrained."

"It is a bit uptight, yes," Jamie admitted.

"It gets easier. You'll like Cowes if you want something more relaxed," I offered.

"Yes but isn't it like... bitterly cold?" She grimaced.

"It can be," Sabine said. "Look, I know it must be a lot to take in. Give yourself a moment. Will you be in London for long?"

"We are off to France end of next week. We're staying with Chloe," Jamie answered.

"Oh, well, then, maybe early on you could come shopping with Maggie and me? We could show you around. Give you a bit of an induction. I bet it's overwhelming. I'm thinking a break to Harrod's and Selfridges couldn't hurt, yeah?"

Sabine was being so genuinely kind to this woman who I suspected did not deserve her charity.

"Well, I don't really *do* department stores usually."

I about recoiled, stifling a laugh. Here was a woman who claimed to be a socialite and "model" telling the niece of Her Majesty the Queen that she didn't slum it with her type. I was about to say something before Sabine, being ever-so-diplomatic chimed in.

"Well, I know. Small shops are fun, but the advantage is that you get a personal shopper who can look you up and down and magically determine the best looks for any occasion. They are like fairy godmothers! And it's not just about the shopping. We'd like to host you for a tea. Teach you about it, you know? Get to know you?"

"Well, I suppose if anyone would know what it's like to be an outsider it's you."

It took me a moment to realise what Jessica meant. I looked at Sabine. Her face fell. She was at a loss for words. Jamie looked at her, also panicked.

"I mean, just because you're not really one of them is all."

I wanted to shout the at the woman. I looked at Jamie, furious that he hadn't already said something to protect Sabine from that hurtful line. Instead, the man looked paralysed and frantic.

"You do realise she is one of them, right? Not you or I?" I gave a low roar.

I tried so hard not to shout.

"Well, I just mean... she's... Jamie was born in, but she was born to someone else. And... you know, that's what matters, right? But it's good. I mean, you're so lucky! So wonderfully lucky to be born into a family like this—"

I stopped listening. Normally-confident Sabine was gone. She turtled into herself. Unable to hear anymore and without her own uncle defending her, Sabine pushed her chair back and stood.

"I'm... I need a moment," she squeaked.

She stormed off.

I shot Jamie a look to suggest he should bloody well do something with this woman and went to somehow mend Jessica the Interloper's harm. I reached the corridor's end, staring in either direction, unsure of where Sabine went. I didn't have to wait long for directions. I could hear a woman's sobs to my right. I turned and found Sabine plopped down by a suit of armour, hiding. It hurt me to see her upset. She didn't deserve that.

"Oh, fuck her, Sab. She's a real bitch." I sat by her.

Sabine collapsed into my arms, sobbing for what seemed like ages. It was slightly awkward. Was I supposed to hold her now?

Was I a genuine source of comfort? Should I act indifferent or not too attached? In the end, I chose to lean into it and to hold her. The smell of her shampoo was comforting. I didn't resent her in the least now. I *wanted* to stand up for her.

"I was just trying to be nice. I know she didn't mean it," Sabine sniffled.

I handed her my pocket square.

"Malcolm, this is silk," she shook her head.

"Oh no! What shall I do! I might need to go to the dreaded department store to buy another," I joked.

She giggled, wiping her tears. "Good one."

"I try. Sometimes, they land, Sab."

"I hate when people say I am lucky," Sabine said. "I hate it. It implies that my birth family wouldn't be enough or that I'm only allowed to be here because people tolerate me—like a charity case."

"You know that isn't true, right?" I asked. "Because your parents love you dearly—all of you. And your aunt is the same. You're wonderful, Sabine. Amazing. So, they are lucky to have *you*."

"I know they love me. And I am grateful my family is so good. But you really think *they* are the lucky ones?"

I brushed hair from her eyes. "Yes, of course. Because you are a laugh. You are too kind. You only want everyone to be at ease. You're also very clever—the cleverest. Of course, they love you!"

I realised at that moment that maybe I might, too. The words weren't a farce. My feelings weren't, either. She was lovely. I hated to see her upset not because I worried I might not get laid later, but because it pained me. She had no idea how much I did like her.

I leaned in and kissed her on the forehead. It was tender, pure almost. There was no ill intent. I just wanted her to know I cared and meant it.

"Malcolm, I—"

She didn't get to finish her thought because Maggie appeared.

"What happened?" Maggie demanded. "Why are you crying?"

"Jessica said something," Sabine waved it off.

"What?" Maggie asked protectively.

"I don't want to get into it, okay?"

Sabine reached out to Maggie, who helped her up.

I stood.

"I'm gonna..." Sabine shook her head, as if getting herself back together. "I will freshen up and see you both again in a moment. Let's just... ignore her, okay?"

We both nodded, watching Sabine disappear.

"That woman implied your sister wasn't one of you. She said she wasn't, in fact. And then told her she was lucky."

Maggie let out an angry groan and paced. She stopped and shook her head, arms crossed. Despite her very small stature, the girl was impressively intimidating when cross.

"I think your uncle should make Jessica apologise. I tried my best to stand up for Sabine and I talked her down, but... it was cruel. All your sister did was offer to show her around and include her in a shopping trip. Jessica was rude and ungrateful."

"How *dare* she!"

"Yes. I am livid right now!"

"I can tell."

"Can you?" I asked.

"The vein in your neck is popping out and your hands are in fists, so yes," Maggie said. "Calm down, prince charming. We'll handle it. I am glad you are taking care of her. In the past, anytime someone found out she could be complicated, they would leave. Even pretty can't overcome crazy or some such."

"What?"

"Men are dogs. I suspect you know that, Lord Ferguson."

I smirked. "Yes, a bit. She is a good person. A kind, good person. Yes, she likes to play it off with laughs, but she's genuine as they come. She deserves better."

"She gets that from Dad. But that self-deprecation? It's a coping mechanism. She goes into full court jester and beats down the pain. Or, rather, she compartmentalises. She can fix all the things around her, but she doesn't want to work on her own things. She never wants to complain. She deserves to be taken care of, Malcolm. I hope you know that."

Maggie's words were terribly direct. I felt like she was a father dressing me down for bringing his teenage daughter home too late from a date.

"Yes, yes, ma'am," I said.

"Do you like her?"

"Of course. Yes."

"Be good to her. Really. Or, so help me, I will come for you. Here's the thing, I don't have to like you, Malcolm. I need no reason to *dis*like you. Got it?"

"Got it. Yes," I said.

CHAPTER 17
Birthday Boy

SABINE

Malcolm and I went our separate ways for a couple of weeks. He was very busy with a court case. I joined my cousins on the family yacht in France. I wasn't bored. Instead, I ended up in bed with one of my cousin's hot air force buddies. Men home on leave were *very* giving and no one seemed to mind the fact that I was *supposedly* in a relationship. It felt a bit exciting to be doing what people assumed was cheating. But, given that my male cousins didn't care. I insisted it was fine, no one said anything.

Thankfully, I was travelling *without* Maggie. That would have been a total buzzkill.

Malcolm and I had stories run around in the press about a legendary breakup. So, we decided to be seen together, out for dinner for his birthday. I even bought him a proper present—a watch since he loved them—and played the adoring girlfriend well. I suspected he was also busy with other people while I was out. Still, I missed our conversations.

"I did miss you," I admitted.

"Oh?" he looked at me, brow furrowed.

"Don't lose your mind over it." I took a long sip of wine. "No, no, darling. It was nothing like that. Instead, it was just a lack of exciting conversation that threw me. I missed our chats, I think. Is that odd?"

"No," Malcolm said. "Not at all. I rather missed them as well. Thank you for arranging this. I feel a bit silly sitting down for a birthday with my much-younger girlfriend, but it is nice."

"Why silly? Don't you know I adore you? And it's nice to talk to you like a friend?"

He grinned. "Yes, I know. It is nice. I miss your wit. I miss gossiping about boring people with you as well."

"Jamie did apologise," I confirmed. "I meant to tell you, but we never got to chat."

"Good. Did Jessica?"

I shrugged. "It was half-hearted. I think she digs in when confronted with the fact that her words have meaning. She views me as a child."

"You aren't," Malcolm said. "Not at all. Look at you. There is nothing about you that screams that. Moreover, you comport yourself with more self-respect than most people twice your age. I admire that about you, Sabine."

I was touched by what he said. Rarely did I receive kudos on that. Most people simply viewed me as wild or divisive. Malcolm appreciated it. I blushed.

"Oh, stop. You know that. Deep down, Sab, you do."

I smiled, "Yes, darling. I suppose. But it is nice to hear it from a man for once—from anyone, really."

"People don't get either one of us."

"That is why we get on so well," I said. "We're both reckless, but ultimately good. The world just isn't prepared for people like us."

He chuckled. "Yes, that's it."

When dinner finished, I asked, "Can I come back to yours?"

He shook his head. "That will be a scandal, Sabine."

"Well, I don't really care, Malcolm."

"Fine. I suppose if we are dating, it's fine."

I shrugged. "Yes. Totally normal. Yes, you are damaging my already dodgy reputation."

He shook his head.

"What? One of us must be the angel and the other the devil. You got the better sister."

"I do fancy taking you, but after a proper drink. I'm in no hurry. I did miss chatting, and I like to wind you up."

Malcolm left an impressive wad of cash on the table as we rushed to our waiting car. Paparazzi followed us for a few blocks before deciding they had what they needed to show we were out together. They'd made their money. I'd told the car to drive towards the palace first before doubling back and crossing the Thames. The press assumed he would drop me off as he had done in the past. Instead, I headed to his.

We arrived at Malcolm's. He decided to make us gimlets in the kitchen. He got domestic for the first time since we started this whole thing. I didn't mind it. I couldn't cook *or* make drinks. I was impressed he was capable.

"Where did you learn this?" I leaned on the kitchen island.

"Postgrad. A man told me I needed to wise up and do it to impress women."

"Does it work?" I sipped the drink.

"You tell me, Sabine."

I set it down and nodded approvingly.

"See, I have some good qualities."

I was about to tell him he had many, but the door buzzed.

Malcolm, confused, went to check.

"Yes, yes, that's fine," he hung up.

"The doorman says there is an old friend of mine down there. She's brought me a gift," Malcolm said, confused. "I can turn her back around if—"

"No, no, it's fine," I agreed.

Soon, a pretty, compact, and well-dressed little blonde arrived on our doorstep. She was not too far off in age from Malcolm, I suspected, and wearing a day dress fit for a board meeting. I was intrigued.

"Sabine, this is Estelle. Esty, most people call her. Estelle, this is Sabine."

"Sabine, lovely," Estelle had a thick French accent.

"You're French?" I asked.

"Ouais."

I switched over to Parisian French, apologising for my accent and that I was rusty. She told me I was darling, and we chattered on. It annoyed Malcolm.

"You know, I'm still here and my French is rather shit," he said.

"Oh, well, she's *lovely*, Malcolm. How did you find her?"

"We were introduced by our parents, of course," Malcolm said.

"I'm the badly behaved sister," I announced.

"She's fine. A riot," Malcolm said. "Can I get you a drink, Esty?"

Esty sat her bag down. She unveiled a bottle of posh champagne.

"Oh, I think we can drink that next," I declared. "Well, assuming I am staying?"

"You're going nowhere," Malcolm said. "Esty, do you want to stay on. Is that alright, Sabine? We were on a date, Esty—"

"Oh, I shouldn't bother you. It's a gift. I was passing through. I had a meeting. Figured I would stop since I never get up to anything. Nor do you ever stay out *too* late these days—"

"Correct. Sabine took me to dinner."

"Well, you really took me. I only planned it."

"Spoken like a woman," Esty laughed. "We do all the work, and they flash a card and take the credit."

I giggled. She was right.

"Please stay. I would love to chat," I said.

Malcolm looked annoyed that I was cockblocking him. I still

intended to shag him, but his friend was fun. And she'd come all this way.

We finished our drinks and moved onto champagne. Malcolm and I were now very lubricated with liquor. Esty played catchup.

"So, how do you two know one another?"

Esty looked at Malcolm, as if asking for permission or guidance.

"Oh, if you two shagged or dated... you don't need to apologise. It's nothing that will bother me," Sabine said. "We're not stodgy like that."

"Well, she's unique," Esty said to Malcolm. "Not your usual bimbo, Malcolm."

I snickered.

"We met in graduate school. And yes. We shagged. In fact, we got up to all manner of things. But now, I think it is safe to say we are friends."

"All manner of things? I want to hear more."

"Sabine, no." Malcolm shook his head.

"What? Perhaps, this is a kink? Perhaps it will work out for you?"

I laughed. "Oh, he'll get his. I invited myself back here."

Malcolm looked about to expire of embarrassment.

"I think it's hot. If he talks about someone else, fucks someone else, I only find it thrilling," I admitted.

"It *is* a kink," Esty said, excitedly.

"Why is that?" Malcolm asked.

"Because you come back to me and give it to me like it is your job," I answered. "There is something gratifying about that. I'm not saying I own you, but in some ways, you are addicted to me. Do not deny it."

He stared at me, surprised.

"Addicted to you? That is high praise, dear," Esty said as Malcolm and I stared at one another.

I wondered what he was thinking.

"It is true I cannot help myself around her," Malcolm said.

"She is enticing. And fun. And I shouldn't enjoy her as much as I do."

"Why not? She's gorgeous. Anyone would say that, Malcolm."

"Because I'm exactly the type of girl he doesn't want and he's terrified of commitment," I said. "As am I. And he's divine. I cannot say a bad word about him."

Malcolm stared at his empty glass. He took my glass and refilled both, bringing it back in silence.

"So, spill," I said, intrigued. "What is the worst you got up to?"

"Don't do it, Esty," Malcolm groaned.

"What, you don't want to tell her about the threesome with the model?"

"You had a threesome with a model?" I scoffed.

"Yes. It was fabulous. She was gorgeous. We were both in London at the same time, went out, and he took this girl home. I was staying with them. We were drinking, not unlike tonight, and somehow the three of us ended up in bed together."

"Well, that's one way to do it!" I announced.

"Have you ever?" Esty asked.

"Esty, be good," Malcolm said.

"What? It's a fair question!"

"No," I replied. "I would. The situation just never arose."

Malcolm's jaw about hit the floor. I assumed it was because he was interested in anything that happened *after* this point. However, he stammered.

"Sabine, you cannot... you never should."

"What? Because the press would find out?" I asked. "Malcolm, I've had sex with women. If that got out, it would somehow be *far* worse than whatever I got up to with two men or a man and a woman."

"I doubt that, but you must be discrete, that is all I am saying."

"Last I checked you weren't my father, nor did you have any say in who I shagged!"

Esty quietly said, "Discretion is part of it. I wouldn't recommend bringing home a model. You shouldn't struggle, though."

"She's... it's complicated," Malcolm said.

Wanting to poke the bear and annoyed that he felt the need to baby me and gatekeep, I stood and walked to Esty's side of the room. I sat by her, staring only at *her*. I had no idea who she was, but she intrigued me. She was hot enough, but I sensed that for both of us whatever we got up to was not what we were after. We were both in this to titillate or irritate Malcolm—possibly both. Neither of us spoke. She played with my hair and then palmed my face before leaning to kiss me.

Malcolm *said* nothing. I felt him watching us, his eyes boring holes into our skulls. After all, he had two women on his couch who he previously fucked snogging like desperate teenagers. It felt good. Did I particularly want to go down on her? No. I wasn't in that head space at present, but it felt good. I could probably get there in time, but this felt amazing. And knowing that whatever I was doing both made him hate and adore me had me running on a high.

CHAPTER 18
The Boundary

MALCOLM

I watched in sheer disbelief as Sabine and Esty disrobed on my couch, excluding me from whatever this was. Every so often, Sabine looked my way. She did so now, panting as Esty kissed her neck. She lay back, Esty kissing her, pinning her to the couch. Esty pulled one of Sabine's breasts out of her bra and sucked on her nipple. That always did it for her. Sabine moaned, looking at me. Part of me hated this. Part of me wanted to join them. Most of me wanted to be there. Esty did like a good threesome. In fact, it was one of the *highlights* of my twenties.

Esty was a lot like Sabine. The difference was she could never have been satisfied with something like Sabine and I were up to. She travelled nonstop and didn't *date*. We partied together and she'd fly through town, fuck me, and move along. We were good like that. She was a businesswoman first. I was a reliable lay who worked too much. We had that in common. I suspected that was what she was up to when this evening began. Of course, now, she was all over my girlfriend and headed south to the border of Sabine's knickers.

Fuck! My *girlfriend*? Was she now my girlfriend? I'd just thought it. Oh, that was a head trip!

Esty asked Sabine in French, "Can I?"

Sabine looked at me, her chest raising and falling quickly and deeply. She looked beautiful like this. It was how I liked her best. By this point, she'd be begging me to be inside her.

"Can she?" Sabine asked.

"Is that what you want?" I asked.

"Well, what do you want from me, darling?" Sabine choked out.

By now, Esty was running her finger around the lines of Sabine's knickers, tickling her.

"I am not going to stop you."

Esty turned to me now. "I just want to make her cum. Then you can do what you'd like with either one of us. Or both. Preferably both."

"Will you let her make me cum?" Sabine panted.

"I will be glad to let you watch. See how it's done," Esty joked.

I wanted to tell Esty no and that she was interrupting my evening, but what straight man would do that? This was a wet dream. It was pure fantasy. I could have *both*. And why wouldn't I?

"Get her off, but I guarantee I'm better," I said.

"Touché," Esty said.

She kissed Sabine again, reaching her hand in between Sabine's legs. Sabine shuddered as Esty pulled back, their lips almost touching. Sabine bit Esty's lip, playfully. They continued kissing. I was rock hard, wishing so badly I could join, but that was all part of what the two of them were doing. They wanted me to suffer.

Esty pulled away, muttering something in French I didn't understand, before kissing her way down Sabine's torso. She removed Sabine's panties and licked Sabine's very swollen clit. It may have been for my benefit in many ways, but Sabine was aroused.

"Oh, fuck," Sabine gasped. "Fuck that feels good."

Esty continued, her arse in the air. She was hot, too, but most of my attention was focused on Sabine's face as she writhed in pleasure. Sabine looked over at me as her breathing quickened. Her face flushed along with her neck and chest. Then, she started to moan louder and louder, gripping the pillow behind her head. Esty continued. And, looking me dead in the eyes, Sabine came. Her eyes then rolled back in her head. Her toes curled and finally, done, her legs twitched and fell.

It was one of the sexiest things—if not *the* sexiest thing—I had witnessed.

Sabine giggled. "Happy fucking birthday! Now, fuck her and take me last. I want to watch."

I wasn't sure how I felt about that. Esty was fun. She was beautiful. But, in this scenario, she wasn't who I wanted.

"Fuck me from behind and I'll continue," Esty said. "Make her cum again."

"Oh... okay," I said. I raced to find two condoms, totally unprepared for the *wild* turn of events that had become this evening.

Returning, I realised they had not waited for me. They were back to kissing. Sabine was now fingering Esty who was braced on top of her, moaning into Sabine's mouth. Again, it could have not been hotter. And, yet I was strangely jealous. Who was this girl? Who was she in that she could fuck someone else in front of me so brazenly and get away with it.

Esty pulled away from Sabine's kiss and let out a scream, swearing in French loudly. She stayed over top Sabine for a minute before Sabine looked over at me. Quite literally, I was there with my dick in my hand waiting.

"See, I warmed her up for you," Sabine said, playfully.

"I can see that. I was worried I may never get invited," I said.

Esty settled back in between Sabine's legs. "You want me, then?"

"Yes, please."

"He tells you please, but I never get such kindness," Sabine pouted as she lay, breath quick.

"You're bad and you know it. This is further evidence. I positioned myself behind Esty.

"I'll be a good girl, I promise," Sabine said.

"Fuck me," Esty said, almost annoyed at our banter.

I pressed my hands into either side of her arse and slid myself inside her. She was wet, no doubt because Sabine had just gotten her off. I was less focused on Esty than I was on Sabine who, again, was engulfed in pure pleasure and whatever this fantasy was.

She stared up at me and moaned, "Oh, Esty, make me cum."

I wanted so badly to tell her off for that, but she was doing it for my benefit more than likely."

Esty came quick, her face still buried in Sabine's pink pussy. God, I wanted Sabine so bad. I needed her.

I couldn't look at Sabine anymore. If I did, I would cum. In fact, if I kept going like this, I would cum. Sabine came again, this time pulling Esty's hair. I could only stare at her hand in Esty's blonde locks as I heard her ramp up and cum hard.

Esty pulled back, somehow satisfied, "Now you fuck her."

I smacked Esty's arse, as I normally smacked Sabine when I wanted her to flip over or do something else. It was old hat at this point.

"Get on top of me," I said to Sabine.

"What will you do?" Sabine asked Esty.

"Watch," Esty panted. "Watch what you do to him. I want to see who makes you cum harder. And who makes you cum more."

"It's not a competition, Esty," I said as Sabine straddled me.

"Well, it could be," Sabine said. "Either way, I win."

It was true. Sabine was winning in more ways than one right now. She took me inside her and bent down to kiss me. She felt amazing. Tight, wet, warm. And her lips pressed to mine felt less lusty and more loving. It was more tender. The view was spectacular, but I tried to look at her face more than anything. If I stared at her tits bouncing around, I would cum in no time.

"Fuck me, Malcolm," she begged. "I've been so good."

"You have been *so* bad, Sabine."

But I did fuck her.

"Fuck me harder!"

I helped pump her until her nails dug in and clinched tighter.

"Oh, God, Malcolm. I'm gonna... I'm gonna... squirt!"

Then she let out a very loud scream they could have heard across the river. She collapsed on top of me, giggling. She kissed me and I smiled at her. I still hadn't cum yet, but somehow it was all good. She was dripping down my balls. We probably destroyed the couch. I didn't care.

She hopped off. I was getting cross at this point. She now buried *her* face in between Esty's legs, where I had just been, and went down to business. I was confused. Did I fuck her? Was I allowed to fuck her. I was jealous and still hadn't cum yet. Sabine turned back.

"Are you going to fuck me?"

"Yes, please." I replied.

"Go on!" Sabine said, impatiently.

I slid back inside. She felt so good this way. But, instead of looking at Esty's face as I had Sabine's last time, I stared at Sabine's milky white arse, noting the familiar mole right below her left hip. It was lovely as ever. I pulled her hair. Sabine came again staring back briefly, but Esty didn't want her to stop, pushing Sabine's head down. The sheer act brought me as close to orgasm as I could come. Still, I had another idea.

I pulled out, tossed the second condom aside next to the first and wanked until I came all over Sabine's arse.

As I did, Esty came, screeching for whatever God she prayed to. Sabine stopped and looked back at me.

"You're dreadful. I didn't tell you that you could do that, did I?"

"No," I answered. "But I was marking my territory."

To my surprise, the two *kept* going. Women were so bizarre. How were they not *exhausted*? So, here I was, trying to clean up Sabine's arse with kitchen roll while she was still going down on my fuck buddy. I should have been grateful, but really wasn't.

It should have been hot beyond measure. It should have been the pinnacle of sexual fantasy. It was. I'd probably think about Esty pushing Sabine's face back in her pussy for a long, long time, but really, I was done. I wanted to cuddle Sabine and talk about stupid things like political scandals and clients I hated. That was what I wanted. Not this nonsense.

CHAPTER 19
The Morning After

SABINE

The morning after our threesome, I was in a good mood. Esty left soon after we wrapped up. Malcolm was unlucky in that he couldn't continue. However, Esty and I did just that for a bit longer. She was hot, I was into it, and Malcolm enjoyed it. Then, Malcolm and I fell into bed together. He held me tight, and I drifted away as I was wont to do with him these days. It was undeniably hot, and I had ticked a box. Esty was not the type to squawk, and she appeared clueless as to who I was. At least she didn't care.

I woke the next morning, kissing Malcolm's shoulder as he slept facing the window. I wrapped my arms around him and ran my hand to his cock. I wanted to make good use of morning wood. He'd be plenty rested to continue. I was insatiable.

Malcolm stirred as I kissed his neck, mumbling, "I have work to do, Sabine."

"What?" I laughed. "It's a bloody Saturday—"

"I've got work," Malcolm did not turn to face me.

Something upset him. He got out of bed and walked towards the shower. Dumbfounded, I followed him.

"Mal, what's going on? Was that not the best birthday present ever?"

He stepped out of his shower. "I felt like a guest."

"Malcolm, you got to watch her get me off. And you got more of me *and* her—"

"You seemed to be enjoying her more. You never quit," Malcolm said. "I came back and the two of you carried on."

"Well, I figured it would be fair," I said. "Was that not... isn't that all men fantasise about?"

"I... uh... I did. I do. I will. But I don't like sharing you. We're not doing that again."

"Alright," I said. "We? Malcolm, the two of us don't own one another—"

"Sabine, you were on *my* turf fucking someone else. There are *boundaries*."

"Boundaries? Malcolm, I asked you—"

"You already started! Would I deny you? And if I had?"

Malcolm's jaw was set and his tone harsh. He was nearly shouting.

My lip quivered and I felt tears coming on. "Yes. I would have. I wouldn't have done something you were uncomfortable with. You said—"

"Well, maybe I shouldn't have. I think it's best you leave, Sabine. Maybe you aren't getting it. It crossed a line."

"Oh... okay," I turned.

I put on my various items of clothing strewn around the living room. I was thoroughly embarrassed. He made me feel cheap. Maybe I crossed a line, though? I thought he was into it. He certainly *seemed* into it. But had I like... forced him? It wasn't cheating. It couldn't be, right?

I left his apartment via the underground carpark and hid under a blanket in the boot to get back into my own house. I felt awful. I was embarrassed. I went straight to bed to hide from Maggie's wrath. She would no doubt give me shit about my poor choices.

Maggie arrived around noon, bursting in, and flopping into bed.

"Where were you?"

"I went on a date with Malcolm," I answered.

"Oh. Well, what happened? You alright?"

I wasn't sure what to say. Were we calling this a breakup? What was it?

"I am hung over. We drank too much," I answered.

"Ah."

To my surprise, she didn't whinge.

"Why are you in a good mood?" I asked.

"No reason. I just got back from Wales."

"Ah," I said. "Did Keir fly you?"

Maggie rolled her eyes.

"Maggie, you are thirsting for him. Just bloody well admit you'd like to jump his bones. Why not make a move? He stays with us when we're out doing these runs. You could have Marilyn set it all up for you—"

"I couldn't possibly! Besides, as much as I find him fit and like our chats, he's older than I am."

"Malcolm is even older. You can manage."

"Well, he's more... experienced, I'd suspect."

"You've been with less people? Who cares. In sex, it's not that crucial. You can learn on the fly. And you're beautiful. He'd be lucky to so much as see you naked. I'm sure he'd concur with that."

Maggie blushed.

"You want to see *him* naked, don't you?"

"I'd rather not tell you things. I don't kiss and tell!"

"Oh, we *must* get you laid. And by the hunky pilot. God, he's gorgeous. And dimples. Such amazing dimples. Yes. You need him."

"He would know."

"Well, who cares if he knows? Some men would jump at the

chance to have you. Many, I'd suspect. You don't have to tell him. You don't owe anyone that information."

"Really? But what if I am bad?"

"You could be having sex for years and be dreadful. Trust me, darling."

"Fine, fine," Maggie agreed. "But I doubt it will come to fruition."

"Well, let's think of ways to *make* it so."

"Okay. But, in the meantime, we have a busy week ahead. And then we must get down to Cowes."

She pulled a face.

"Yes, oh how *horrid* that shall be." I rolled my eyes.

"I don't want to be around Jessica," Maggie protested. "I loathe her."

"You are incapable of loathing someone, my love."

"Not true! I can loathe! I hold grudges!"

"Well, I do, too, but I don't have one against her."

"Malcolm does. Mark my words. I may have had misgivings, but he will come for her."

My stomach fell. I wanted anything but to think about Malcolm right now. Still, I wanted him to apologise so we could have hot, hot makeup sex. But maybe we were over now? Maybe we were done? If he decided that, it was fine. He was allowed to. I wasn't supposed to be invested. However, I'd never been dumped before... much less by someone like Malcolm. The fear of being cut off hurt. And, to my surprise, it wasn't about the sex or even a concern for how it appeared on a social level. It felt like I was losing something big. I didn't want to lose him.

CHAPTER 20
Grovelling

MALCOLM

After Sabine left, I didn't hear from her for a week. I had to sit with what I had done. She rarely ever rang me in any circumstance, but to hear *nothing* from her was odd. To make matters worse, I was supposed to host her family at our home in Cowes for dinner in a few days. Moreover, she was supposed to stay with *me* during the week. I was supposed to drive us to Goodwood. Those was the plans, but now what?

I arrived in Cowes second, after Kiersten.

"So, is the Princess staying with you? Or should we prepare another room to insinuate you aren't up to something?"

She referred to the fact that I had my own room at Windsor when we stayed for Ascot. I never slept in it, of course. No, I would much rather have been in bed with Sabine. I didn't care about keeping up appearances now.

"Stop it with that. Just call her by her name."

"Oh, someone is cross. Trouble in paradise with your child bride?"

"Kiersten, stop it. I realise that you think she's too young for me. That makes two of us—"

"Then why?"

"I don't know how to explain it," I said. "I feel completely and utterly invested in her. I don't get like this. It's some sort of magic. I am not sure if it is good or bad."

"You're in love with her!"

I shook my head, in denial.

"Uh-huh. That's why you fall all over yourself to impress her and make us behave ourselves within an inch of our lives when she's around. It's so disorientating! My scoundrel of a brother acting like a good boy for the sake of impressing who? The Duke of Kent?"

The Duchess. I didn't fear Simon. I feared Bethany. The woman was *fierce*. She could make or break me. Thankfully, our parents got on. It was the only thing shielding me from Beth's evil eye. She put up with me. I had yet to put a foot wrong before her. However, I expelled her daughter from my house after a threesome went awry. If Sabine squawked, then I was a dead man walking. Luckily, I suspected Sabine wasn't vengeful and had her own self-preservation to worry about.

"It's no matter. I think I've angered her."

"Sabine? Is it possible?"

I glared. "Kiersten, Sabine has feelings. Just like you or me. Why are you being such a bitch today?"

"I'm not being a bitch, you wanker!"

"You're acting like it. Leave Sabine alone."

Kiersten drew a long breath. "Sorry. I get protective of you because I think she's up to something. She seems... calculating. Dodgy."

"She is anything but dodgy. She's kind, generous, and gracious, Kiersten. She's not up to anything other than trying to fit in every day of her bloody life in a way her sister doesn't have to worry about. And the minute anyone points it out—that contrast, it makes her turtle inward. I added to that insecurity somehow and... I don't know how to say I'm sorry."

"Well, have you said you were sorry?" Kiersten asked.

"No," I replied.

"Well, don't be a knob. Ring her and apologise. And send her a gift. For the love of God, learn to grovel."

"Grovel?"

"Oh, I'm sorry, you are thirty-four and still haven't learned this rule. When a man angers a woman the way you seemingly have, he should learn to lay at her feet and beg for forgiveness. If you want to see her again or get back into her bed, you must try."

"I care to be back with her—not just be in her bed," I clarified. "That's not what this is about."

And, as I said it, I realised where I was. I wanted Sabine—really wanted her. My overreaction was unwarranted but justified by the fact that I loved Sabine. I loved her. It was the first time I had admitted to loving *anyone*. I always found myself pulling away. I always thought I was irreparably broken and unable to get attached. In fact, I didn't see that as a liability. I thought it was a superpower until now when I stared down the reality of living without Sabine. I didn't want that. I wanted her. I suddenly didn't care about the issues of her station and all of that. I just wanted *her*.

I wasn't willing to tell her I loved her yet. I chocked that up to the fact that I still feared my confession would run her off. I was frightened she'd destroy my fragile heart. This was new and terrifying. I wanted to have her to myself. Even that might be too much, but the idea of sharing her with anyone ever again if we were a thing was unappealing. It wouldn't work. The more I tried to make it work, the less I liked it. The more I wanted it to change.

I had two days to get this into gear and make her not hate me. I rang her to apologise, but Maggie fobbed me off. So, Maggie knew something was up. Great. I wasn't sure whether I feared Beth more than Maggie at that moment. They were both intimidating in the worst way. Who knew that I could fear women so tiny in stature? The truth us, they were easily addled and protective. The family always protected itself. I was a rank outsider as much as any man on the street. It was humbling. I had *no* leverage in Sabine's world.

So, without any luck getting her on the line, I did the next best thing. Sabine loved to be spoiled—deserved it now. So, I pulled out all the stops and prayed it would work. I spent a great amount on my misstep. I told myself it was a learning experience. And then, I could only wait. She'd either ring me or not.

Twenty-four hours later, I heard nothing. I was worried she wasn't on her way. I was unsure how to explain this to my family. How could I even explain it? Yes, so we were fake dating, but now I wanted to *really* date her. And yes I acted out after a threesome I should have gone mad for. I lashed out and sent her away when she was most vulnerable. And, really, who does that? A monster. Malcolm Ferguson was a monster.

At this point, I was certain Sabine was never coming. I paced; my parents concerned about how I acted. Still, I never bothered them with my worries. I was afraid for their reactions. And, if she showed, it would all be better. Around three, a Mercedes pulled into the drive. I noticed the head of a pretty ginger poking from the drivers' seat. Sabine came.

My heart leapt. She'd come! Then, it fell. What if this was all about keeping up appearances? She was the best sort of actress. She could tolerate anything to save face. So, maybe it meant nothing? I stood there staring until my mother whinged.

"Malcolm, what is wrong with you? Go help her with her bags!"

I froze. My feet felt leaden. I left to assist her, panicked. The next few minutes felt monumental. Whatever happened now meant everything.

CHAPTER 21
Cowes Week

SABINE

"Hi." Malcolm approached, looking like a kicked puppy. He was contrite.

"Hi." I smiled slightly.

"So, are we doing this? Really doing this?"

I chuckled. "Malcolm, I am still a bit cross with you, but you grasped your behaviour was unacceptable. So, I'm here. Yes. We are doing this."

He nodded, dumbfounded.

I leaned in to kiss him, slowly. I had missed him, as much as he hurt me. Everyone got a mulligan, right? He'd sent me a lovely gift. I didn't need to forgive him, but I could see that he tried. He'd taken time and given me the same. In the past, men tried forcing the issue. That was when I pulled away. So, I kissed him to let him know I accepted his apology.

Malcolm smiled. "Thank you."

"You're too darling for me to complain about, Malcolm," I assured. "I loathe you for that. Making me feel like that."

He grinned cheekily. "Same for you, baby."

It was the first time he used a genuine term of endearment for me. I didn't mind.

"The gift was a nice touch. Even Maggie had a laugh."

"So, she doesn't want to punch me?"

"I tried not to poison that well. I told her very little. She figured it was a normal lover's quarrel. Which it was."

Malcolm delivered me a delicate Cartier watch inscribed, *I'm a knob. -M*

He knew he was. He admitted it. I relented.

"Don't think that's all I expect," I reminded. "I will need more of an apology later."

Malcolm kissed me. "Yes, yes. I plan to grovel more later. Whatever you want."

"I'd like a lot of things," I said.

I looked over his shoulder to see his entire family peering through the front window of the cottage.

"Darling, we have an audience. Maybe we should take my things in the house, yeah?"

Malcolm turned and shouted, "Go away!"

I giggled and hoisted my duffle bag. He took my large suitcase.

"You packed light," he joked.

"The rest of my luggage is coming down to Goodwood with my mother's and sister's. This *is* light," I said.

"Dreadful being a girl, isn't it?"

"Not really. I can get off endlessly when you're already spent."

It was true. We proceeded to his room, and he kissed me, as if we were separated for a year rather than a week. It felt amazing. I couldn't explain why it always put me into this dreamy, girlish headspace, but it did. I wanted him. Unfortunately, we knew the entire house was listening to whatever we were up to. So, we broke it up.

"I just want to change quick," I said. "I want to continue this later; I can assure you."

"We will," Malcolm said.

I hung up my wardrobe from my duffle bag and took out a

summer dress for dinner. Malcolm's family hosted mine for some fabulous thing. They were trying to impress us. If only they knew that my parents were most impressed by a good barbeque. We were simple people. Meat and fire were all we needed to have a good time. Malcolm zipped my dress, unprompted. It felt strangely *real*. We knew one another much more than two engaged in some sort of relationship plot had any right.

He kissed my neck, delicately, and spoke soft. "Can I ask you something, Sab?"

I turned. "Sure."

"I wanted to explain why I behaved badly the other day. It doesn't make up for it—"

"No, it doesn't."

"But I should explain. Sabine, I don't want to share you. I cannot share you. Whatever this is, it's crossed a line. I can understand if you don't want this anymore. I didn't intend to fall for you, but I think I have. I don't need you to give me an answer right now. Still, I want you to know where I'm at. I don't want anyone else."

"I did that for you, Malcolm. I enjoyed myself, yes, but... I saw an opportunity to make your birthday lovely."

He confused me. I thought this was male fragility, but it was more.

"I know. I should have been over-the-moon. It was a fantasy—the hottest thing a woman has ever done for me. It was good. But in the end, I felt *bad*. It wasn't you or Esty. She's fine. We had lunch. Same as ever. But even after that, I thought I'd feel better. I didn't. I only wanted to speak to you. I only wanted *you*. So, I cannot share you. I know that probably upsets you—"

I took a deep breath. "I guess it's fine."

"Fine?" He looked disappointed.

"No, not fine, baby. I mean, I'm fine with it. Malcolm, we said if one of us fell for someone, they'd be released from our previous agreement with no hard feelings."

"But I fell for *you*."

I wrapped my arms around his neck, interlacing my fingers tightly.

I looked him in the eye. "I know. Maybe it will take me a bit longer to wrap my head around it. I wasn't looking for this, but I think you could be enough. I worry about the end of summer with my school and workload. I'm not giving that up—not for you and not for anyone."

"I am not asking that, Sabine."

"I know," I said, convinced. "You don't own me."

Malcolm nodded. "Of course not."

I smiled. "Malcolm, you make me feel things. Wonderful things. I don't know if that will be enough long-term. I have neither a crystal ball nor a knowledge of what love feels like, but I can give it a chance."

He smiled. "I feel the same. I've never really loved anyone, Sab. This feels different. I'm not saying I love you. I am not ready for that, but if it happens, it happens."

I kissed him. "Good. For now, I am genuinely yours if you are genuinely mine."

"I am," Malcolm promised. "I don't deserve you."

I giggled. "You really don't, but I'm a sucker for an underdog story."

"So now what?" Malcolm asked.

"I guess we continue. Do the same thing for now? Reassess at the end of the summer when life gets mad again?"

Malcolm agreed. "That's wise. I feel so much better. I wanted to be honest with you. I needed to tell you."

"I appreciate you being honest, Malcolm. I will be honest with you, too."

It felt good. Something felt *right*. I felt like I could fall for him. I wasn't ready to confess that. I wasn't brave enough or prepared, but I meant it. I meant that for now, I thought we could be happy as we were. I thought that maybe, just maybe, I could fall for this hopefully reformed earl of poor repute. I trusted him. I believed he would be true. He knew better.

CHAPTER 22
Giving In

MALCOLM

If anyone told me I would end up *back* at Balmoral in August with Sabine, I would have said to fuck off. While summer was tumultuous, I left my work for a few days to join her at her aunt's castle. That was where it began. And I was somehow nostalgic. We'd spent the past few weeks together, virtually obsessed. I never saw anyone so much as I had her in these few weeks. I'd make excuses about work. Now, I was going to use the fact that I was partner to fuck off a bit. Sabine pointed out that what I wanted was to make Queen's Counsel—or QC—for the uninitiated. It was true. Her suggestion was to work smarter, not longer or harder.

And, while I never thought I'd agree, I gave it a try. I wasn't the desk jockey I was, but I was happy. There was more to life than keeping score of people I fucked over or cases I won. I could be a shark and lean into loving Sabine. Of course, I hadn't told her that *yet*. The end of summer bit at our heels now. In a few short weeks, London would be alive again with MPs and more court dates. Sabine would be on a law course at LSE. I knew how demanding that could be for her. I was only supportive, but protective of the time we *did* have.

And on the first morning of our few days in a moratorium from the real world, I was keen to spend the morning in bed, touching every bit of her. I wanted to devour her. It'd been only five days since I saw her last, but it was five days too long.

There was something different about this morning. I could pin and watch her give into the slow roll of pleasure. I could relish the way she looked at me. It was new somehow. Still raw. Still magnetic, but somehow sweeter in a way. It held meaning. Sabine's wild ginger hair fanned out. I kissed slowly, taking her in. It started out sweet, but she soon pleaded with me to pick up the pace.

Yesterday evening, I cared about our volume level, but I gave in. I would give her what she wanted, even if everyone knew what we were up to. Somehow, our feelings now legitimated gave me licence to take her any way I saw fit. And, anyway, she wanted it like this.

Sabine dug her nails into my back, her eyes rolling. Her back arched. It was always so good when she completely lost control. She came back down from the high, going to jelly. She'd reaching whatever pinnacle she climbed. I kissed her, unable to help myself. Her heart raced, and she breathed heavily, but she kissed me back. I pulled away, knowing this wasn't going to last much longer.

"Fuck, Sab. Fuck," I said, breathless.

I fell on top of her, spent. I didn't want to leave. It felt too good being inside her.

"Good?" She smiled at me as I perched above her.

I kissed her. "Yes."

I finally pulled myself together, dealing with the obligatory post-coital rigamarole. Part of me wanted to ask if we could just get rid of the bloody condoms now? We used them inconsistently at best, anyway.

When I returned to bed, I wasn't thinking about my desire to be in her unadulterated. It was the way she lay on her side, her arse facing me, her long hair now behind her like a red cloud. I couldn't help but want to crawl back in bed next to her and scoop her up. As I did, I felt the strongest urge to tell her I loved her. It was frightening. She would run. I was certain of it.

Instead, I pushed it off. "That was fabulous, Sab. You are the best."

Sabine bit her lip. She ran her finger down my chest. "It was great. Thanks for not going easy on me."

"Nah. I know you like it rough."

She looked down, closing her eyes. I felt her smile as she buried her head in my chest and held me tighter. The smell of her hair was intoxicating. It smelled like lemons. I hated to admit that I enjoyed it so much that'd I'd have slept in the same sheets for weeks to keep it that way when she was off to some far-flung place. It was odd. I never thought I would care about that.

"What shall we do today?" Sabine asked.

"Nothing," I chuckled. "Can we do nothing? Can I stay in bed with you all day? Keep you here naked?"

"Much as that would be wonderful, I think we are expected to participate in *some* sport apart from this, Malcolm."

I sighed. "I'd rather not."

"I know, darling. God, that would be the life. We can take a 'nap' later, I suppose."

"There will be no sleep."

"No. No sleep for the wicked."

I kissed her head.

"You really don't want to get out of bed?"

"I need nothing but you here like this," I said.

It was the truth. I wanted nothing more.

"You sound lovesick, Mal."

I was.

"I'm a simple man, Sabine. And any man would prefer this to just about all else, baby."

She looked at me. "Darling, you are silly. There is much to do here. We could go out on a ride."

"*Must* we?"

"You don't want to see me in a pair of breeches? Besides, we could get up to no good out there, too."

I knew we wouldn't. It was frigid. There is no way I wanted to fuck bare-arsed in a field. She would have to wait. I knew if I told her no to riding, she'd pout. And the pouting would work. It *always* worked. She was all too good at it.

"We can go out on a ride, fine."

We dressed and grabbed a quick breakfast. Maggie gave us the evil eye. She always knew what we were up to. I wondered if this was just the fun of having twins. I couldn't imagine having two sets. Her parents were mad as hatters. In the stables, Sabine chose us mounts based on my laziness and her adept riding skills. I marvelled at her arse. I did that practically every day, all the time. I couldn't help it. Any man would and I was weak.

We mounted and took a hack out on the expansive estate.

"Why do you loathe this, Malcolm?"

"I find horses troublesome, expensive, and heart-breaking," I said.

"Heart-breaking?" Sabine asked.

I took a deep breath. "Don't take the piss, okay? I have feelings, too."

"Sure. You're allowed feelings, darling."

"I had a horse when I was a teenager. A horse I loved. That was rare for me. I am not much for horses. They are unforgiving beasts."

"They demand the best versions of us, yes."

I chuckled. "You always prefer them to people."

"They are less troublesome than people, Malcolm. If you are good to them, they are generally good to you. They will be good to fault."

I nodded. "He was like that. We were bonded. I took him up. He was a fine hunter. He taught me a lot. He was one of my father's rejects. He'd been born one of my grandmother's favourites. That made him special to me, too."

"That's darling, Malcolm."

"Maybe a bit. Well, he got injured on a hunt. We hit a hole in a field. We went down. He fell in a way that protected me. I think he did it on purpose. But it led to him unable to stand. I was there, pleading with him to stand. I was in tears, frustrated, thinking that if I could just get him up, all would be well. He stood for me, but he was in such pain. Papa doubled back—"

"You call him Papa sometimes. Rarely. I noted this."

I blushed. "It seems ridiculous—"

"It's not," she chuckled. "We did the same growing up. It's not Dad in Quebec, so we used to always call him Papa. We still do if we speak to him in French."

I was surprised. "Well, he came back round. And he assessed things. We called out the vet. We couldn't bring him back. He couldn't walk. And I saw the pain in his face—"

"What was his name?"

"What does it matter?"

"It does to me. He was special."

"Harry," I said. "My grandmother always called them by people names. She was a bit mad."

Sabine grinned. "I can get behind that. My aunt does the same."

"It runs in the family. They were distant cousins."

Sabine nodded.

"We had to put him down in that field. I stayed with him to the end. And after that, I never wanted to get attached to an animal again. It was the worst feeling. You love so many of them. I couldn't be like that—so attached. I see them as bloodstock."

"That's sad, Malcolm. Love can hurt, but it's a beautiful part of life. I do care for many of them," Sabine said tenderly. "But you must love. Love makes life better even if it frightens us. I do love horses more than people. I'll grant you. Losing one is dreadful, but loss is a part of life. You cannot run from loving someone or something because of fear of loss."

Her words were poignant, whether she knew or not. I wanted

to tell her I loved her, but I beat it down. It wasn't the right time. I worried she'd take off to the stables. I avoided the words.

"Let's race," she changed the subject, sensing I was holding back.

I was glad for the reprieve.

CHAPTER 23
Scheming

SABINE

Margaux sat on the couch by me. She put her head in my lap and let out a long sigh before looking up.

"I loathe you," she grumbled.

"What did I do now?"

"You spend all your time with Malcolm. It just reminds me how devastatingly single I am."

"And if you had tried to impress sexy pilot and actually chatted him up, would you be so single?"

She grimaced. "It's not so easy."

"It really is."

"How did you charm Malcolm at that snap of your fingers then?"

I thought for a moment. "I stared at him."

"Stared at him?" she giggled, sitting up.

"Yes. We made eye contact. I dunno. I sense this sort of pull. Sexual chemistry is undeniable. And you have it with sexy pilot. Don't waste your chance. *Tell him.* We must be in bloody Cardiff for four days. Tell him."

She groaned. "Let's not think about work. We have another two weeks off. I'd like to enjoy it. Where is your boyfriend?"

"He's out with Papa and the boys on a hike."

"Heaven help him."

She said it because our father was known to outpace anyone. Simon Bouchard was tall and moved at an alarming speed. We spent our childhoods whinging about it. Mum almost didn't accept his proposal on the top of Mount Royal. She griped at him and was sweating profusely, something she hated. Still, she said yes because she loved him dearly. I hoped that if any man *ever* proposed to me, he would pick a moment when I wasn't an absolute mess.

"He'll be fine."

"Well, I will go out for a ride? Will you join me?"

"No. Cramps. Staying in today. That is why I did not give into Malcolm's pleas."

"Well, sucks to be you two. I forgot we're in sync again. Fuck our lives, right?"

"Oh, darling Mags, just don't sleep with *man-babies*. That is *not* a dealbreaker for everyone," I said.

She pulled a face. "No thank you."

"Don't knock it till you've tried it."

She shook her head and left.

I continued my quest to read by the fire like old days. As a child, the two of us curled up with books, competitively trying to eliminate everything from our reading list in the few weeks we stayed here. God, I loved it. Everything about it felt right. Malcolm rubbed my aching back to sleep last night. The way he looked at me this morning with nothing but care and affection, this book, my warm mug of tea—it was all perfection.

My mother and aunt appeared, laughing about something.

"Where is your sister?" Aunt Greta asked.

"She went to the stables. I'm waylaid by cramps. And the boys and Malcolm went out with Papa."

"Poor Malcolm," Mum said.

Aunt Greta snickered. "Has Maggie gotten less sour then?"

"No. She's bitter, possibly in love, and refuses to do anything about it."

"Love?" my mother asked. "What do either of you know of love?"

"She is completely head-over-heels with our pilot. She gets all silly and mumbly around him. She stammers and either says nothing or cannot stop her verbal diarrhoea. She's beyond help. He fancies her. I *know* he does. The way he looks at her and always comes back to talk... it's not average. He pretends to care I am there to keep things up, but... he's there for Maggie and Maggie alone. I wish I could move it along. I made him our permanent pilot with Marilyn's help, but Maggie is so useless."

"She's like you," Mum said to Aunt Greta.

"I eventually did make a move," Greta said.

"How? Can Maggie learn?"

They giggled.

"We had a power outage. Uncle Gary ended up back at ours. Remember, he was on staff for your grandfather? Well, we brought him back to ours. I went to ring Simon—"

"She was up to no good!"

"I came back to find them snogging like children," Beth said. "And never mind that he was *much* older and staff."

"We drank too much, Bethy."

"Yes, well, you may have, but you finally let your guard down. The power outage removed all the distractions. It made us start a fire and drink and chat. It made the difference."

"So, I should cause a power outage and get them drunk? I feel as though on a plane that's reckless," I said.

"No, no. Just help her."

Our cousin Christian passed through. "Have you seen my mum?"

"Uh Carrie went out to shop with Chloe," my mother replied.

"Oh. Brilliant. She told me to come find her after lunch. I got invested in something else and now—"

"Hey, Chris, question?" I blurted out.

"Yes, Sabine?" I was annoying him.

"That pilot of ours—Keir McDonough. Do you know him?"

"Everyone knows him. He bloody well outranks me. He's a star. Giving him preference to fly you lot around has not helped my star power at all. The guy can do no wrong."

"Brilliant. Maggie is in love with him. I am sure of it. How could we set them up?"

Chris stared, confused.

"Oh, that's a brilliant idea," our aunt agreed. "Chris, how would that work?"

"There's an officers' retreat. One of the other Scots is taking people camping. It's a bit of a drive and I don't much *want* to bring my baby cousin to tag along, but I am sure I could call in a favour from one of the girlfriends of another officer and say she's along to occupy the women or something."

"Oh, would you?" I asked.

"If I am doing this, I am getting laid. Your damn sister lacks any skills when it comes to dating. And she will not be the reason I don't—"

He looked at my mother and our aunt. "Shit. Sorry. I forgot you all were there."

"It's alright. Maggie is useless with men. I'll grant you. She's beautiful but painfully shy," Mum said. "It's why I *told* Malcolm's mother it would never work out. Of course, he took a liking to you, so it wasn't all a loss."

I blushed.

"Fine. I will ask her to come," Chris said. "But she loathes camping—"

"Malcolm and I are going to bore her. Tell her there are sexy young officers and you want to introduce her to your friends. Do not—under any circumstances—mention Keir will be there!"

"Why?"

"Because she'll run," Greta sighed. "I agree with Sabine."

"You owe me, Sabine." Chris left.

I beamed.

Mum was chuffed. "That was brilliant. Well done! She will never appreciate how much you love her."

"She will. Someday," I said. "We are always there for one another. We know that."

I knew that was true. Even if Maggie would be reluctant to tell me, she loved me more than anyone. She would eventually love me for this, too. I wanted my sister to be happy—happy like me. Or at least, how I was in that moment. Then, it all came crashing down.

A footman rushed in, looking nervous. "Your Majesty, Your Royal Highnesses, may I ask where Lord Ferguson has gone?"

I furrowed my brow. "He's out walking with my father."

"He is needed in Edinburgh, ma'am."

"What for?" Mum asked.

"His father is ill, ma'am. His sister just rang. The Duke had a heart attack. They would like him to return."

I was in total shock. Niall had a heart attack? But he was so well the last time we saw him. That wasn't but two weeks ago. How? And now, what happened. I stared at my Mum.

"You should drive him," Mum insisted. "He shouldn't drive himself."

"He doesn't have a car, so he cannot," I said. "I will go find him."

CHAPTER 24
The Worst News

MALCOLM

I made out Sabine's figure as she paced towards us through the garden, a cardigan wrapped around her. Her hair was wild in the humidity, but she was beautiful as ever. I wanted to swoop her up in a kiss after surviving what could only be described as a hike on speed. Her father was a mad man. I was dying, as were her brothers. In my book, hikes were relaxing strolls. Simon had other ideas.

But, as we approached, I realised her expression was drawn. She looked aggrieved. Something was wrong. My smile fell. She trotted up.

"Malcolm, you must come with me immediately."

"Oh, leave him. God, can you not even give him an hour?" Hugo whinged. "He's knackered."

"It's... it's an emergency," Sabine said.

"We were going to have a drink. You can join us," Simon said to his nervous daughter.

She said something to her father in French. He backed off.

"Malcolm..." she searched for words.

Sabine took my hand and led me to the side.

I stood, panting, trying to get myself together as the words poured. *Hospital. Edinburgh. Heart attack.* I was so confused. My blood ran cold. This wasn't what I wanted today to look like. I wanted to lie in bed with her this evening and make jokes about stupid chat shows. I wanted to fall asleep with Sabine in my arms, thinking the world was fine and we would be okay, but, right now, it wasn't.

When we arrived back inside, my bags were packed away inside a Range Rover that was waiting to whisk me three hours south. I'd like to say it was a delightful road trip with Sabine. Normally, it would be. However, this time, I said little. She said nothing apart from reassuring me she would get there fast as she could. She drove like a bat out of hell. It was as if everything changed and neither wanted to say it. One of us had to call it, but we were in a daydream. We'd been living a beautiful fantasy. Now, reality hit hard.

We arrived at the hospital, and I kissed her goodbye.

"It's... it's going to be complicated and frightening," I said. "You should be home with your family."

"I can help, Malcolm. Get people tea—"

"Don't take this the wrong way, baby, but you're going to be a distraction," I said.

She knew it, too.

She was tearful. "Tell your family I send my best. And... tell your Dad to get better soon. I will be thinking of him. We'll keep him in our prayers. He's going to be okay."

"Yeah," I said. "Sure."

"Malcolm, ring me. Later?"

"I will," I agreed.

I would but had no idea how that call would go.

I left the car and stood, staring at her, shaking my head. She cried. This was hard for both of us. I loved her with every fibre of my being. I knew it more than ever. I wanted to tell her that I loved her, and we would make this work, but I was a realist. There was no way I could manage whatever else I faced and her. She was lovely. She deserved a future that did not end with a horse farm and estate. She deserved a lively life in London, one I could no longer give.

I closed the door and took my bags. I found my sister and mother in father's room. They explained he had fallen over in a stable aisle only hours before. The ambulance rushed him to hospital, but the prognosis was uncertain. He was in surgery. Twenty minutes after I arrived, a doctor who looked about twenty entered. I was doubtful of the man's credentials when he said that my father had handled surgery well but that the damage to his heart was great. He was lucky to be alive, but he was experiencing heart failure.

"I expect he will have about a year," the doctor said.

"Until he is better?" I asked.

"No, sir. Until he passes," the doctor responded. "Heart failure."

My head fell into my hands. My mother and Kiersten sobbed. The room was suddenly very, very hot. I got up to walk. I roamed corridors trying to clear my head. My father was *dying*. He was lucky to be alive. I felt selfish and wrong for worrying about myself, but I was about to lose everything—my life in London, my job, and my girlfriend. I would never be able to keep Sabine like this. It was over.

I called her for a moment later that evening and told her my father survived surgery and no more. I was too tired to break it off and listen to her cry after spending an evening listening to the other women in my life sob. I was now in charge. My father needed me to be The Man. I had pretended I was until this point, but I had no idea what I was doing.

All of me wanted to climb into bed with Sabine and hold her impossibly close. I wanted to smell her shampoo and feel her warm body pressed against mine. I wanted to feel the calm rise and fall of her chest. I wanted to feel everything I had only hours before. Yet, all I felt was *pain*. I could not have her. We could not be. As soon as I had found the only woman who made me feel as though I wanted nothing else, I lost her. It wasn't even my fault. It couldn't be helped.

Two days later, I rang Sabine. It hurt more than anything to hear her cheerful voice on the other end—dear, sweet Sabine. I was only a few hours away, but it felt like an ocean between us—greater than ever.

"So how is he, darling?"

"He's... he's sick, Sab."

"I thought they made him better?" She asked it with childlike confusion.

So sweet and purely intended. It made it worse.

My voice broke, "They did... for now... but his heart is failing. They've given him a year to live, Sab."

"Oh, Malcolm, I am so sorry. How did that happen?"

"He never told anyone. He never... he never... he didn't want us to know. He wanted to carry it all around. And I'm sure he was waiting for us to stop being fuck ups, get married, and all that but... joke's on me, right?"

Sabine wasn't laughing. "Malcolm, you're not a fuck up. Don't say that."

"I am. And I'm even worse because what I am about to say... it's going to hurt."

"What? Why?"

I took a deep breath.

"Sabine, I can't do this. Not now. Maybe not ever. Maybe someday when things have settled, I can ring you like this and ask you out, but... sweetheart, you deserve better than what I can give you right now."

"Malcolm, I—"

"No. It's complicated and messy. I must give up practicing and move up here and—"

"So, we will just... make it work."

"Sabine, that will never be. Just admit that it will never be. I care about you too much to put you through that—"

"Don't do this," she cried. "Malcolm Robert Ferguson, do not—"

Her invocation of my middle name only made it worse. There was something so *normal* and *domestic* about her using it. Only someone serious would do that. No woman—apart from my mother—had ever done that.

"Sabine, it's for the best. You must trust me."

"Why do you think you should make decisions for me?"

"Because I have an idea of what is best."

"Malcolm don't do this! Please do not do this! Please don't!"

She sobbed. She pleaded. It hurt like nothing else. It was *this* that I had feared. I knew this would break us both, but in the end she would be better off. She was young, pretty, and had a life before her. I was old, bitter, and didn't deserve someone as wonderful as Sabine.

"I've got to go," I said. "Goodbye, Sabine. Take care."

She cried. I hung up.

I sat down the receiver and muttered. "I love you."

It was as if I needed to say it. I thought I might feel better about it. I didn't. It only burned more.

CHAPTER 25
Everything's Over

SABINE

I practically threw myself into my mother's lap, sobbing hysterically as I had not since childhood. I was so sad. So embarrassed. So everything. She was confused but settled me with quiet shushing. She rubbed my back and told me to breathe. I couldn't breathe. I couldn't calm down. I'd been crying for half an hour on my own, unable to come down.

"Sabine, my darling, what is the matter?" she asked.

I sat up, unable to speak without whimpering. "Malcolm just broke up with me."

"What?"

"He... he says that he... is... sparing me," I hyperventilated. "That he has to... give up his practice... and move back home... and we can't make it work."

"Oh, darling, how? Why?"

"His father is dying. Within a year. He's very sick. Malcolm says he doesn't want to burden me or some such."

My mother fell silent.

"I can handle something like that. I could make it work—"

"Sabine, you are much younger than Malcolm. He's lived more life than you have—"

"And I just..."

I looked for the words. I loved him. Did it even matter now? I loved Malcolm Ferguson. I knew it. I hadn't known, but I did now. I wanted to wake up with him every morning and go to bed with him every night. I didn't want anyone else. I wanted him to make me laugh. I wanted him to be grumpy with me. I wanted to gossip and joke. I just wanted him back. More than ever.

"He's doing what he can to protect you, Sabine, before it gets really... serious."

"Mum, it already has," I insisted. "We already—"

"I think this is the first time you've ever had a grownup relationship. And, as such, you're finding it exciting and wonderful—"

"Mum do not patronise me! Do not do that."

"Do what?"

"Baby me! I realise that I sought out comfort, but... I am a grown woman. I want to be in a relationship with him. He's not some old creep who needs to spare me. I am not a princess in need of saving from myself. I know what I want. Why is everyone trying to 'spare' me suddenly? Spare me from what? Happiness with someone who understands me and doesn't see me as damaged goods?"

"Oh, darling, no one sees you that way—"

"Mum, people absolutely do. Everyone whispers. Fuck! I mean, Jamie's girlfriend doesn't stop jawing on about how different or lucky I am. I get it from all sides. All Malcolm sees in me is pure perfection. He adores me. He spoils me. He sees me as an equal. Or, at least, he did until he tried to go all paternal to 'spare me' from whatever!"

"There are other men—"

"I don't *want* other men! I want him!" My voice echoed through my mother's sitting room.

It was unexpectedly powerful.

Mum furrowed her brow. "Sabine, you have never said that. I... I assumed it was just a summer thing."

"It may have begun that way, but... he wanted me for me. I wanted him for him. We were divine together. Yes, everything about it was fun and exciting, but it was also just... normal. Intellectually, he can keep up with me. And he's something good to look at. Do you know how hard it is to be both of those things and not be a lying wanker?"

Mum chuckled. "Yes. I know. Your father was a rare find."

I slumped into her lap. "My heart is shattered."

"I know, darling."

"He says maybe in a few years, it could work."

"Don't wait around," Mum said. "Really. Live your life. If it is meant to be, it will be. If it is not, it will not be. Maybe Malcolm just wants to get his affairs settled before he brings himself back to London and sees you again? Grief is complicated, sweetheart. And when you lose someone in a flash or find out they will be gone quickly, it is hard. It was impossible for Greta with Cecilia. Think about how complicated things were."

"And for you and Maggie."

"Yes, but those were growing pains. It doesn't compare to losing a child. And it didn't compare for me to losing my mother suddenly in my childhood. It wasn't easy. Malcolm isn't *that* old. I don't think he expected to be a duke so fast. He had a life in London—"

"Has a life. Can he not just... manage it from afar?"

"If it wasn't a working operation—one that prints money at present with its prospects going off to America—it would be fair to say it was a hobby and he could live on his inheritance. That isn't how his father ran it. I suspect even if Malcolm resents it now and feels out of place, he will take pride in keeping it up, Sabine. It's in your blood. It's the same reason we all stepped up after Cecilia died. It's why you always wanted so badly to care for Maggie. It's family. So, Malcolm had to choose his as we often choose ours. It's not that he doesn't care for you."

"But he—"

"Sabine, he is tender with you. Completely enamoured of you. His parents have never seen anything like it. You were a *godsend*. But Malcolm is right. If you go back there to him, you'll be expected to marry him and take over the estate as the current Duchess of Lauderdale. That isn't what you want. You have a bright future, darling. He's right. I hate to say it. I know it hurts, but he's right."

I knew it seemed easy this way. That he could leave. The hope was I'd move on and meet some other bloke who made me happy, but I knew that wouldn't happen. I would not feel this way about anyone else. I was convinced that I would still feel just as much for Malcolm in a year as I did that day. And that didn't change in the coming months.

CHAPTER 26
Sweet October

MALCOLM

I was a weak man with poor coping skills. Normally, I'd run off to scoop some random girl home after a breakup. That was complicated in more ways than one. One, I was back in the village where I was born. I didn't know most people. I stuck out like a sore thumb. And I wasn't about to get involved with some farmer's daughter only to see her daily for the next 40 years. London was a world apart where one could be anonymous. Here, everyone knew your business.

This was demonstrated when I agreed to run to the tea shop for my mother. I thought I was helping. Instead, I ended up answering questions about Sabine, my girlfriend. Yes, the girl I just dumped. Yes, the girl I just told it was better to live without me. And, yes, the girl I wanted back more than anything.

My normal distractions didn't work. Moreover, I didn't *want* them. I could only find myself filing through the *Mail* and *Sun* for pictures of what Sabine was up to. She launched a ship in Glasgow in the most impeccable blue dress. I thought about what a fool I was. She was statuesque, affable, and a laugh on any day. They didn't make people like her. And I had turned her down.

While that hurt, it was excruciating watch my father come home from hospital a shred of his prior self. He was down two stone, barely hanging in there. The nurse who came to help with his rehabilitation said he would get stronger. I doubted it. My father had been a force of nature. Now, he was a shell. He was confined to a wheelchair and, rather than try to build up his mobility, he was angry with the world.

In October, he was finally well enough to go down to the barn and check on his best horses. I returned from packing my apartment, set to sell in the coming weeks. I was back home, bored, and missing Sabine. I resisted ringing her the entire time. While I was proud of myself, I was weak. I wanted her as much as ever now. The smell of her hair would have been a great comfort as I waded through financials, calendars, and leases with farmers. I didn't know anything about any of this. She would have been the greatest distraction.

"Malcolm, when will you invite that girl up here?" Father asked. "She's not been around. You're living like priest—unless you are up to something down at the cottage I don't know about. You must be lonely."

"She's busy, Dad."

"With what?"

"A law course," I answered,

"And she cannot get away for a moment?"

"Dad, I don't—"

"Life is far too short to spend with her down there and you up here alone. Malcolm, if she's the girl, you'll run her off into the hedge by ignoring her. A woman like that needs to be taken care of."

He wasn't wrong. It was true. Sabine required regular care and feeding. She *deserved* it. And that was why she was down there, and I was up here. I couldn't give her my best. I couldn't promise her much of anything now. He insisted we could make it work. I wasn't about to disrupt Sabine's life and school for some selfish desire to have her in bed regularly. A year ago, I would have wanted to do my own head in over that, but Malcolm now was convinced that was a selfish prick move.

"Dad, we're not together anymore."

"Since when?"

"Since September?"

"Since September?"

"Yes."

"Why?"

"Because all of this is too much. She would feel obligated to help and the distance is more than miles, Papa."

Dad looked back. "Malcolm, did she dump you?"

He appeared to relish the idea she had.

"No, I broke it off."

"Why on *Earth* would you do that, son? Do you not love her?"

I took a deep breath. I didn't want to admit that I *did* love her. I refused to say that I doubted my decision every day and that I woke up most mornings wishing I had done differently.

"I do love her," I said, unable to lie. "But I didn't burden her with that."

"Son, telling her the truth is no burden."

"It is for a girl who is twenty-two and deserves a world of happiness, rather than being tied down with me up here."

My father pulled a face. "Is it that dreadful?"

"She wants to study law. She wants to work. She wants to take care of her sister and be there for her family. She cannot do that up here."

"Last I heard, Malcolm, the head of state was still Sabine's aunt. Same here as there. Bullocks. You fled. You got frightened and you fled!"

I swallowed hard. "Dad, if she's still single in a few years... after things settle..."

"Malcolm, you need a partner. You need a girl who can keep up with you. You need someone who loves these horses enough to put up with living up here. I think she's all those things. I know your mother and I hoped it would work out. I won't be around forever—"

"Papa, please."

Listening to him talk about his death was impossible. It hurt. It killed me.

"No. I will go someday. Sooner, rather than later."

"I wanted to give her a fighting chance, Papa."

"Do you think she's a baby who can't make choices for herself, Malcolm?"

"No, Papa. She's a grown woman."

"Then, why make choices for her?"

I didn't have an answer. I pushed him through the aisles. He greeted the horses. I stewed. I loved her. Even now. I loved her. In fact, I loved her more knowing how precious she was when I didn't have her. Sabine deserved all the love in the world. I held firm to the fact that I did her a favour.

I delivered Dad to the castle and returned to my cottage at the bottom of the hill. I rang a friend of mine who mentioned he saw Sabine and Maggie out opening a film at the cinema on Russell Square. I wanted to scream at the thought. I fought myself from rushing to purchase the papers the next morning, only to do so. I hated myself. There she was in a beautiful jade green dress, much like the one she wore when we met.

Sabine was still the most beautiful woman I could imagine. She was perfect. She was out of my league. I didn't deserve her kindness or love.

I wallowed. Then, I spotted the bangle I gifted her. Was it a sign? Was it a signal she loved me still? If she ever did. I hoped she had. Still, there was the bracelet. She must have had dozens of options, and she chose *that* one? It was a sign. I had hope. I had no idea how to move the ball forward, but I would try.

CHAPTER 27
Love Sucks

SABINE

By the end November, I swam in essays and prepared for exams. Meanwhile, my sister drove me mad. She suffered a mental breakdown after Keir unexpectedly shipped off on a deployment. She sent him emails daily. The two talked about everything and she wanted me to know it. She was the annoying friend who upon losing her virginity, thought she had keys to the castle and knew the meaning of life.

She was in love. *They* were in love. My gut was correct. They were golden. Maggie had never been as happy as when she talked about Keir's boring, predictable fucking flights around the world. She thought it was exciting. I did not. I was happy for them, but irritated because I was lonely. Not just a bit lonely, but *very* lonely.

Normally, I'd try to pull a boy. This was different. Finding someone like Malcolm seemed a losing battle. He was gorgeous. He was perfection. He was everything I needed him to be. He was rough when I wanted it, sweet when I needed it. And here we were. Maggie lived out her dream while I was jilted and resentful.

When my mother and aunt suggested I take a solo engagement and spend a few nights on the road, I was relieved. The problem was that I was far from home and in *Scotland*. Being in the same country as Malcolm suddenly felt too close. Damn him for making me feel this way!

On night two at Holyroodhouse, following a day of engagements, I received a call.

"Your Royal Highness, the Earl of Lauderdale is on the line," a footman said.

I was irritated. Did he think that I was down for a booty call? Besides, he'd waited two months to get back to me? Why should I care? I wanted the footman to tell him to die in a ditch.

"Ma'am, he says it is an urgent matter."

I doubted that. His dick wasn't an urgent matter, but I digressed.

I sighed. "Put him through."

The switchboard transferred the call.

"Yes?" I asked, annoyed.

"Sabine?"

"Yes, Malcolm. It is me."

"Hi."

His voice was quiet. He sounded knackered. So, this was no booty call after all. I wondered what it was about. I immediately wanted to be with him. If he asked me, I knew I'd run off. I wanted nothing more than to see him. It was like nothing changed. I went from anger to longing.

"Sabine, my father had a stroke. He's back in hospital."

"Can I help?"

"No," Malcolm said. "Well, not him. He's going to be alright. I mean, as alright as he can be at this point. I just got home."

"You must be exhausted."

"Knackered."

"So, why are you calling?"

"I don't know, Sab. I wanted to hear your voice. I needed to hear it. I know that's unfair."

I played with my bangle. It stayed on more than it came off. It was terrible. Maggie gave me such shite for wearing it all the time.

I couldn't part with it. I felt closer to him, even now, wearing it. I knew it was toxic and painful, but I wasn't ready to completely let go of the idea we could be together.

"It's... it's okay. This sort of thing must be hard, Mal."

"Sab, could you... would you... come out here? Could you?"

I groaned. "Malcolm, we promised one another—"

"It's nothing dodgy. A chat with a friend. I just... I don't want to be alone tonight. It's selfish, but there is no one I can talk with like I can you, Sabine."

I knew that feeling. I felt the same.

"Can I ask you about my torts module?"

"You can ask me whatever you want, Sabine. I'd be glad to be distracted with torts about right now."

"I'll come, but don't expect—"

"I'm not." His voice was steady, but excited. "I just want to see you. I need you."

I needed him, too, but not the way he wanted me. I needed him to tell me he loved me and regretted our break. I needed him to promise he'd never leave me again. I needed him to choose me. I wanted that more than anything. Malcolm still made me happy. My heart swelled as I drove to his father's estate. It was vast. A private road wound up to the castle. But, based on his directions, I was to go left, not right and head to a line of cottages. Malcolm's was first on the left. Why he stayed at a cottage, I did not know. While I did not make out much of the castle, I assumed there was plenty of room there.

I pulled into a tiny slip next to a cottage. I stepped out of my car and stared at a tall figure in the doorway. It was him. It was Malcolm. I approached, unsure of what to do. Did I hug him? Did I kiss him? I didn't have to think about it, though. Malcolm pulled me in for a tight hug, holding me so close in the threshold. I wanted this. I needed this. He did, too. Malcolm gave me a kiss on the top of the head and invited me in for a drink.

"Malcolm, I really cannot be drinking. I must drive back this evening. I have morning meetings."

"Fine," Malcolm said. "Just sit, then? How is your course going?"

"Don't you want to talk about your Dad?"

"I'd much rather hear about mundane things," Malcolm answered. "And I miss those days."

"It's going well," I answered. "I'm good at it. I got to do a moot court battle. I was brilliant at it."

"I am unsurprised. You'd make a shark of a litigator."

I blushed. "You don't have to be nice. You're no longer beholden to me."

That hurt. His face twisted.

"Sorry, I didn't mean to say it like that, Mal. I just... I wanted to make it clear you don't have to compliment me."

"I want to. You're brilliant, Sabine. I believe what I say. If I didn't, I wouldn't have felt bad about asking you to leave it. What you are doing is important. You'll do beautifully. I trust that as clever as you are, you will excel. I am glad you are."

"I hate torts," I laughed.

"You either love or hate them."

"You love them."

Malcolm chuckled. "Bread and butter, yes."

"I wish I were so flash, Malcolm."

"Meh. What do you think of your other course?"

"Humanitarian law is much more entertaining," I answered.

"I couldn't do it. I have no compassion for that."

"I think that's ridiculous! Malcolm, you are back here taking care of everyone. You are carrying this weight on your shoulders because you love your family. That's compassion and empathy. You are a good person, Malcolm. Maybe you need to hear that?"

He looked at his glass.

"Malcolm, you are a lovely soul. You love your family. I know this must hurt. My heart breaks for all of you."

"That means a lot, Sabine, but you don't owe me—"

I said, voice wavering, "I didn't break this off, darling. I didn't want to. I know you think you saved me. I feel like I still owe you that much. I still care about you—very much. I miss you like mad, Malcolm. You don't want to hear it, but I'd be lying."

"Sabine, I don't want to hurt you—"

"Why would you hurt me?"

"Life is complicated."

"My life is complicated. It started when I was eight weeks old. It started before that when I was born to an unwed mother with few resources and a history of drug use. Malcolm, my entire life has been one crisis after another. This is not a crisis for me. I don't see it that way. I would rather be here."

"I cannot ask that."

"You aren't asking. I am offering."

He looked at me and shook his head. "This pains me so much, Sabine. I love you. You know that?"

He stunned me. He *loved* me?

"Why did you—"

"I was frightened. For ages. And then when you dropped me at the kerb, I looked at you and wanted to say it. It felt wrong to burden you with that one before our lives changed—before I possibly hurt you. Sabine, I love you. I do. I wish I didn't. I never meant to. It killed me deep down to be without you, baby. Still does."

"Malcolm, if you feel that way, why would you not want me around? Why not go for it? Why not tell me!?" I raised my voice.

I was livid. I popped up. I went from empathy to wanting to strangle him. How could he be so stupid as to ignore the fact he loved me? And if he *did* love me, why would he then let me go? It was maddening.

"Because I didn't want to hurt you—"

"That is bullshit, Malcolm! That's a lie!"

"It is not."

"Spare me all the paternalistic bullocks, Malcolm. Don't be a wanker! Get your head out of your arse! You didn't tell me because you didn't want *your* heart to get broken. You were being a selfish prick!"

Malcolm looked hurt, not cross. It was like my words cut him.

"Sabine, I was never trying to be selfish. It was the opposite."

"You're afraid of commitment. Both of us are broken like that."

"I'm not. I thought I was. But, Sabine, you are the only woman I can say I have cared enough about to spare such trouble. I want you to move on. I want you to have a beautiful life rather than be tied to me here. I know you're better off without me."

There were tears in Malcolm's eyes. He was honest. I fought tears. I tried hard to be strong, to resist the urge to run to him and sob. I didn't want to give in. He hurt me. As much as I wanted him, I couldn't stand the idea of more loss. I felt tears rolling down my cheeks. I couldn't hold it back, but I would not run to him.

"Baby, I know you feel it, too."

"Don't *baby* me!"

"Sabine, stop deflecting."

"How would you know?" I demanded.

"Your wrist," Malcolm said. "You have been wearing that bracelet all the time. You wear it everywhere."

"Have you been stalking me?"

"A bit. To torture myself, yes. But I see it and I know there is hope. I don't want to know it, but you'd not wear it if you were completely over me. Just like if I were completely over you, I wouldn't have phoned you and asked you to come here. I would have moved on. The truth is, I needed you."

I was speechless.

"Sabine, I don't have answers. I don't know. I *do* know you, baby. I know you so well. And you know me. And I know I still love you. And I think you love me, too."

"What good does it do to tell you that? So, you can break my heart again? No, Malcolm, I'm not doing this. You're pissed and grieving and—I haven't the time for this!"

I grabbed my handbag and strode towards the door. I couldn't face him. I couldn't do this again.

CHAPTER 28
Temporary Ceasefire

MALCOLM

"Sabine, come back here!"

"No!" Sabine shouted at me. She stood by her car, tears glistening in the light from the doorway. She looked broken.

I was at an impasse. I could tell her I loved her, but I didn't know what to do with that. Finally. Too little, too late. And she was about to leave my life forever. Except, she'd *never* be gone forever. She'd marry another socially appropriate man. He'd steal her away in a few years and I would spend years regretting my decision to break it off, knowing she was all I ever wanted.

"Please," I pleaded.

I never pleaded.

She stared, dead on, jaw set. "You just dumped on me emotionally and left me nowhere to go. Why the fuck should I come back?"

I shrugged. "I don't know."

"You tell me you love me *after* you break it off and tell me this is impossible. You never asked me how I felt. You don't care. This is all about you. It's all Malcolm Ferguson's world and we're just fucking living in it. I feel like this about everyone in my life. I am *never* the main character. You did this to me. I'm my sister's sidekick. I'm yours when you want me, but never—"

"Sabine, I want you every day."

"Then why not make it that way?" Sabine demanded. "You had ample opportunity—"

I was crying. She was crying. I never cried. I would have been mortified if I wasn't so distressed at the real possibility of losing her forever.

"I don't know. I don't have answers. I refuse to trap you here and, much as I would love to, I am selling my place in London."

"Don't act like that is a serious impediment when you have a bloody Lear jet and a house on Regent's Crescent at your disposal, Malcolm! You make so many excuses. Either you love me, or you don't."

"Give me a month. Give me until Christmas," I pleaded. "To get things in order and think about how we could make this work without disrupting life. And to give you the time to figure out what you want, Sabine."

"I know what I want, Malcolm. I want *you*. I... I love you." Sabine's voice was strained. She was tortured but she said it. She loved me. *I knew it!*

"I love you, Sabine. I love every bit of you. Please, just give me time. Give yourself time. I need to adjust. I'm in a dreadful, sad place right now. I need space, but it doesn't change the fact I love you. I didn't think I could ever feel like this about anyone, but I do."

Sabine's outline changed. She approached, burying her head in my chest and sobbing. I wasn't sure what she indicated, but I assumed she wanted me. She wanted *us*. She wanted whatever might be in the new year.

"We will readdress in the new year," she sniffled. "Get through Christmas. We'll both be mad busy. And you're right. I have exams and essays out the arse right now."

I tilted her chin to mine so I could see her in the light. "Been there, done that. I get it."

"It's frigid out here. Can we go back inside?"

I nodded. "Of course."

She tossed her handbag aside and kicked her boots off, making herself more comfortable than before. That was a good sign. I wished she could stay forever.

"I love you. And you hurt me." Sabine sat on the couch. "Don't ever do that to me again."

"I won't," I promised. "I am waiting for your signal, though. I want you to seriously consider what you are agreeing to. This place... it's a huge thing, Sabine."

"I know." Sabine nodded. "But I don't want to talk about that. Not now. Next year. Let's do it next year, alright?"

I agreed to that. I leaned over and kissed her. I took in the feel and smell of her. I had been waiting months for that. I had been torturing myself and thinking about it. Now, she was here—in the flesh. She took my face in her hands and scooted closer. Slowly, she leaned in and kissed me. I kissed her back. It was like coming home. She was the only person I trusted at that moment. I bore my soul to her, and she reciprocated by being the sweetest thing I'd ever know.

I told myself we'd not do anything more, but things got the better of us. We disrobed, never leaving the living room. Sabine climbed into my lap, kissing me. I wrapped my hands tight around her arse. I kissed her neck as she grinded, teasing me. All I wanted was to be inside her. I wanted it so badly, but she didn't want me to beg. She wanted me to tell her how it was.

"What are you doing? Just jerking me around?" I asked her.

"What do you want?"

"I want to be inside you. I want to watch you lose your mind."

She smiled slyly but didn't move. I slapped her on the arse playfully. "Do you ever listen, Sabine?"

"No, darling. I am dreadful. I'm disobedient."

"Get on your hands and knees," I said.

I took her over the arm of the sofa for a bit. It felt wonderful. It felt amazing, but something was missing. Even as she screamed my name, cumming hard, it wasn't right. I wanted to watch her. I knew we'd never have tender sex. We would never be up to lovemaking. However, I wanted to watch her now. I need to see her face.

"Get on top of me," I said.

"Why should I do all the work, Malcolm?"

"Because I want to see you cum. I want to see what I do to you. I want to watch you come undone," I said.

She obeyed, climbing astride. I slip into her warm, wet pussy again. It felt amazing, but even better now that I could look into her eyes. She was beautiful, her hair now an utter disaster. She was wild and determined. I unwound her bit by bit.

She came again, digging her nails into back of the couch for dear life. "Oh God, Malcolm. I love you."

It couldn't have been sweeter if she tried. Never did I think I would be the type to say "I love you" during sex, but I became that person.

"I love you, Sabine."

The smile she gave was *unmatched*. After two days of hell and worry, it was a balm. After feeling hopeless, Sabine's grin and the light in her eyes made it better. It wasn't all better, but it felt liveable. I had her back. Maybe not in a forever sense, but she was here now. She wasn't gone forever. I had salvaged a second chance. I wanted to avoid fucking up. We had a ceasefire. What was a period was now an ellipsis. I could make it work. I could give her the space now. And by trusting in it, I would get her back and never wonder if she came back out of obligation. I gave her the choice. If she came back, as I thought she would, it was meant to be. Deep down, I knew it was that.

CHAPTER 29
The Rabbit Died

SABINE

"Am I terrible if I go buy lingerie? Do people do that? Is that something people do?" Maggie rambled.

I adored my sister, but she was unusually on my nerves this morning. On this day, we had been all over London. We would lunch and then resume. It was about a week until Christmas. Maggie received word that Keir was home on leave for a month. She had *plans*. She wanted me to know. Meanwhile, I wanted my sister to shut up about her sex life.

I didn't understand why I was so irritable. I wasn't exactly a prude. We shared like this. We didn't have boundaries when it came to sex talk. She was the prude. I was the oversharer. However, I had been so irritable. My head hurt and I felt off.

"Sabine! Earth to Sabine!"

I shook my head.

"Sorry. Yes. Yes. Some men like lingerie. But, given that you two got up to it in a tent the first time and didn't have anything but wet clothes, I think he'd be game for anything."

"But doesn't Malcolm like it?"

"Malcolm likes me in anything and everything. It's neither

here nor there. He appreciates suspenders. Many men do. They are dreadful and annoying, but worth it to feel like a sex goddess. I doubt he will *mind* if you go there."

"But what if it's like... trying too hard?"

"Margaux, you won't be trying too hard. I promise. He is home on leave. After months of celibacy, his hot little love interest will be a welcome relief even in a bloody flour sack."

"Love interest. What am I?"

I was the wrong person to ask. Malcolm and I were everything and nothing at once. We had gone from having hot makeup sex and confessing our love for one another to radio silence. We both agreed to it. I wanted him badly. I knew I would say yes to him. Whatever it brought after that, well, that was for me to decide. We would make it work. I would see him less than I wanted, but when I finished my course, we could readdress it. Something about it felt so right, so decided.

"Well, you should ask him. Determine if you two are exclusive."

"How?"

"Just ask him. Dear sexy pilot, can I lock you down? Please and thanks. He'll say yes, Maggie. He adores you."

"Or he'll run. We don't know one another that well—"

"By the end of Christmas break, you will be painfully aware of one another, trust me. The two of you send messages back and forth like an old married couple. It's fine. Let it go, Mags."

"He calls me Magpie. I love it. God, I hate myself for thinking that is cute. He's adorable. I love him."

Maggie covered her mouth. "Oh, no. I said it!"

"It hits you, doesn't it?" I murmured. "Darling, just give in. You two spent months of angsty pining only to hook up and then go back to angsty pining. You deserve happiness. I told you, sometimes you find love in unexpected places."

"And Malcolm?"

"I don't have any news. I will report back after the new year."

"I don't understand this."

"He is giving me the chance to have an out, Maggie. It's important that I come back to him free and clear. This is a big choice."

"I don't get it. Why?"

"He'll run the estate—he does. Things will be expected of me. I want to finish school. I really do. I don't want to give that up. We'll have to make it work in the meantime. I love him, Margaux. It will be fun for a bit, but we'll make it through. I will show you all I can finish something. I can be me and be with him."

"I know that's important," Maggie said. "I'm so proud of you. You're so good with this whole balancing everything with school. I'm jealous."

"You work so much, Maggie. You deserve a medal. We're both doing well. We're both kicking ass."

Maggie squeezed my hand as we pulled to the service entrance. It was time for a lunch and back to the grind in the late afternoon. We took lunch in the small dining room. There was a French onion soup—my favourite. However, it didn't appeal today. I picked at my food.

"You alright, darling?" Maggie asked, concerned.

"Feeling a bit odd today. I think I didn't sleep well. I have this headache that lingers. It's driving me mad."

"You should take something, darling."

"I know. I know, but... I feel I am whinging."

"You look pale. Maybe you're sick?"

"I hope so. I'd love to get out of Christmas."

As a child Christmas at Sandringham was magical. As an adult, it smacked of boredom, the old people getting too drunk, and being on parade to attend church on Christmas morning. I was over it already. I was run down. I was exhausted after my exams. I wanted and needed a break, not to be on parade.

"I think I'm tired."

"You should find out. I could stay back and take care of you?"

"You're dreadful," I laughed. "I think I'm just a bit knackered."

"Take the afternoon off."

"I cannot do that. I won't just kick my duties aside. I am trying to be reliable, Maggie."

"You should see the doctor. I want to have him get you out of work. Because then I can take a break. Think about it, we could sit around and watch Christmas movies. Do nothing else. C'mon."

I rolled my eyes. "Sweet Maggie, you are anything if not scheming. I will go see him if only because I feel a bit feverish. I don't want to get anyone sick."

I went to visit the palace physician. He worked on the ground floor. It was an absolute luxury to have one. He took care of us, kept our secrets, and provided good reminders to eat our vegetables and stop drinking so much. The minute he saw Margaux and I coming, he looked panicked. The last time we had bothered him, it was because we wanted IVs to help with a hangover. I am sure he expected the worst.

"How can I help you, Your Royal Highnesses?"

"Sabine feels ill. We want to get her checked out."

"Ensure it's not catching," I added.

"Of course. Sit, sit."

I popped up on the exam table. He took my temperature and looked in my ears and nose.

"My stomach is upset," I said. "I have this headache. And my back aches."

"Do you have chills?" he asked.

"No. Not really. Just what I've mentioned. I feel bad, but it's not easy to pin it down."

"What was the date of your last menstrual period?"

Maggie stared at me. I stared back. We both panicked. We had periods at the same time. I hadn't had mine. The look on her face indicated she *had* her period. *Fuck!* I tried not to meltdown and think about the worst.

"Uh... the 12th or so?" I asked my sister.

She nodded. The doctor looked confused.

"Mr. Williamson, she and I... we have cycles at the same time," Maggie explained.

"So, last week?" he followed up.

"No. Last month," I replied. "It's... late."

"Are you often late, ma'am?"

"No," I replied. "But I'm on the pill, so—"

"And do you always take your pill at the same time every day?"

I shrugged. "Mostly. Same day."

"Similar hour?"

"That matters?" Maggie looked alarmed.

He nodded. "It's paramount you must take it at the same time. Even a few hours can reduce the effectiveness a bit. Sometimes that bit is enough to let it fail."

"Yes, but she uses protection," Maggie insisted. "And you haven't even had sex—"

"I have and..." I cringed. "I usually do."

"What? How!?"

"Maggie, I'm not getting into this here," I said in French. "Later."

I hadn't told her that Malcolm and I had made up very much off the cuff in his cottage in Lauder. I hadn't had time. I'd told her we'd spoken and agreed to readdress in the new year. I didn't mention that we had fucked like rabbits on his couch.

"We should do a test, ma'am. To be sure. Since you have had unprotected sex, I think it is best. Do you know about the timing or was it... frequent?"

I was offended by this line of questioning. "It was the once. A few weeks ago. We usually use protection but it just... happened. I don't appreciate the slut shaming!"

He stared confused. "I do apologise, ma'am but if you are pregnant—"

"Just give me the cup. Let me get this over with."

I had a wee in the sample jar and handed it to the good doctor.

"Brilliant. You know, when I was a child they had to kill a rabbit to get this result."

"Kill a rabbit?" Maggie looked faint.

"Yes. Dreadful. But this is fast. I'll be back in a few minutes."

The physician disappeared into his little lab and Maggie demanded more information. "How did that happen? You haven't even—"

"I went to Edinburgh. Niall had a stroke. He called me in a weak moment. I went to see him. We made up—of sorts—and shagged. It was beautiful. Of course, now I am regretting it. I am sure I took my pill just fine. I am sure of it."

"Good reminder for me."

"Always, always. Malcolm loathes condoms. Every man does. Still, they are necessary."

"I am sure it's nothing," Maggie said.

I was sure it was, too. We had sex *once* in months. I took my pill every day. So, what if we had unprotected sex *once*. Lots of people did that every day. We'd done it before and nothing bad happened. In fact, I'd been more reliable with my pill than ever. I took it every morning before leaving for class. It was a fluke. I was stressed. This was nothing. It would be a sick joke if true, but it wasn't true.

The doctor returned, a far less cheerful expression on his face. My stomach sank.

He stared, dumbfounded, at me. "Would you like to speak alone, Your Royal Highness?"

"No," I replied. "I want my sister here—no matter what. Whatever you say to me, you can say to her."

He swallowed and his voice shot up nervously. "The test is positive."

"So, it could just be a false positive?" Maggie said. "She cannot be."

"Ma'am these are very reliable. I can run a blood test that will say the same," the doctor said. "They are no more reliable, really. Comparable. I could run another test?"

I felt like all the air was knocked out of my lungs. I wanted to vomit. In fact, I did. I ran to a bin in the corner which held recycling and vomited for what seemed like an hour. It was uncontrollable. All I could think was that my family would disown me.

"No," I said. "It's fine. Please, can you keep this secret?"

"I can for a bit, yes. But it is my job to report to Her Majesty—"

"I will tell her," I said, fighting tears. "I just need a couple of days to figure out what is going on and... how I will handle it."

"Can you give her an abortion? Do you know someone who can?" Maggie asked.

"Margaux!" I shrieked. "Why would you ask that?"

"Obviously, you're not going to *have* it, right?"

"I don't know. That's a conversation for another day," I confessed. "My decision and mine alone."

Maggie went to the nervous place where she spit balled. She wanted to make everything right. She wanted to fix everything.

We climbed in the lift, silent. The doors shut. I broke into nervous tears.

"It will be okay, Sab. I promise you, love, it will be," Maggie pulled me close.

Her tiny body held me up somehow.

"Mum and Auntie will disown me, Margaux. I will be out on my ear. Malcolm's family will want nothing to do with me. I have dishonoured us all."

"That's not true, Sabine. No one would love you less for this."

"It is bad. Maggie, you know it is bad! It's why you rushed to suggest I needed an abortion!"

"Well, it's a legitimate choice. I support a woman's right to choose even if it is a morally grey area."

"It's not morally grey. The church is against it. And I may not give a flying fuck what the Archbishop of Canterbury is on about, but you must be aware—"

Maggie put her hands on my shoulders. "Sabine, you are my sister. I will always choose you over some man in a stupid hat. Do you hear me? You would do the same for me. I will be here for you. I will defend you."

"I need to talk to Auntie—"

"You need to talk to *Malcolm*."

"I owe Malcolm nothing right now. It's damage control for the family, first. Malcolm will come second if I decide to keep it," I murmured.

"Sabine, is that wise?"

"Margaux, it's always us versus them. It's always the family first," I said.

She nodded as the doors open. We both knew it too well.

CHAPTER 30
Bad Decisions

MALCOLM

The problem with being back in London was knowing that I was only a couple of miles from Sabine's door. We still felt forever apart. Thankfully, I had some time to catch up with old friends. Or, rather, I was guilted into going out with my mate Jason because his wife, Belinda, was pregnant. We ended up at the same place we used to go when we felt posh in our early years as associates. We *were* posh, but also tried pretending we were every man. It was a balance Jason thought he perfected. It was a balance I cared nothing for.

Jason whinged because he had once again knocked Belinda up. The poor woman was miserable, but Jason felt sorry for himself. The way he described it all was dreadful. Of course, the way Jason told it, women relished pregnancy so they could torture their men. I figured that was far from true.

I was not the most evolved man on the planet, but I knew better than to take the piss at the expense of a pregnant woman. That was low—even for me.

"She just whinges. It is nonstop, Malcolm. Everyday. All the whinging. All the problems."

"Perhaps, Jason, she's miserable because she's pregnant and sick?" I asked.

"It's not that bad. I am certain of it. Women wax nostalgic about it. They want *more* babies. It's madness. I can only blame myself because we drank too much wine, and I gave in and said, 'What the fuck?' But don't be like me, Malcolm! No. Don't be like me!"

"I have no intent to have children soon, much as it pains my parents. Kiersten and I are useless."

"What of the girl?"

"What girl?"

"The Princess!"

"Sabine?" I played dumb. "She's hardly a girl. It's not as if we discuss such matters. We're not in that place. Neither of us is in a hurry, Jason."

I conveniently avoided the fact that we were about to have some very tough conversations about what happened after Sabine's course was over. That was if—and only if—she chose to stick by me. She owed me nothing. I loved her. I wanted her more than ever, but she didn't owe me her time.

"Good. Don't be. The next time you find yourself between her legs, she's bound to be trying to do it all over again. You'll get a couple good weeks and then back to square one."

"Don't make it sound ghoulish. She pushed out one baby and must prepare to do it again for another."

"Are you defending her constant whinging? I'm so tired. The baby keeps us up all night. She cries nonstop. They get *so* hormonal."

Back home, we geared up for the first babies of Spring. It was my father's favourite time of year. The anticipation buoyed him at a time he needed it most. I'd had cameras installed on every foaling stall. Close circuit footage played into a bank of screens in his office. He could stay and wait for the new foals until his heart was content.

I didn't get it. What I did understand having watched it

happen enough times was that it was quite literally bloody and painful work.

"It's hard on them. She's given you a child and will give you one more. Your parents must be happy. Ring them and pawn the baby off."

"You think it is that simple? Women go mad. They don't want the baby to go away for the evening."

I saw someone approach. It was dark. We were sitting in a corner of the bar far from the action, down to the last third of our drinks. Finally, I made out a face.

"Esty." I stood to greet her in surprise.

She stopped, kissing both my cheeks. "Malcolm. How are you? And Jason!"

"I'm good, thanks. Jason is whinging about Belinda. Buckle up. It's a doozy."

"She's pregnant and unreasonable."

I rolled my eyes. Esty sat.

"I do think you should cut her a break. Our bodies are complicated. She has given you a child."

"You sound like Malcolm."

"He's pissed. Ignore him," I chuckled. "What are you doing here."

"Last run before the end of the year. I wanted to drop by for nostalgia. And then to find you both? It's fortuitous. How is the girlfriend?"

Was she? I didn't know.

"You met her? Even I haven't properly met her!" Jason said, annoyed. "You never bring her around."

"We've both been up to other things. It's not that I do not think she and Belinda would get on."

Except I very much thought the two would not get on. They were completely different people, came from different backgrounds, and Sabine would have nothing in common with her.

"I invited myself over for his birthday," Esty laughed. "That girl is divine."

I moved uncomfortably in my chair. I did not want Estelle to tell Jason that she and Sabine had gone at it like animals on my couch or that I had them both in one evening. It was cruel to Jason and embarrassing for Sabine.

"She's nice, yes," I said.

"Nice. Malcolm, you fawn over her. She makes you overprotective and all manner of things. Stop being ridiculous!" Esty laughed. "Where is she? Is she on house arrest?"

"Sabine is busy with work. She will be until the new year, I suspect."

"And you just let her go. You trust her?" Jason asked.

"Yeah, I do. She's overly forthcoming and not someone I worry about," I admitted.

It was true.

We drank for a bit longer. Jason wanted to continue drinking. By that point, I was a bit pissed and willing to go forth. So, was packed up and continued out to the next place, a posh cocktail bar. Jason talked off the ear of the very pretty bartender. It was harmless, if not annoying for her. He seemed entertained.

"He's very Jason," I sighed.

"Look, I get the sense that we're not okay," Esty changed the subject. "I didn't mean to—"

"It's okay. She and I... we took some time and... it just made me realise I loved her. And she loved me. And that looked very different from how I thought it would. She is simply... freer. But no hard feelings towards anyone. It's alright."

"She's hot. You know that? She's too good for you—"

"Well aware. And yes. She's fit and beautiful. But she's also everything I could want. We're both mental. Neither of us makes good choices most of the time, but I don't know what to do without her. Lord knows I tried."

Esty smiled. "Malcolm Ferguson is finally in love?"

"I suppose it has to happen to all of us at least once."

CHAPTER 31

Seeking Guidance

SABINE

"What is it, sweetheart?" Aunt Greta asked. We sat in the part of her office taken up by two velvet tufted couches and an antique coffee table. It was chic, but warm. She always had the best office. I held onto Maggie's hand, shaking like a leaf. I didn't want to do this alone.

"I... I got bad news," I said.

"Bad news? Has something happened to you?" Our Aunt's expression pulled tight, straight into concern.

I realised she thought I was ill or something. I didn't want to trigger some unresolved grief.

"I'm not ill, per se."

"Alright. That is good."

I looked over at Maggie. Maggie nodded. She squeezed my hand, telling me to persist.

"I have..." I struggled for my words. "I have... fallen pregnant."

A SUMMER WITH THE EARL

Aunt Greta did a double take. "But, Sabine, I thought you were again single and—"

"I was... I am. Sort of and sort of not. Malcolm and I decided to table things until the new year. He needed time to get his affairs in order. He wanted me to have time to decide if what he could give me was what I wanted. I want him. Or I thought I did."

"They had a moment," Maggie insisted. "A bit of a moment."

"We usually are much better but threw caution to the wind. He'd just told me he loved me. I reciprocated. We lost our heads a bit," I rambled.

"Oh, I can understand. We've all done that. Of course, you're just able to *have* babies. Much like your mother. Your father could just look at her and she'd fall pregnant. Me, it was nearly impossible."

I looked sad. Maggie grimaced, horrified at the mention of our parents having sex.

"I am sorry, Auntie."

"No, darling. Do not apologise. This is... unexpected, but you are loved. We will manage. It is happy in the end. Or it could be. What would you like to do?"

I shrugged. "I don't know."

"What does Malcolm think is fair? Is he frightened? All men are at first I think—"

"He doesn't know." I flushed red hot. "He doesn't know, and I don't even know where to begin."

Maggie looked sympathetic. "You must tell him, Sab. I think he will handle it better than you imagine."

"Malcolm needs to have children. If anything, his parents would be over-the-moon at this. As would we if it pleased you both."

I stared in disbelief.

"What? You think you are the first princess to fall pregnant before her wedding? Oh, Sabine, that is far from true. Malcolm is not the first man to cause a moral panic. Not by a long shot."

"You won't disown me over it?"

"Sabine, you could shoot a man and I'd still come to see you in the witness box testifying. I'd still love you even if I disagreed with what you did. Having a baby is a wonderful thing. Well, if that is what you want."

"I don't have a choice—"

"Oh, Sabine, there are many things that can be arranged. I don't have to know about them, but they can be arranged."

"I have... a choice? And you won't disown me?"

"Sweetheart, you two are the lights that keep your uncle and I swimming. Since Cecilia died, we have struggled mightily. It has been watching the two of you grow and thrive that brought us much happiness. It is bittersweet. Cecilia cannot be here. We don't see her take these steps—finish uni, start a postgrad course, find love—but we get to see you both do them. You two have always been precious to me. From the day I held you the first time, Sabine, I knew I adored you. And that was even before you were my niece. You were so tiny."

"Really?"

"I have loved you so. Both of you. When we struggled for years before Cecilia, we lost so many babies. Your mother always gave us free access to dote on you both. And now, seeing you grow into beautiful young women, it's precious. So, no, Sabine, there is no bone in my body that could judge you for this. You are struggling because this is hard. It is hard for someone your age. Things are complicated for you and for Malcolm."

"I know. There is no good choice."

"If you love him and can imagine yourself happy with him, you should go," my aunt said. "But your life will be forever changed. You will have to grow up even faster, Sabine. He will, too."

"Mum will be so cross."

"I will not say anything to her if you want to say it first. And I think you should, Sabine. This can stay here."

"She will want me to end it. I... I just don't know if I want that. I don't want to feel like that is my only choice."

"It's not, darling. And no matter what she says, this is your life. You are a grown woman. He is a grown man. It is a choice you must make about your body and together if you choose to stay together."

"But if he doesn't want me and I want to keep the baby?"

Aunt Greta took a deep breath. "Let's cross that bridge when we come to it. In the meantime, you should go speak with him. Try to figure it out."

I was relieved and surprised by her response. I knew deep down how much my family loved me. I knew what I had to do. I returned to my room. My heart beat fast as I rang Malcolm.

It was anticlimactic. I got told to press a given button to be transferred to the main house. I pressed, assuming maybe he was there with his parents. Then, I feared the worst. What if his father had died? What if they were at hospital? My fears abated when his mother answered.

"Yes, hello?"

"Uh. It's... Sabine. I'm searching for Malcolm."

"Oh, Your Royal Highness. Hello. He's not up here at present. It is good to hear from you. Are you well?"

The plot thickened. I didn't like a plot that thickened.

"Brilliant, thanks," I replied, lying. I was anything *but* brilliant. "You and His Grace?"

"We're fine, darling."

I heard a man's voice, assuming that was the Duke.

"Yes, it's Princess Sabine. She says she is well, darling," his wife said.

"Tell him I send my best," I said.

"She sends her best, darling."

"Tell her to come visit sometime," he called back.

I chuckled. Oh, if only he knew what I was about to tell everyone. He'd second-guess all of that. They wanted to have a casual chat. I was losing my nerve. To keep up this steam and motivation to come clean, I needed to find Malcolm. Where was he?

"Ma'am, where can I find Malcolm?" I asked, ignoring the Duke's polite invitation.

"Is it an emergency?"

"I have a question for him," I said. "No burning fire, but I'd like to run something by him. A legal question... related to my course."

She hated law and all that. It would end the follow-up.

"Oh, well sure, darling. He's in London. At The Embassy."

That was the house on Regent's Crescent. I was relieved and horrified. I couldn't do this via phone. I'd have to go over there. I should ring him first, but he was probably turning in for the evening. Maybe I should wait? No. If I waited, I would lose my nerve.

"Thanks. I'll ring him there," I said. "Have a lovely evening and stay warm."

I hung up the phone and gathered myself, throwing on a coat. I stopped, staring in the vanity mirror as I ran a brush through my soon-to-be-second-day-curls. Malcolm loved my hair like this. I wouldn't stop him from mooning over me if he wanted to. Right now, feeling so off-kilter, I'd welcome any attention he'd relish on me. I wanted him to say he wanted me and this. I needed that confirmation. I needed us to choose one another. I needed that more than anything.

I called a car at the service entrance. I didn't ask Maggie to come along. I wanted to have her there like my emotional safety blanket, but this was a conversation Malcolm and I needed to have on our own. I couldn't bring Maggie with. I was a grown woman. I would do this on my own.

The car pulled up at The Embassy. I took in its beautiful chalk white facade. It was the stuff of prestige period pieces. I felt like a confused character in Austen. By this point, I was a marked woman. Did that make Malcolm my Mr Wickham? It was unclear, but I loved him. I was doing this. I would wait as long as needed to speak with him. I ducked under the front door's overhang, avoiding the dreadful rain. I buzzed the door.

It took a moment, but a butler appeared in a dressing gown. He opened the door and looked as if he had seen a ghost. I'd surprised everyone.

"I need to speak with Lord Ferguson," I avoided any pleasantries.

I had no time. I'd lose my nerve.

"Ma'am. It is late."

"I am aware of this, but it is pressing—urgent."

"Let me reach him."

The butler disappeared. I waited, nervous, along with my detail in the foyer, annoyed I'd not be brought properly to the drawing room. I wondered why that was. Looking around, I took in the grand surroundings. If wealth could be reflected in a place, it certainly was here. The gold leaf darting the intricate ceiling was perfect. Everything was neat. The marble was perfection along with grand staircase. A woman with a familiar brow stared down at me from a grand portrait at the top of the steps. I grand tiara sat atop her head. She had a sash, which I recognised. This was Malcolm's late grandmother, Princess Rikhild.

"Sabine," Malcolm emerged, confused.

He looked a bit pissed. It made sense if he was back in London. He'd probably gone out.

"Hi. Can we talk?" I asked.

"Sabine, I cannot—"

"I must speak with you," I insisted.

I looked down the hall off the entry and saw Esty peering out. Somehow, I began to expect the worst. He was entertaining *her*? Were they sleeping together? Was this some sort of thing now? Was he cheating on me? Was it cheating if we weren't together? Were we broken up? Was this how I found out about it?

My expression gave away my displeasure.

"Esty and Jason dropped by," Malcolm explained. "We were out drinking."

"I ran into them," Esty said. "You look... well."

She was lying. What else were they lying about?

"Is Jason here now?"

"He just left," Malcolm replied. "We rolled him into a car. He's feeling a bit sorry for himself and got blazingly pissed."

"He thinks it's like old times, but we're all old now," Esty giggled. "Look, I should go, Malcolm. Nice seeing you, Sabine."

Esty departed, by my angry gaze never left my face. She ducked out, giving him a kiss on both cheeks. She suspected that touching me was a mistake. I suddenly saw red.

"You know what Malcolm, if this is some sort of sign and you are done with me, let me know and I can just... cut this short."

"Esty and Jason weren't up to anything nefarious. I wasn't, either. We were old friends catching up. Besides, even if we *were*, we agreed—"

"I don't care about that. Life has changed for me in an instant and I need you to talk to me."

"Well, go on."

He was cross. I suspected he thought I didn't trust him. Perhaps, I didn't? A day ago I did. Now, I was feeling low. Esty's presence challenged my sense of supremacy. I didn't like it. I knew I was a hypocrite for saying it, but I couldn't make sense of anything right now.

"I can't do this right here."

"I'd invite you in, but it's late and you've been clear."

I took a big breath. "Malcolm, you don't want me to do that."

"I do." Yes, he was cross. Impossibly cross.

"Malcolm, I'm pregnant." There it was.

CHAPTER 32
Cruel Joke

MALCOLM

The words were simple. They were life changing. She was right about that much. I fell speechless. I couldn't comprehend what Sabine said. She was *pregnant*. Was it a cruel joke? Her face suggested it was real. This was never supposed to happen. How had it? And was it the worst thing that ever happened to me? What did it mean? Was it good? I figured if this had happened several years from now when we were properly together, would feel like a relief. Tonight, I was drunk and standing in our foyer, unable to speak. I felt the wind leave my body and not return.

"If you think it's not yours, I don't want to hear it. It is. I haven't been with anyone since our little interlude with Esty. And I can assure that doesn't get you pregnant."

There were tears in her eyes. I wanted to cry as well, but I couldn't find the strength.

"And if you're done, that's fine—"

"I'm not, baby," I finally spoke. "I just need a moment."

"Can you properly invite me in, Malcolm? Because I'm standing here and... I'd like to sit."

I shook my head as if resetting my body. "Come in."

She followed me into the drawing room, observing that there were three glasses. She believed me now, I assumed. I saw the way she reacted to Esty. Sabine was jealous. I never thought I'd see that day.

We sat on the couch, Sabine nervous. I hadn't reacted at all to her immediate concern. I needed to. It was dreadful to see her so upset. She was frightened. I'd never seen her frightened before. She feared my retribution. I had none to give. I wanted her to know that much.

"Malcolm, I know you don't want this," Sabine said. "Neither of us did or does."

"No, baby," I shook my head. "I... I didn't want this. Nor did you. But here it is. Like this."

"I can get an abortion, but... I am not sure I want that."

"No." I shook my head. "It's too risky, Sabine. If anyone found out—"

"Well, if it's a choice between people potentially telling me of eternal damnation in the pits of hell or certain eternal damnation in the press and social circles, I will take my chances with hell."

I chuckled. "Sabine, you needn't resort to that. That's all I am saying."

"It's my body. I get to make my own choices."

I nodded. "Yes. You're quite right, Sabine. However, I don't think you want that. That's my read. And I don't think that's the best solution."

She rolled her eyes. "It's the cleanest one. And we can. Auntie Greta basically promised she'd look the other way and help me. It is the easiest solution."

"Assuming we get away with it. But that's not what I'm asking, Sabine. What do you want?"

She looked down, tears running.

"I want to have this baby. It's a pipe dream. And, yes, I know what that means. The thing is, I want the baby. I cannot explain it to you. You won't understand."

"Try me," I said.

"Malcolm, I have lived my entire life wondering if I looked like my mother. If I shared her mannerisms. And now that I might have someone to share these with… it matters. You'll say that is silly. My family loves me. My aunt told me nothing could stop her from loving me, so why bother?"

"It's not silly."

"I looked at that portrait of the person I'm sure is your grandmother. She looks like you, Malcolm. Every day, I am surrounded by old portraits of people who resemble my mother and siblings. I don't get that. Something tells me to protect this thing—whatever it is. And I cannot explain it. I feel so different now than I did this morning. Everything has changed. I was bursting to tell you I chose you, that I loved you and would love you. I wanted to try to make it work despite the distance. I wanted that. Now, I cannot get that."

"Untrue, Sabine," I said. "You must get that now."

"I don't want you obligated to choose me. I want you to choose me because you cannot live without me."

My face softened. I wanted her to see how much I loved her. "I was always choosing you, Sabine. This is only makes it clearer. Like crystal."

Sabine shook her head at me. "You don't want to be a father."

"The timing is off, Sab."

"So, maybe I get an abortion and we do this again in a few years?"

That seemed silly. Why bother? Marriage and a baby would solve a multitude of our problems. We'd have some sense of clarity. Was it frightening? Yes. Was this a sign? I was certain of it.

"No, Sabine. I think that's a poor choice. If I get any chance to suggest some solution, that's not in the list for me."

"It's easy for you to say. You're not agreeing to leave uni to move far, far away from your family and manage an estate. I'm twenty-two years old, Malcolm. What should I be? A duchess by twenty-three. It's ridiculous!"

"Sabine, I cannot stay with you... we cannot have this baby if you and I aren't married. We must marry—and soon—if we're to continue this. I cannot accept any other solution if you keep the baby. It will cause us both reputational ruin. Your parents will want to kill me. My parents will kill me—for certain."

She rolled her eyes. "Don't be hyperbolic."

"I'm not. My father is on death's door. We could either scare him senseless and leave him thinking he raised me completely wrong or make his day and life by letting him know the estate would continue. Please, Sabine."

"What? Agree to marry you for now and forever under duress because you want to save face and be a good boy for once? That is so selfish, Malcolm!"

It was. It was the way to save us both. The *only* way. Sabine was young and idealistic. She had no idea what the stakes were. She underestimated her mother's ire. I didn't want to point out that her mother would want the same. Her aunt would demand it. If she kept the baby, we needed to be married. It would be a major scandal for my family, but it would be epic and disastrous for hers. The press would have a field day with her. She was the adopted one. I didn't mention this. It would hurt her. It wouldn't be helpful. Sabine needed love and compassion, not my strategic opinions.

"It is, perhaps, but we've done this once before. What is the difference?"

"Doesn't it occur to you that I might want the whole thing."

"The whole thing?"

"Love, a proposal, a family. Properly dating. You wanting this with me. I wanted you to fall head over heels with me. If we were to do this, I wanted a proper proposal, not whatever this is. I have always thought if I did marry, it would be in front of a proper audience—not one that is aware of my indiscretions. I don't want a sad shotgun wedding. I know I'm a bad person, but Malcolm, I want a happy life. I don't want to feel like I was the next-best choice. I want to be everything. That is the thing. I want happiness. I want all of it."

Tears flowed like a river from her blue eyes. It killed me.

"Sabine, I love you. More than I ever imagined I could love a person. I love you unendingly. You already *are* everything. When I do not have you, I'm lost. I need you. That will not change. This is unconventional. It's problematic, I'll grant you. I also think it's the best idea I have."

"I deserve better. Not than you. I think we are about as perfect for one another as two flawed people could be. But I deserve better than a messy wedding and a non-proposal-proposal."

"I can promise you much better than that."

"Don't be ridiculous!"

"I can be remarkably romantic, Sabine."

"Uh-huh."

I chuckled. "I am not known for it, alright. Neither of us are."

"You don't want to be a husband or a father."

"No, I didn't. I feel altogether differently about it."

"What a ridiculous thing to say! You feel different out of obligation, Mal!"

"Sabine, I felt different ever since I realised I loved you and didn't want anyone else to ever have you. Yes, that sounds bad. But I never loved anyone, Sabine. Anyone but you. This is different. I didn't want to mention any of it because I knew you needed —wanted—to finish your course."

"What does that matter?"

"It comes from not wanting to tie you down. For wanting to give you space, Sab."

"Malcolm, it comes from not trusting that I know best. I am a grown woman—"

"I know that! No, you're saying you want all this and that you don't believe I do. I do. I wish we could announce our engagement and I could do this big proposal and all the fanfare would hit, as you want it to. I wish I could give you a year to plan the biggest, most ridiculously spendy wedding in eternity, Sabine. I wish I could say we conceived a child under better circumstances than on my couch in the cottage. But it was very hot sex."

"Fuck off, Malcolm! You cannot possibly think about that right now!"

I could. I always could—especially with her. She was right, though. There was no time for waxing nostalgic about a makeup sex session.

"I love you, Sabine. That is all. Nothing about us has been average, for better or worse. Give me some time to make this feel better and less rushed. Do you trust me?"

She groaned.

"You must trust me, Sabine. If you don't, this won't work."

She sighed. "Fine. I do. I must. I haven't a choice. You're probably right. It's the only way to save face. And if we were going to do it anyway, it's risky to put off the inevitable at risk of ruin."

"I love you, Sabine. So much," I said. "And I want you to be happy. I need that for you. The rest will just... It will have to work out. I will make you happy. I will do my damndest. I promise you."

The sides of her lips curled as she half-heartedly smiled. "Okay, Malcolm. I trust you. We're doing this. Commence marriage plot and save the world?"

I chuckled.

Unable to help myself, I leaned to kiss her. "Commence marriage plot. If anyone can pull it off, we can, baby."

CHAPTER 33
God Only Knows

SABINE

Malcolm and I came to my family first. We were a day out from leaving for Norfolk. My mother and father looked unimpressed. My aunt and uncle were there for moral support. I was grateful for their unending confidence in my abilities and unending love. It felt right. It felt as good as it could. We were frightened. Malcolm put on a brave, relaxed face, but he feared my mother most of all. By now, he knew Aunt Greta was the calm one. My mother had a temper. She was the protector of the entire family.

"We have news," I looked over at Malcolm.

"Please tell me you are not engaged. Do not be ridiculous!" Mother started in, steamrolling.

I set my jaw, determined. "We are."

"Congratulations," Aunt Greta said.

Mum glared.

"It is happy news! Let them be happy, darling!"

"She's a child. He's preying on her somehow."

"Bethany, stop it! I won't hear it. Sweetheart, that is good news. I do worry it is... fast... but so were your mother and I."

Beth glared at Papa but knew she would be put on her arse if she protested much more by both my aunt and father.

"We know it's a surprise and not ideal. And if there were more time, ma'am, I would have come to ask for your blessing. I should have done the same with Her Majesty," Malcolm said.

"You have it, dear," Auntie said. "I can assure you."

"Thank you."

"We have done something, and this is the best way forward," I continued. "You will agree."

"Sabine fell pregnant. It was an accident. We tried our best for that to *not* happen, but it did. I don't think it changes anything for us... apart from the abbreviated timeline." Malcolm squeezed my hand. "But our feelings don't change."

"You two broke up. How did you manage that?" Mum asked.

"We got back together," I embellished the truth, but what did it matter?

This would be acceptable. It would make things better.

"We didn't want to say much until after her exams. I regret ever breaking up with Sabine. I did it with good intentions, but it would be my greatest regret. I would never live with myself."

"He loves me. I love him. This is the right thing, Mum. It was inevitable. Who cares if it happens a year or two too soon?"

"You're twenty-two years old! It's ridiculous!"

"She's a grown woman, Bethy. Leave her alone. I, for one, am happy for them."

"Margaret, you knew about this, didn't you?"

"I knew Sabine was pregnant. I didn't know their plans. I encouraged her to tell Malcolm and let them figure it out."

Mum fumed.

"That is protocol, Beth." Uncle Gary finally spoke.

"Perhaps for a married woman. A sensible, married woman."

"Any woman. And she is a sensible woman who will be wed soon... I am assuming?" Aunt Greta asked.

Malcolm winced. "Unfortunately, we have an abbreviated timeline, yes."

"Because you impregnated her," Mum said.

I fell into a puddle of tears. "Mummy, I know I am a massive disappointment, but can you just please stop talking about it like that. We're having this baby—whether you accept the baby or not—and I would just like you to act like you loved me."

My words broke her. She searched for something to say. There was no comeback. She, too teared up.

"I am sorry. I... I couldn't ever not love you. I was there the night you were born. I loved you from the minute you were born. I held you and fell for you. And you are mine. You're always my daughter, my baby."

"So you won't cast this baby aside?"

"Of course not, Sabine. I could never do that. And... I will support you. I am doubtful about Malcolm's role in this."

"Maybe I am not everything you dreamed for in a son-in-law, ma'am, but I will always do right by her."

"As you did when you destroyed her, broke her heart, and left her to pick up the pieces in September?"

"Bethany, let it go," Papa said.

Malcolm took a breath. "It's fair. It's fair. But can I not learn to do better."

"Yes, so typical. You'll step up, a reformed man because she's pregnant."

Mum dug in. She wouldn't go easy on him.

"I love Sabine. I love every bit of her. And this doesn't change it, ma'am. It's not about her pregnancy. I was willing to commit—did commit—before we found this out. While I'd like more time with her, selfishly, before we did, I know life is messy and fleeting. It's not guaranteed. Happiness isn't, either ma'am. In a way, Sabine is our saving grace. She makes me happy. She has given me such love and support when I needed it. She is everything I never thought I would find in someone. We're an unlikely pair, but I couldn't ask for more. I am certain of it. My family adores her. This will be happy news at a time we need it most. I don't know why it happened like this, but... I am grateful in a way."

"Fine," Mum relented. "I will say congratulations and warn you that if you put a foot wrong, I will rain down on you like the fires in hell."

"I am aware, ma'am."

"We can discuss plans and timeline over Christmas, then," Aunt Greta said cheerfully. "You'll attend with us."

"Uh... my family might take exception to that."

"It's non-negotiable. You will announce your engagement on Christmas Eve. That is a must."

Mum glared at my aunt and uncle. "This is your doing, Gary. You had an emergency plan in place."

Gary the Fixer gleefully spoke. "I hoped they would do this so we could implement it. That's all."

Back before he was with Aunt Greta, Uncle Gary was the palace spin doctor. He relished this.

"Be grateful."

"I am not sure your family can attend, given your father's health, but I would like to extend the invite, Malcolm."

"I should go speak with them imminently," Malcolm insisted. "I don't know their thoughts. They'll be over-the-moon about the wedding and baby, but I don't know about Christmas."

"He can do the announcement and photo call with me," I said. "And then go home for Christmas. This is the last Christmas he'll have with his father, more than likely. I would like that for him."

"I will report back," Malcolm said.

We left the White Drawing Room and back towards my room.

"That went better than I anticipated. I kept both eyes," Malcolm joked.

I nodded in agreement. "Yes."

We continued, unsure what to say.

"Malcolm, did you mean all you said in there?"

"Yes. Why?"

"That I've made you happy beyond measure? That I'm a saving grace?"

"You are baby. You are. Of course, I did. I should say it more."

He stopped and kissed me. He meant it. I was convinced. I melted at his touch. We hadn't been much for romantic gestures in the past twelve hours. Neither of us slept much. We'd fallen asleep on the couch in Malcolm's sitting room. I was so knackered. It was odd. We'd made this huge, romantic commitment. I'd imagined this happening in a different way and ending with passionate sex. It didn't.

"I must return to Scotland and discuss this."

"I can go with."

"You have a life here. Engagements. I know that. The carol service tonight. Take care of yourself. Nap and look rested. Be your most beautiful self. Let me explain what is happening. I promise the next time I see you I will have more for you than promises."

Malcolm kissed me again.

"Okay," I agreed. "It's best you handle it. I don't want to impose."

"You never would, but I want to handle this on my own," Malcolm said.

"I love you. Come back soon." I kissed him goodbye.

CHAPTER 34
For Better or Worse

MALCOLM

"Malcolm, you didn't have to rush back," Mum said. "It is fine for you to go out. You need breaks, too."

I sat around my father's dining table. I arrived as dinner started, having come north on a whim. It had been a whirlwind day. I wasn't sure anything would work out.

"It's fine," I said.

Yes, it was fine. Totally fine. Nothing to see there. It wasn't as if I were about to tell my parents that I was getting married, my girlfriend was pregnant unexpectedly, and, oh, her parents are insisting we announce our clandestine-until-now relationship-cum-engagement on Christmas Eve. Oh, and I have no ring. That part didn't occur to me until I was on the jet headed back. I was fucked. Royally fucked in all ways.

"Did you see that girl of yours?" Papa asked.

"What girl?"

Both sat their forks down and glared.

"The Princess. Obviously!" Mum rolled her eyes. "I mean, really, Malcolm!"

"Yes. When did the two of you get back together?" Papa asked.

"Oh... uh... I suppose last month."

"And you said nothing?"

"She had exams. You were in hospital."

"But that was because of the medication. He's doing so much better now."

It was true. In three weeks, my father had been happier and healthier than he had in months. It was a surprise second wind. I was grateful. I hoped my news would not send him right into a tailspin.

"How did you know?" I asked, confused.

I had not told them. How did they clue in on this starting up again?

"She rang you at your place. The phone transferred here. So, we answered. The staff were all in bed. It was late. She seemed upset and looking for you."

"When?"

"Last night," father replied. "Really, Malcolm, you are so cryptic and odd. Did she find you?"

That was how she came to find me in London. I wondered how she had, but I didn't ask. It was small potatoes.

I nodded. "She came by late."

"And is she alright?" Mum asked.

I grimaced, unable to lie. "Yes. Sorry, no. I mean, it's a bit of both."

My parents stared, confused.

"She's pregnant," I replied. "And a bit under the weather."

"She's... pregnant," Mum stammered. "With a baby?"

"No, a foal. Yes, mother, a baby!"

"Don't snipe at your mother. You've just uttered something massive, Malcolm!"

I winced. "Sorry. I realise it's unexpected, but there is no easy way to say that."

"Well, to clarify, it *is* yours?" He followed up.

"Papa! Yes! It's mine."

"How? She hasn't even been up here, has she?"

"She may have come round at a particularly weak moment while you were in hospital. I was beyond help and she was in Edinburgh, so... yes. And... it's mine. If anyone here ever questions her, I'll have their head."

"No, no, it's fine. We wouldn't assume ill of her. I just needed clarity. She is a lovely girl, son."

Mum added, "Yes, too good for you."

"Mother!"

"She says it as she means it." My father shrugged. "So, Malcolm, what is your plan? To shirk? Is she keeping it?"

I hated that he assumed the worst, but I couldn't blame him. A year ago, I would have offered to pay for an abortion and prayed that was what she chose. Now, I was only trying to figure out how to do Sabine justice. That was the difference between having random, meaningless flings and finding the person you could rely on and talk to. You cared what they thought. Sabine's happiness was what mattered now. My current level of discomfort was minor.

"I will do right by her, don't worry. I always have, Dad. She's amazing and she's worthy of my time."

"She's remarkable. Again, you don't deserve her. Your mother is right. We don't deserve her, perhaps. How could you be so daft?"

"Daft? I wasn't daft!"

"At your age, you know better. Although, given your history with women, I am surprised it has taken this long."

"Dad, Jesus H Christ! I didn't come here for a browbeating over poor life choices. I am here to tell you that I plan to marry Sabine, to have this child, and that I need everyone here to support us—mainly her as I am not currently pregnant. She's the one who must move her entire life up here and have a baby."

"And she wants that?" Mum asked.

"She wants to be happy," I answered. "She wants to have a

baby with me, yes. She chose that. And we both know this is the best way forward."

"It certainly makes things better, yes. I cannot imagine that her parents and aunt will approve of this—"

"I emerged with all my limbs from the meeting we had this morning with her parents and aunt. Surprisingly, Her Majesty was very supportive and overwhelmingly kind. Sabine's Mum wanted to tear me apart, but everyone else restrained her."

"I don't blame her. You took away the girl's virtue! You should be held accountable," my father said.

"Trust when I say, I did not take her virtue or anything, father. Nor should anyone mention such a thing in a day and age when women are also allowed to have indiscriminate sex. Do not shame either one of us. I love her. The very thought of having here to help has me feeling such relief. I need her."

"And what are her thoughts?" Mum asked.

"It's not like she is over-the-moon about the way this all went down."

"What does that mean?"

"That it is complicated, Mum. That she wants a beautiful proposal, all the happiness in the world, and a lovely wedding. And, at this point, I can give her none of those things."

"Why not?" Father asked. "Last I checked, you weren't destitute, and neither were we. And if anyone can make anything happen, it would quite literally be her family."

"There are certain things money doesn't help, Niall," Mum said. "Girls dream of fairy-tales and exciting moments in their engagements and weddings. They don't imagine they will fall pregnant and must settle for a half-hearted wedding to a man who maybe loves them all because they fell pregnant at an inopportune moment."

"Mum, I can assure you I do not maybe love her. I do love her. Very, very much! And if you say that again—."

"Watch your mouth, Malcolm," Dad warned, "Watch your mouth."

"I will," I murmured.

"He loves her, darling. He told me in the most tortured way that he missed her. I know he does. It's the only time I've seen him so uncomfortable over a woman. We have a ring for her. Or, rather, you will."

"What? I just realised I should get one."

"Yes, that's essential when you're proposing." Mum rolled her eyes again.

"Your grandmother's ring is in the vault in London. Gerrard can size it."

"They'll need her measurements."

"I am sure if they do not already have them, son, they will get them swiftly. The Queen uses them."

"It's a beautiful ring," Mum noted.

"Well, I'm here. She's there, and there is yet another complication." I cringed. "Her aunt and mother are quite set on timeline. So, I should say they plan to do the engagement release in a few days—on Christmas Eve. She will leave for Norfolk in the morning after hosting the carols tonight."

"It's on telly. We can watch it," my mother said. "Or will that be odd to see her?"

"Mother, everything about dating a princess is odd. This is nothing new. I find Christmas carols dreadful, so I will be down at my cottage ignoring it."

"So will you go to Norfolk?" My father asked.

"I shall. I must be there for my own engagement photo call, I'd assume. Can they size a ring like that?"

"Oh, I would imagine. She's going to love it," Mum beamed. "They can send it with a courier. For the Queen, they'll do anything."

That was somewhat a relief.

"So, they want to invite you for Christmas, but I told them with Papa's health—"

Dad cut me off. "No one has told me I cannot fly to bloody Norfolk. It is a short flight. I'm a dying man. If the Queen is inviting me for Christmas and my son is getting engaged, I will be in attendance. And your sister will be, too, if she'd like."

"Papa, your health is most important."

"Malcolm Robert Ferguson, I didn't ask for your opinion. I didn't ask for your acceptance or permission. I am not long on this Earth. Do you know how hard it is for me to know you're going to have a baby and, more than likely, I won't ever meet that baby?"

I shook my head no. I couldn't possibly understand what that was like. I couldn't appreciate it. I didn't like thinking about it. The thought of losing my father cut so deep that I spent days compartmentalising it in total denial about the future. On one hand, everything was a blaring reminder my life would change. On the other, I wanted to go until it hit me like a brick wall.

"I want to see you married. I want to see you happy. I want to know you have someone to do this with. Your mother has been the greatest gift. She helps me in all ways. We do things together. I'm never alone. It pains me to think she will be. Of course, with Sabine around, she will probably have more light in her life."

"Nothing will replace you, Niall," Mum said, choked up. "But a baby could be a blessing in disguise."

"I hope you make it," I said. "I do. I want that for you."

"I want to die a happy man, however that happens. So, go all out. Do whatever she wants as far as the wedding goes. Be happy, Malcolm. That is all I ask. Be happy and make her happy. You have a lot more life to live together. I will take solace in that."

"I will try, Papa."

"I love you," Dad admitted. "And I know you will do right by her if you promise me you will. But you're going to need to take care of her. She's not used to all of this. It's a great deal for someone her age to take on."

"Trust me," I said. "If anyone can pull it off, it's Sabine. I don't doubt her. If anything, she knows enough about horses to keep this place afloat. She's a godsend."

CHAPTER 35
The Unproposal

SABINE

Malcolm arrived in Norfolk two days before Christmas. He did so with his parents. Despite the stroke and being mostly confined to a wheelchair, the Duke was in bright spirits. He was happy for us, as was the duchess. Kiersten was absent, choosing to ignore us for the South of France. I wanted to read it not as a snub but as a relief. We never got on. She was always a bit irritated with me. So, it was better we do the announcement in peace.

I was relieved to see Malcolm. I missed him in a way I didn't know I was capable of. We had been so close, yet so far. And it wasn't about lust, as I was so knackered, I had little desire for anything beyond a nap. It was borne out of feeling most comfortable with him there. We were united in the face of adversity. We were on the same team. I was surprised—in the best way.

The minute he saw me, I wrapped my arms around him tight —too tightly. Being pregnant was many things, but mostly uncomfortable. My tits felt like someone was stabbing me anytime something or someone touched them. I winced and pulled back.

"What?" Malcolm asked, concerned.

"Sorry, nothing," I said.

He bent down and gave me a glorious kiss. It felt real again. I was reminded that we were doing this. Despite all my complicated feelings about how it came about and everything, he was mine. He was here and was mine. Our lips remained pressed together for what was altogether too long a time, interrupted by his father clearing his throat.

"Yes, Dad, can I help you?" Malcolm turned with a chuckle.

"You should come up for air, Malcolm. That's good for the both of you."

I snickered.

Carolyn gave me a bear hug. Again, I winced, pulling back slightly.

She furrowed her brow, worried. "You alright? Or did I just break protocol. I know I did! Shoot!"

"No, no, it's not that. I'm... tender. Everything is just a bit... off."

"Oh, I forgot all about that. Yes, it can be. Babies do a number on the body from the very start."

"Sabine was the best pregnancy I never had." I heard my mother coming down the hall. "Perfect baby in that way—in many. She was such a good baby."

I shook my head and blushed.

"Hello again, Carolyn and Niall. Niall, you look much sprier than anyone led me to believe."

"I fought back like a bat out of hell," Niall declared. "You know me."

"I do, yes. So, welcome. You all should make yourselves comfortable. Greta is wrangling dinner. There was a snafu, but shortly, we should be ready."

"I'd like to freshen up a bit before, if that is alright, Beth?" Carolyn asked.

"Yes, please. Do all you need. I will show you both to your room."

The parents filed off, leaving Malcolm and me. We didn't speak for a moment. Malcolm stared, as if taking me in.

"I'm real," I giggled. "I'm here."

He cupped my cheek. "I know. I'm glad. God, the past few days were hell. We had two mares colic, a gelding broke his cannon bone, and the entire place was so covered with ice, I wasn't sure we'd make it out."

"I am glad you are here safe and sound. And the horses?"

"The gelding will be lucky if he can stay alive to be a pasture ornament. A terrible waste. Papa was rather unhinged over the loss of such a promising horse. The mares are fine. Both are still in foal. I think the cold snap had some of the particular ones a bit nervy about the automatic feeders. Or, rather, that is what I was told. I am not sure that's a thing."

"No, it is. Can be. We had a mare who would only drink water from home. We had to transport it in a big jug."

"That is madness!"

"Horses are just like people. They all have their neuroses."

"You can manage all that chaos when you move up to Scotland. Aren't you excited?"

"To have a fleet of horses to lavish with adoration? Yes. But I plan to bring some of my own, too. So, I will need to figure out stabling them."

"I think I can manage that," he said absentmindedly. He tucked a piece of hair behind my ear before leaning in to kiss me again.

If a bomb went off, I probably wouldn't have left him. I pulled him towards me, backing towards a closed door off the corridor. He pressed me up against it. I went from zero to sixty, my body yearning to have him. I would have shagged Malcolm right there if not for his own sense of self-preservation.

"Okay, before I get completely wrapped up in that, I have bad news and good news. Which would you prefer?" Malcolm asked.

"Malcolm, just take me upstairs," I pleaded.

He chuckled. "No, baby. I must do something else. Bad or good?"

I grumbled, "Bad then good."

"Fine. I don't have a big, beautiful, bold proposal. I just don't. I can work on it, but I don't have it yet. I've been barely keeping my head above water."

My heart sank because I really *did* want that magic moment. Now, I didn't get it.

"Oh, my love, don't look sad," he said. "It will happen. I promise that what I tell you next will cheer you right up."

I crossed my arms again grimacing as soon as the pain shot up my breasts.

"What is going on with you?"

"My tits feel like they are on fire—in a bad way. This is normal."

"Normal for what?"

"Pregnancy. Early pregnancy. So, don't touch them."

He looked disappointed. "Oh, well. Now, come with me. I had a minion help me with this bit."

"Who is the minion?"

"A person you love dearly."

"You schemed with Maggie?"

"Shh! Don't focus on that!" Malcolm laughed.

"Come with me," I said. "You're headed in the wrong direction, darling."

I led him back to my room which was across the hall from Maggie's. She had slept in my bed last night. We had joked that it felt like we were both waiting for our men to come home. Neither of us wanted to be alone. We fell asleep watching a Christmas movie, a plate of Christmas biscuits on the side table. It felt like old times. It felt normal. Now, looking down the nose of announcing an engagement I wasn't prepared for tomorrow, it all seemed odd again.

"Sit and close your eyes," Malcolm said. "Go, on the bed. Eyes closed. Otherwise, I will be required to punish you quite severely."

I bit my lip. "And I should dislike that?"

"You stop it! Go!" He gestured towards the bed. I sat, cross-legged, covering my eyes.

"Good girl," Malcolm said. "Now hold out your right hand."

I held out my free hand, still covering my eyes with my left. Malcolm pressed something in my palm and closed my fingers around it.

"Open your eyes," he said.

I opened my fingers to reveal a breath-taking pear-shaped diamond solitaire. It was huge.

"Malcolm... this is... wow."

"Good. Wow is good."

"It's mine?" I asked.

"It's yours if you want it. And I hope you do because I don't have a backup ring."

"It's lovely."

"Put it on. They sized it for you."

I slid it on my finger and gasped. My left hand sparkled in the light. It was impressive. It was beautiful. It was much better than I anticipated it would feel to have such a symbol on my hand.

"I love you, Sabine. I just want it to be good. It's an important piece. One of our most significant ones."

"It's breath-taking. I love it, Malcolm."

He sat by me, perhaps relieved I liked it. I gave him a sweet kiss.

"I think it's beautiful on you. But it's very special as well. Just know that my father insisted you have it. That was notable. I didn't think he'd let me have it."

"It's lovely."

"The ring was my grandmother's. My grandfather was tasked with finding her something beautiful. Diamonds weren't common then like they are now. Moreover, Norwegians still don't give such things out very often. It was a rarity, but she was a rare gem of a woman. And, if I am honest, you remind me very much of her."

I blushed.

"Sabine, I promise I will make up for the unproposal. But I want you to have this. I want you to know how serious I am. This is all a mess but asking you... that's not a mess. There is no concern in my mind about you. You are perfect. I can only hope you think I am good enough."

I patted his cheek. "You're quite good, yes. We're both flawed, but this does help."

CHAPTER 36
The Not-Prince

MALCOLM

For Immediate Release-

The Duchess and Duke of Kent are happy to announce the engagement of their daughter Her Royal Highness Princess Sabine of Kent to Lord Malcolm Ferguson, Esq, Earl of Lauderdale. The Princess and Earl became engaged when he proposed at his family's home in London. The two began dating earlier this year.

Lord Ferguson currently manages his family's estate in Lauder, Scotland, but was previously a partner at Nitter, Parker, and Ross. He is a graduate of Oxford University. Lord Ferguson is the son of the Duke and Duchess of Lauderdale, friends of the Duke and Duchess of Kent.

Princess Sabine and Lord Ferguson are expected to wed early next year, due to concerns for the Duke's health. Both families are excited to celebrate the marriage of their children and wish them the best.

A photo call will take place this afternoon at the Sandringham Estate. As this is a private family matter, there will be no public interview or public wedding festivities.

* * *

The photo call was convincing. Sabine did well. I didn't have to try to love her. I did. I could not hide my enthusiasm. And, given my father's sheer glee about this happy occasion, I floated through the day. We did the photo call in the garden, freezing but happy. Sabine beamed. We were relieved when we went to bed. Sabine had fallen asleep on my chest. It felt warm and perfect, just right.

Now, the morning we needed to pull it together to make it to the little church on the edge of the property, she was anything but right. Instead, I held her hair as she vomited into the toilet. It sounded painful at this point.

"Don't let her hair get messed, Malcolm. I will strangle you!" Maggie was also there, adding to the fun.

"I spent all that time on my curls," Sabine sobbed. "I will look dreadful."

"No, no, Sabine. You couldn't if you tried, baby. No. Your hair looks lovely."

"Don't lie."

"I am not lying, Sabine."

"Does it look dreadful, Maggie?"

"It doesn't look dreadful. Stop! Deep breaths."

A fourth person arrived.

"Drink this," Beth said. She held out a cup and saucer.

Sabine pulled a face and sat against the wall. I sat by her, trying to hold her. She looked pathetic, so miserable. She was exhausted and defeated. Gone was the beaming, beautiful bolt of a girl who had been there yesterday. She was down. I hated this for her.

"What is it?" Sabine pulled a face.

"Ginger tea. It will settle your stomach."

Sabine sipped the tea, handing me the saucer. She wasn't about to care for convention right now. There were no manners when you were on the toilet floor trying not to vomit.

"It's not terrible," Sabine noted.

"I'll bring her a biscuit," Maggie insisted.

I could hear one of the twins outside asking Maggie what the matter was.

"Go away and stop asking questions!" I heard her shout.

"Do they not know?" I asked, aware the boys may not know their sister's condition.

"We have a house full of nosey people, Lord Ferguson. I am not about to tell them. They are still young and unaware. Poor Sabine. Poor darling. You don't need more stress."

"By full of, you just mean Uncle Jamie's fiancée."

"Stop calling her that! It makes me want to punch a bloody wall. And Malcolm loathes her as well."

Prince Jamie proposed to his American new age girlfriend at the formal Christmas Eve dinner. It was like a kick in the teeth for me. Sabine had been too happy to care but did remind me of my obligation to try to impress her before dropping off to sleep. I tried my best. Fuck him for upstaging me. And fuck his meddlesome soon-to-be-wife for her comments about *my* soon-to-be-wife!

"I don't loathe her."

"You and Maggie are united in her hatred of her, Malcolm. Don't lie to me. You're dreadful at it," Sabine said.

"The fact that she is already calling herself Princess-to-be is abhorrent and smacks of how out-of-touch she is!" Beth declared.

"The what now?" Maggie returned with a roll of chocolate-dipped digestives.

"Whatsherface," Sabine groaned. "Oh, I feel so lousy. I'm so hungry."

"Eat slowly," I said. "Don't do too much."

Sabine, ignoring me, shoved a biscuit in her mouth. "She wouldn't know, Mum. Jessica is American. They all think everyone is a bloody princess. They'd think Malcolm was about to be a prince."

I was glad to be spared that atrocity.

"What will happen. Will Aunt Greta grant you a title?" Maggie asked.

"I doubt it. I will have Malcolm's title."

"But also your own," Beth said, proudly. "You can be styled as Princess Sabine of Kent, Duchess of Lauderdale someday."

Sabine looked about to go again. Instead, she let out a tremendous belch. I expected her to be mortified. Instead, she and Maggie burst into a flurry of full-body laughter. They laughed until crying.

"Malcolm don't look surprised. Girls are dreadful, too," Beth said. "You could have the least-dainty little girl on the planet by September."

"Do you want a girl?" Maggie asked.

"Well, it's not what I want that matters," I replied.

"That's a cop out," Sabine grumbled. "You sound like a bloody politician."

"You do," Maggie piled on.

"Do you two always do this?"

"They do," Beth confirmed. "Get quite used to it. They will always be together and always unified."

I was unprepared for this. In a week, I had gone from a man pining for the girl he never expected to fall for to a man marrying into the royal family despite all his protests. I hadn't expected the photographers, my family being so excited, or to inherit a loud group of siblings. And I never expected that I would be a father in less than a year. Yet, as I sat with Sabine, I didn't care.

"I must get dressed, as do you, Maggie. Come along. I will be back to check on you in a bit, darling," Beth said.

Maggie gave Sabine a sympathetic look and left with her

mother. In a way, I was petrified because I didn't know what I was doing. Still, I was glad we had our room back and some privacy.

I squeezed her knee. "I'm sorry you feel so shit, baby. I feel guilty."

"It took both of us to do this. I do curse you a bit since you don't deal with the full effects of this pregnancy. Yet, I know it's a bad time in more ways than one for you."

"I think they say there is never a good time."

She leaned her head on my shoulder as she sighed. "Yeah. True. I am happy. Surprisingly happy. I am cross about Jess and Jamie. I'm livid about how hard life is for no reason because of stupid societal rules. I just wish it had unfolded in a different timeline, but I am so happy to have you back here every day. I didn't realize how much I missed this. Just us living like we're together... it's beautiful."

I smiled, wrapping my arm around her shoulders. I kissed the top of her head. "It is good. It's fabulous."

"I am sorry things have been... not at all sexy and not all that exciting."

"It depends on your idea of exciting," I said.

Yes, I did wish there had been a hot round of reunification sex. I thought there would be time for it two days ago, but it was a joke. By the time we were alone again, she was knackered. I couldn't fault her for it.

I continued, "Press fever was madness. I never thought I'd see such a thing. I didn't like it, mind you, but it will do if I get to keep you."

"I don't intend to take you 'round, Malcolm. You've made it clear you aren't interested in royal work. We should probably discuss that. We haven't."

"Well, I won't be a prince. I'm just going to be Malcolm."

"Yes, of course. Oh, darling, that will never be the case. But you are correct."

"And there is no need for a title, as they will have their own house," I insisted. "And I don't think they are eligible?"

"If Mum outlives Aunt Greta, as I anticipate she might. Or, alternatively, if Auntie abdicates, Mum has the right to confer titles to all her grandchildren. In fact, it is expected."

I grimaced and pulled away.

"You don't want that?"

"I don't. I have no desire to have children with royal titles, Sabine. That sounds ridiculous."

"I didn't say she would. I don't believe we'll receive additional titles. I've made it clear to Auntie I didn't think you'd like that. And... I'm fine just being the Countess of Lauderdale. That suits. We can cross the title and bridge when it comes."

I nodded. "It's not what I expected. I don't know what I am doing."

"I often still don't. Maggie lives in another world. The good news? I'm not held to her standards. I never will agree to that. And, as long as we're together—hopefully forever—I will ensure you are allowed to exist as you prefer. I love you, Malcolm."

"You don't have to protect me," I said.

"I do. You have no clue. The family is a black box. It's unrecognisable to outsiders. It's our favourite defence."

Sabine's stomach settled after she devoured an alarming number of biscuits. She finished her makeup and changed into her little outfit for church service. I reluctantly pulled on the suit my mother insisted I wear, unable to cut the cord. The truth was, I hadn't the heart to tell her no. They wouldn't walk with us down to the church. They would stay here. The suit was her way of giving me—and us—support. She had little control over life right now. None of us did. Still, she found pleasure in preparing us where she could. And, no doubt, they'd watch the coverage from the comfort of a sitting room here.

I finished more biscuits along with desperately needed coffee. No time to sip tea. I needed energy. That was it for breakfast. While tending to my pregnant fiancée, I missed the official breakfast. I couldn't whinge about it, either. I knew better.

As we approached the church, people called for us. Sabine and

I were remarkably popular. I loathed pomp and circumstance, but Sabine thrived. She carried me through. She was the day's star. I realised I spent little time in her world, but whenever I did, people were captivated in her orbit. In a way, I always had been, too.

CHAPTER 37
The Dress Dilemma

SABINE

A bride needs a dress. I needed a fabulous dress with only two months to find one. I needed a brilliant one, in fact. In all my dreams, I had thought about a fabulous, classic style. Not a big fluffy princess dress. No. I wanted something chic but timeless. It had to be big *enough* but not imposing.

There was little time to create something. Choosing something off-the-rack felt cheap. That wasn't fit for a princess and future duchess. I rarely cared about such things. However, this mattered in a way I hadn't anticipated. I suddenly cared a lot about my wardrobe. I wanted to look perfect. I wanted to look back on our wedding photos in thirty years with my child and think about what a beautiful day we had, rather than think about how I was pregnant and embarrassed by the disaster of a dress I had been squeezed into.

I sat in my mother's office with my aunt and sister, trying to brainstorm. Who might be able to turn a dress over so quickly? At first, the idea had been that I was sample size so we could pull something couture from a bridal collection I liked. I wasn't restrained only to British designers like my sister would be someday. I could be broader. I had more choices. This was a private affair, not a matter of state. By the time I was 14 weeks pregnant, I doubted I would fit in a sample. Moreover, if we let a designer in on the fact that the bride had a bun in the oven, we opened massive wormholes.

My aunt's staff were aware of my quandary. They were trusted with all manner of secrets. So, we had them. They could only do so much, though. Without a dress, they could not work magic.

I paced, longing for this all to be over. Here I was, alone again. Malcolm went home to sort things out for my arrival—whatever that met. I was now here in London by myself. Last night, I had listened to my sister and Keir go at it like bloody animals. Meanwhile, I hadn't gotten laid since Malcolm and I conceived the thing causing me terrible sickness. It was all a cruel joke. I wanted to climb in bed with Malcolm and block out the world.

I stopped at a photo of my mother and aunt. It was my aunt's investiture as Princess of Wales. She was newly twenty-five and glowing. My mother, her lady-in-waiting for the occasion, was similarly beaming. The photo was candid, not the official one released with my aunt, grandfather, and all the rest in official attendance in Wales. God, they had been so beautiful. They still were. I thought my mother was a stunning woman at any age. Maggie would be lucky to age so gracefully. My aunt, too. However, they were in the prime of their lives. And they were sisters, always a united front.

It reminded me of my own sister and how much I was about to miss her every day. I pulled the photo frame down from my mother's shelf and cried. I held it to my chest, confused by my sudden grief. Was it grief? What was this feeling?

"Sabine... are you... alright?" Maggie asked, concerned.

"I don't know why I'm crying."

"Because you're pregnant and you'll cry at anything."

My mother stepped up and took me by the shoulders, guiding me kindly back to the couch.

"What do you have there?" She pointed at the frame, turned upside down, in my hands.

"A photo of you and Auntie."

"Which one?" Aunt Greta asked.

"You at the investiture together."

My mother held the photo out. "This is one of my favourites of us. We were so happy on that day, weren't we?"

"We were," Greta said. "Goodness, those were the days!"

"I don't want to go," I sniffled. "I cannot go."

"Oh, sweetheart, is this about leaving?" Mum asked.

"I have felt so lost here. In this place," I gestured. "Not that you haven't been a lovely host, Auntie. But it never felt like home. The only thing that made it bearable was Maggie. Maggie, I don't know what to do without you."

"I'm sorry, darling, but you're getting married. Generally, that means you must move." Maggie sat on the other side of me.

We hugged tight. I did not want to let her go.

"The thing is," our aunt said, "sisters are never so far apart. No matter where you go, she will always be there for you. Just like when you were in Canada. It's no different."

"Oh, it is. This is final. I was always coming back," I said. "I always knew I would return. But when I did, it was all different. We were grownups and... everything changed. But now it does forever. Because once I move... I'm not in this family anymore. I'm... his."

"He doesn't own you, love," Maggie laughed. "I would fight him over that. I think I frighten him, so he knows better than to think that."

I giggled through tears. "You do. A lot."

"I should. I should."

"You will always be our family, Sabine." Mum squeezed my arm. "You will always be ours, always be my baby, and always be a part of this. As will Malcolm. Malcolm and the baby will be a part of us, too."

"You will find your place," Aunt Greta said. "You will find

what you love there. You will fall even more in love with him than you ever imagined. And when the baby arrives, it will feel even bigger. I promise you that while it is frightening and soon, you never feel completely at peace when you make a change."

I shrugged. "I dunno. I keep feeling like I am his problem, his thing to solve."

"Well, he is responsible for taking care of you because you are the one giving up so much and moving to a strange place. I don't think he views you as a problem—any more than I viewed hosting you here as one. I spent the last week and a half trying to avoid thinking about you leaving, sweetheart. Your uncle would strangle me over it if he didn't love me so much. It's unfair for me to be so selfish, but I want you here."

"Why? Did my running around with Malcolm not bother everyone?"

"No," Aunt Greta answered. "No. Never. Seeing you and your sister fall in love has been such a blessing. And now, you will be married and have a child. I will never get grandchildren, Sabine. I will never see Cecilia walk down an aisle on her father's arm. So, I live vicariously through your mother as she gets to see it all. And I hope that you will let me be the over invested aunt who dotes too much."

"I will." I cried more. "Auntie, you only ever welcomed me. You believed in me. You still do, even though I might not. I would be so honoured to have you in the baby's life. Rather, I insist. I want her to look up to you and Mum and Maggie. Well, or him. Either way."

"She wants a girl. Malcolm doesn't," Maggie sighed.

"Malcolm doesn't care. I do. And either way, I don't get much of a choice in the matter."

"It works out either way," Mum said. "Although, daughters are wonderful, as are sons."

I looked at the photo. "Where is your dress?"

Everyone looked at me, confused.

"Auntie, this dress. The white dress. Where is it?"

My aunt's investiture dress was a beautiful satin with gold details. It was every bit as classic as any I sought. And it was something from my family's history. It would be perfect. I made a snap decision.

"Which dress?"

"The investiture dress?" My mother was keen to clarify, pointing at Aunt Greta's dress.

I nodded. "The white dress."

"It would be in the archive. Why?"

"Well, with pumps, could I make it work?"

"You hate pumps," Maggie pulled a face.

"Yes, but my feet are already swollen. You will understand someday."

"I can ring the dressers and see if they can pull it. Sweetheart, it would require some alteration."

"I know, but no more than something off the rack and disappointing, right?"

"You really don't have to do that."

"I want to," I insisted. "It's beautiful. It's classic. It's an heirloom. Unless you are opposed?"

"I am a fan of breathing new light into something." My aunt smiled. "I would be so honoured, Sabine. You really would like that?"

I nodded. "Theoretically. Let's see what happens."

CHAPTER 38
The Lady of the House

MALCOLM

"Sabine is pregnant." I confirmed to my sister.

She'd been told the bizarre news of our engagement but had no context. It felt unfair to keep Kiersten in the dark when she should know the truth. The other adults did. I expected her to poke fun on me and move on, but she was surly.

Her face pulled tight, and she snarled, "On brand, huh? I feel sorry for you. Glad she trapped you."

"Trapped me!? Kiersten, this wasn't intentional. Neither of us was expecting it."

"And yet an abortion is still freely-available and affordable."

"I let Sabine choose," I said. "Because it's not my decision to make. The two of us did choose to get married and have the baby."

"So, that's why there is now a plan for an express wedding? Very classy."

"Kiersten, be nice to your brother," Mum said. "He is navigating a great deal right now. We should support the two of them, not cast stones."

"Moreover, I would have this no other way. I'd like to see one of you happy with a partner," our father said.

"Yes, well, it's nice she gets to take the family ring and run off with it. She's a child, Malcolm. This will not last. You may have done something stupid and knocked her up, but let's hope you have thought about the implications of losing something that's been in the family for three generations."

"Papa offered it. I didn't take it. Sabine never asked for it."

"She wears it well enough."

I set my jaw. "It is her engagement ring. I should hope she doesn't keep it in a drawer."

"It was his to have. She will be the lady of the house in short order," our father said.

"Papa, please," I said. When he mentioned contingency plans, it always made me feel ill. "Is it not cruel to Mum?"

"Sweetheart, I need the help. I'd like to focus on your father, not social obligations, and village-related expectations. I'd love to not be the point person for horse-related matters. We deserve time together just to grieve. Sabine is a welcome relief."

"Putting all of that on her shoulders is unfair."

"Life isn't fair, Malcolm," my father said, curt. "And you two will find out soon enough after that child arrives. But there is good in it, too. And Sabine is plenty good with people. It has been her job, has it not? Let her take some pressure off your mother."

"I am not about to throw her to the wolves up here. I will not have her beholden to village obligations when she is quite plainly pregnant and in need of rest."

"She's twenty-three and in great shape. She'll be fine."

"Yes, as you remind me, I am missing her bloody birthday right now and must plan something spectacular. I am out of ideas—first for birthday and then the proposal I still need to do. No bloody pressure! And we're all pacing around waiting for mares to foal out. At least she'll be pleased with that. Sabine is insistent all she wants to do is play with foals. I don't quite understand it, but at least I can make one of her dreams come true."

"Malcolm, you will find your footing, but there will be changes," my father said. "Kiersten, there is much to be done to welcome your sister-in-law here. I expect you to be kind to her. No rude behaviour will be tolerated."

Kiersten rolled her eyes. "I'm fine, thanks. An angel."

I highly doubted that.

"Sabine will need a staff. She's been painfully obvious about it. She needs a lady's maid or some such."

"Of course," Mum agreed. "I think that is fair."

"And she is insistent we leave the bloody cottage. I am opposed, but I don't think I will win that battle."

"The cottage was ridiculous, and she should be insistent. It's two bedrooms and you have a baby on the way, Malcolm. You need help and staff close by. Moreover, we would like to see you both," Mum said.

Dad nodded. "You'll lose that battle. She's right. Kiersten, we will move you to the other side of the wing."

"What? Why?"

"Because that room is of similar space, but theirs is closer to ours I would assume Malcolm and Sabine might appreciate privacy."

"Give her one of the other guest rooms. I am not giving up my room."

"Kiersten, you don't live here. This doesn't matter," I said.

"They need a bigger wardrobe and there are adjoining rooms. The baby could be in one room," Mum said.

"When is this child coming? It will be months—"

"Kiersten, your brother is right. I pay a pretty penny to keep you living in Edinburgh. I bought you an apartment. You live quite well there. When you visit, you can stay in the room on our side of the castle, and I won't have protests about it."

"She gets a staff and a better room. I am cast aside! I'm your daughter. She took my engagement ring, too!"

"I don't see any point in keeping your ring when you aren't

anywhere near engaged. And it was willed by your grandmother to Malcolm!" My father's voice was short.

I didn't understand this. Kiersten could be petty, but not cruel. Then, just when I thought it could get no worse, she threw down the gauntlet.

"I think it's funny you all are bowing down to a girl—a child—who isn't even a real royal. All because what? She has a title? She's not even of good breeding, which is what you wanted, right? And why? All because she opened her legs and Malcolm is too weak to resist her?"

I jumped from my chair, hands gripping the side of the table to hold me back.

I bellowed, unleashing all my anger. "Damn it, Kiersten, if you so much as utter a word of any of that ever again, I will disinherit you the minute I can!"

"Malcolm Robert Ferguson!" My mother declared.

"No. You do not get to talk about her like that. No one here does. No one! Anyone who brings up her biological origin story or implies she is some sort of cheap whore is getting the boot. I will stop paying your expenses Kiersten. I already have control of those, lest you forget. Do you want to continue spending bank at Harvey Nichols, or is your opinion on this matter too precious?"

Kiersten looked at me, stunned. I'd never spoken this way to her. We'd rowed though never over a girl and never like this.

"Malcolm, sit down," our father said.

I sat, only because I wanted to listen.

"You have every right to be upset. Kiersten, please. I agree with Malcolm. No member of this family should ever speak that way about another. I do not think we should resort to desperate measures. It should be enough that a sensible, kind person would never suggest Sabine was unworthy or less-than because she was adopted or because things happened out-of-order. Your brother is as guilty as she is in that and there is a child at stake."

"A bastard, yes."

"Oh, Kiersten, please," Mummy whinged. "Please, darling, just let it go. This is Malcolm's child, his heir, my grandchild, and your niece or nephew."

"Don't go all moralistic on me when you are as bad at dating and commitment as I was," Malcolm said.

"And how is that working out?"

"I am in love with someone who understands me, doesn't feel the need to control me, and supports me. I don't know many women who would sign up to take on an entire estate like this while also experiencing an unplanned pregnancy."

"She's a saint," my father added. "Kiersten, I think it makes sense for you to go to your room. Sabine will be arriving. Take some time to think about how you want to handle this. I will not make the final decision here. I'm not long for this world. Your actions have consequences and Malcolm is now the arbiter of those."

Kiersten looked dumbfounded.

"Come down when you can speak nicely to people," Papa said.

He admonished her like a child. Kiersten, angrily sulked away and I stared at my parents, dejected.

"Why is she being like this?"

"Everyone is talking about the happy news. You two have been all over the papers," Mum answered. "She is usually our star. Now, we have the two of you taking up a lot of space. Sabine will take over. Kiersten will have to curtsy and speak kindly to someone a decade younger than her and someone who now helps you manage this place. You and Sabine are a team. Kiersten feels left out. And, moreover, she's now the only unwed one. People will pressure her about men and children."

"Yeah, the way you did me," I grumbled. "I feel for her there."

"Well, it worked," my father said.

"No. Sabine worked. It didn't work."

If only he knew that we had started this thing as a game. I'd never admit to doing it. It seemed to cheapen what Sabine and I had. What it began as bore no resemblance to what happened now. Sabine was everything I could want in a woman—even things I didn't know I wanted or needed. So, I would fight like hell to make sure she was happy and protected from vitriol. That included my sister's ire.

CHAPTER 39
A New Life

SABINE

I finally related to Margaret Tudor. I now understood the jarring transfer from English Princess to Scottish Duchess. No, things were nowhere near as brutish or hostile as they had been, but things were different. The atmosphere was too relaxed, the temps basically polar, and I didn't know anyone.

While Malcolm and his parents never admitted it, his sister loathed me. It was bloody well obvious. When I entered a room, she'd make herself scarce. Malcolm said she didn't live there. Yet, there she was. Living there. She was constantly about. It was so awkward living with someone who obviously didn't want to see you but was ever-present. I had flashbacks to my first-year suitemate from hell at uni.

Wedding planning took over every facet of life, along with the conference room in the bank of offices on the castle's ground floor. Conference calls with my sister, aunt, and mother always happened.

I couldn't say I was bored. It was the contrary. I had never been so busy in my life. I wondered if this was how Maggie and Mum felt every day. If so, I bowed down to their ability to keep pushing. I was exhausted on all fronts. When I felt too overwhelmed, I hiked to the barn in the freezing cold to check on the babies. Foals were beginning to fill the barn. I was in love with them.

Whenever I spoke to Maggie, she would laugh that I was more obsessed with the foals than with my own pregnancy. That was true. The pregnancy felt secondary to the waves of nausea that hit me like a brick wall. Morning sickness was no joy. My breasts feeling like fire weren't, either. I had no libido, I was knackered, and we had yet to meet our baby. I mostly prayed all was well and counted down to our first scan.

Still, I was lonely. I hoped someday soon that Carolyn and I would grow closer, and I might feel a bit more at ease. And I hoped that Kiersten would eventually come around to the idea of me being there. I knew that with her dad's poor health, things were complicated. It was all so much change.

Thus, when a stranger arrived a bit early—before Malcolm returned home from conducting business in Edinburgh—I expected that it would be more of the same. I would be just getting by, awkward and exhausted. Instead, it was a treat.

Malcolm's friend was an American who dropped by to look at a colt. Ralph Thomas was charming with a divine accent. He was older than Malcolm, but still handsome enough. I wondered why in the hell he was single. He seemed compassionate, taking great care to find what to say and asking kind questions of Malcolm's father.

Niall was the only one left in the house. Upon hearing that Ralph dropped by, he came down to the drawing room to say hello. Carolyn was out with a friend. Kiersten returned to the city with Malcolm this morning and was, thankfully, gone. She wouldn't glower at me. I was glad for a distraction.

"What did you bring us then?" Niall asked. "Before Malcolm makes it back from the solicitors."

"No, no, I won't fall for it, Niall. You can't get away with stealing the best stuff before Malcolm gets home."

Ralph had a bag. I wondered if it held something fabulous. I was about to find out.

"Come on, I'm a fragile man," Niall said. "Be kind."

"Let's ask the lady," Ralph said. "Or rather, the Princess. What do we call you?"

I giggled. "Sabine, obviously. Not sure I qualify as a lady. However, I do like the idea of nicking whatever you have from Malcolm. It will make him quite cross. I rather like to poke him."

Ralph shook his head. "You're too much."

"She matches him toe-to-toe," Niall said. "But you heard the girl. C'mon."

"I'm sure he'll be back soon," Ralph said.

"Knowing Bodie, could be ages. The man never stops talking. Malcolm struggles to leave. Doesn't want to be rude. And, anyway, the boy misses shop talk."

"C'mon, Ralph. We won't tell if you won't," I said.

"That's how you have him over a barrel? You bat your eyelashes?" Ralph's joking tone meant no harm.

"That and outargue him. He likes it secretly, whinges publicly, but I have his number. He's alright with that."

"Well, I think it might be time, then."

Ralph reached into the package. He pulled out a bottle in pristine, expensive packaging. American whiskey! It was like the one Malcolm brought to my parents as a peace offering.

"You're the bloke with the bourbon!" I declared, excitedly.

Ralph was confused. "We own a distillery."

"You may have single-handedly saved Malcolm's arse, Ralph. He brought a bottle of the good stuff to impress her parents."

"Papa was over-the-moon," I laughed.

"Is your Dad American?"

"Canadian," I replied. "Close. But he only gives out Canadian whiskey as a joke. It's swill in comparison."

"Oof, you are cruel to his countrymen," Ralph chuckled.

"I'm a dying man, Ralph, let's bust this out before Malcolm

A SUMMER WITH THE EARL

gets back. Glasses are over there." Niall gestured to the stocked liquor cabinet.

Ralph grabbed three glasses. Niall rifled through the collector's box. He was like a kid in a candy store. He reminded me of my late grandfather. There was little better than a good bottle of booze.

"Ladies first." Ralph sat a glass before me.

Niall burst out laughing. I stared, deer-in-headlights.

"Ralph is basically family, sweetheart," Niall explained. "She can't drink."

Ralph looked at me. "Some sort of condition?"

"Yes, sort of." I blushed.

"Clearly, Malcolm didn't tell you the whole story when he told you about his life events."

"He told me nothing, Niall. I learned about his surprise engagement the same way everyone else did. It was far from the first time I'd heard of her, though. Sabine, he was *smitten*. Don't believe anything else he says."

I blushed. "Oh, well, I hope it's all good."

"So, when is the big day?"

"August," I replied. "By early September."

"I thought I had the date as the 6th of March—"

"Shit. Sorry. I thought you were asking when I was due. No. We're getting married on March 6th."

"Oh, you're pregnant?"

"That was the insinuation, yes?" Niall laughed. "A happy accident of sorts."

"Well, a double congratulations are in order. That's amazing! I'm surprised. Malcolm will have a learning curve."

"We both will. My brothers are twins. All I remember is Mum and Papa being exhausted nonstop. The only one who could settle them sometimes was our grandfather. It's ridiculous really. Mum had bad depression. She called him one day and he came over with Granny and just... watched us. Cancelled it all."

"Sounds like a good man."

"He was. He could also be stubborn as a mule and terribly overprotective."

"I don't think the old King would have gotten on with Malcolm. He would have strung him up by his entrails, I suspect," Niall said.

"Well, he nearly did Uncle Gary. Uncle Gary was staff—Grandfather's staff—prior to that news coming out."

"You're talking about a king?"

"My grandfather, yes," I answered. "It's weird to think about it like that. To us, he was just grandfather. My Granny is still alive—Grandmother Georgina. But she was a good fifteen years his junior when they wed. She's still in good health. And very excited to come up here. She's mostly down at her castle near Salisbury."

Malcolm entered. By now, his tie was undone, and he removed his jacket. His five o'clock shadow was dashing. I smiled at his approach. He stopped, giving me a quick kiss, and sat. He stared across at his father.

"Papa, you nicked my whiskey?"

"She gave us your blessing, son!"

I giggled. "Niall. You're dreadful! But I did tell them to go ahead. I do wish I could partake, but alas."

"I am aware of the great secret," Ralph said. "Should I congratulate you?'

"It stays here but pray for me. I need it."

Malcolm poured. "Brodie is a madman, Papa. A damn madman. And I can barely understand a word the man says."

"That's what you get with that posh accent of yours. That and all your friends, present company exempted, hen."

I nodded. "Of course. Technically, I was born in Canada, so I'm a little odd either way."

"She speaks French. Two dialects. Did you know?" Malcolm said. "Fluently. It's very annoying."

I snickered. "We speak French at home with my father."

"Ain't that something? As a person 'with an accent' I can relate to this man's plight."

"Oh, I could listen to you talk all day. It's a darling accent," I mooned. "I must get to Kentucky. I went once with Mum. We went to Three Chimneys."

"That's a nice barn."

"It was like a horse palace. I was amazed."

"The man is from Glasgow. Dreadful to listen to," Malcolm said.

"I think those accents are fun," I shrugged. "They don't compete with a Highland lilt, but I could find it charming if I were pissed."

"Darling, you find many things charming when pissed," Malcolm chuckled.

I smacked him on the arm. "Be nice!"

"Yes, Princess," he relented. "How are you, my love?"

"I am knackered. I helped Paul let the horses in. It was good. I saw the florist. Guess what?"

"What?"

"My taste in flowers reminded her of a 'sad funeral', so I am not getting what I want. I settled on dozens of roses. Typical."

"It will be fine. It won't matter at all, Sabine," Niall said. "The whole of it will. The sum of it. Its parts? Nah. You'll remember the day fondly. That's all that matters. Beyond that, you'll forget if it was roses or lilies and what have you. Much like you forget how sleep deprived you were with the first child and proceed to have a second."

"Let's survive baby one," Malcolm said. "Just get through this one."

CHAPTER 40
In One Piece

MALCOLM

"Sabine, come on!" I called into what Sabine referred to as her 'happy place'.

It was her walk-in wardrobe; the one Kiersten loathed her for. It was as if she were in a C.S. Lewis novel. She'd disappear in there and not return.

"I need to look less pregnant!" She called.

"Sabine, you really don't look pregnant."

She didn't. At least, to me I couldn't tell. She was lovely, either way. Sabine fussed over her appearance, as never before. I worried she was falling into the same trap I saw women fall into everywhere. That they weren't enough. I couldn't understand it.

She emerged in a jumper and jeans. Why that took an hour, I didn't know.

"Ready?"

"As ever," she said.

"You're nervous?"

"Malcolm, it could all be so wrong. It could be dreadful news."

"Sabine, it won't be. It will be good news."

I hoped that was the case. This was our first scan. We were only a few weeks from the wedding. Sabine was feeling nervous, but nothing like I was. It wasn't that I doubted my choice. I figured if I was to marry anyone, it would be this wonderful creature—even if the idea of standing before a room of people and doing the thing was fucking with me. I made a living talking in front of people. When it came to personal things, it was different. Tomorrow, we had to meet with the minister presiding over our nuptials. I hoped he didn't ask too many questions.

As we drove away towards the city, Sabine softened. "I love you, Malcolm. Thanks for coming with me."

"Sabine, I would always come along. Good lord. This is my child, too. Our child. I would never want you to do this alone. Jesus!"

"Don't get offended. A lot of men still don't go along."

"Well, those men are knobs."

I meant it. Perhaps, I softened to the idea? Maybe I was less frightened and more entertained by the idea that we'd have a child? And maybe I tried not to think about losing my father, hoping that this baby could make it in time for him to meet them. I was all over the place.

Due to Sabine's situation, we entered through a service lift. We ended up in a room off a hallway no one travelled. This was life with a Princess. And finding out that she was pregnant would have earned the press billions. Anyone could do simple math would know better after the wedding when we finally released the announcement about her pregnancy.

There two women helped Sabine onto a table where they would conduct the scan. We'd waited long enough for this. Sabine was nervous. I felt a little tightness in my chest as they pulled up something on the screen and pointed. The woman who I now knew was the midwife explained what was going on. Still, I didn't want to think about it too much.

"And there is baby's heartbeat," the technician said.

A fast 'blub, blub' played over the machine.

"Is that too fast? Was he running a marathon?" I asked.

"No, that's how it is. They are different from adults," the midwife said.

"Everything looks good. That is your baby."

Sabine blubbered. The poor thing cried all the time. I gave up trying to stop her. Even her mother explained it was pointless. She was a bit emotional. I got choked up, too. I expected a baby to look more like a tadpole or something. Instead, it had a head, body, arms, and legs. And even from here, I could see its profile.

"It has your nose, Sab," I said.

"Yeah," she snickered. "I have a baby that looks like me. Like *me*."

It was sickeningly sweet, and I adored it all. God, call me a sap, but there was nothing like knowing you had made something so tiny and still impressive. And in a few months, the baby would be here. Perfect, I was sure.

We left with a few photos of our little soon-to-be-bundle. Sabine could barely contain her excitement. Her nerves faded to what could best be described as love for something neither of us knew. God, I loved this baby. How could I love something I didn't know already? My happiness soon faded back to fear. When we returned home, we found the worst surprise. There was an ambulance waiting in the drive. I felt as though my entire body might shut down.

"Malcolm," Sabine said. "Deep breaths."

She knew already.

I put the brake on and left the car, still running, rushing into the house. I figured Sabine could take care of the car. Inside, I heard the voices of several people talking. They were loud. People shouted. And then, I heard a person shout.

"Move! Move! Coming through!"

A man rushed by. My father, on a stretcher, was about to be loaded into the back of the ambulance. I watched in horror. Kiersten stepped next to me, tears in her eyes. My father was moving.

My mother followed, ignoring me completely. I didn't know what happened or what to think.

"He just fell over," Kiersten said, horrified. "Clutching his chest. He was fine this morning."

A man slammed the ambulance door shut.

"Are you tailing us?" he asked.

"Yes," I replied.

"I'm riding with you," Kiersten said.

We jogged back to my Jag.

"Get in. I'm chasing that ambulance," Sabine said. She'd flipped into the driver's seat by now.

Kiersten climbed in back, and we peeled out. Sabine drove like a bat out of hell again. It occurred to me now that I'd never let her drive anywhere except a hospital. Last time, I didn't notice it much. I was in shock. This time, I was holding on for dear life as she hugged every turn like a Formula 1 driver, following the speeding ambulance.

"You're amazing. This is terrifying!" Kiersten giggled. "Malcolm is seeing his life ending."

"Shut the fuck up, Kiersten! Now is not the time!"

"And hold on," Sabine shifted as we merged onto the motorway.

"Mind the speed, baby. We will get pulled over—"

"You assume anyone will stop me?" Sabine asked. "Oh, sorry, officer. It's a medical emergency and my aunt is the Queen. No one cares."

We swerved through traffic, Sabine laser-focused on the ambulance doing the same. She was remarkably calm. I bent to pick up the ultrasound print out which fell off the dash. I hoped I wasn't about to die.

"What is that?" Kiersten asked, being nosey.

"The baby," I handed it over.

I fully expected her to say something nasty and was unprepared to fight in our current state.

"She has Sabine's nose."

"Or he," Sabine said. "We don't know. We won't know."

I rolled my eyes.

"Malcolm, I know you are rolling your eyes. I get to choose. I chose not to know."

"I love you, so yes."

"Aww. That's exciting," Kiersten said. "Bring it. Show it to Papa. He'll adore it."

He would. I could only hope he was still on this Earth.

"If he... died... would they turn the lights off?" I asked.

"Malcolm, darling, don't torture yourself. He's a fighter," Sabine said. "Both of you, deep breaths. I will get you there in one piece."

We arrived at hospital where a doctor ran us over everything they did for Papa He needed changes in medication again. But I could see the wheels turning. Dad wasn't going to last. They were hesitant to do too much now. God, I hated that. He was like an old horse. Better to do as little as possible.

Sabine stepped away to call her anxious family about the baby. She still couldn't tell them much, but she explained Papa was sick, and we were at hospital. Everything else was cryptic as all get out. On the phone, she talked about The Foal. If a call was ever intercepted, it was above board.

"He'll be alright." The doctor noted my expression as I waited in the hall.

Sabine used a phone in an office off the main ward. I was giving her some space.

"But for how long?"

"It's end of days, you know? But, if you are worried about the wedding, don't be. He needed an adjustment. He's alright. Frightened you all, but he talked our ears off about your wedding. If you want my advice, live like each day could be his last, but don't worry that every day will be."

Sabine emerged.

She asked, "Any update? More news?"

"No, Your Royal Highness. He is resting comfortably. There is not much more to be done."

"Good. Thank you, Mr Burrows," Sabine said.

Her tone was so held together, so strait-laced. This was not the woman who once told me she was dying to sit on my face until she rained down on me like a monsoon. There was Princess Sabine and Sabine the Girl. Sabine the Girl was very different.

"You should go home. Take her home. She's been out all day," my mother said. "Sabine, you need rest."

"I'm fine." Sabine pulled the ultrasound photos out of her handbag. "But we both probably should go manage things at home in case something happens with the foals. Niall would want that. When he gets up, Carolyn, show him this."

Sabine handed the ultrasound pictures to Mum. Mum stared at her, tearfully.

"Oh, this is wonderful, you two. Look at that!"

"Healthy as... well, a horse," I said.

"Just beautiful. Absolutely beautiful. Niall will be beside himself."

"Maybe we should wait then?" Sabine said, nervous.

"No, no. He will adore this, Sabine. It will be good for him. It will put some wind in his sails. He needs that."

I rubbed Sabine's back. I wanted her to know it was okay, even if for now it was touch-and-go. I was relieved to see my father in one piece, resting and breathing. I was excited for whatever the future held. I tried not to focus on the terror I'd felt hours ago. Rather, I tried to be grateful for what was left. We had Dad for a bit longer. The wedding would happen. The baby would come. Those were the good things I needed to make it through.

We left the hospital in some semblance of silence, returning home. I suddenly knew exactly what Sabine and I needed. It may not make a lot of sense to her now, but hopefully it would shortly. I only prayed she could suspend her disbelief long enough to let me attempt it.

CHAPTER 41
The Declaration

SABINE

Malcolm drove home, seeming much calmer than when I drove us to hospital. He seemed lighter. We were both grateful Niall was still with us. I had a gut instinct he would be. The man had a flair for the dramatics and kept us on our toes. He was tough as nails. I knew where Malcolm got his incredible stubbornness.

I napped a bit. I was knackered. Between my concerns about the baby's health and now Niall, I was tapped out. Pregnancy drained my reserves like no other. Thankfully, the longer I stayed with the Fergusons, the more I realised I did have help. Malcolm's mother was an angel—like any good mum—and his father was a nice conversation partner. We lazed about together watching telly. Malcolm, too, was becoming dutiful as ever. It was different than it had been. I couldn't have managed otherwise. My exhaustion was ever-present.

Malcolm woke me as we pulled onto the castle's private drive. I perked up, still sleepy-headed.

"Where are you going?" I asked.

"Just roll with it," Malcolm said.

I rolled my eyes. "I need a proper dinner, Malcolm."

"I will make sure you are properly fed and watered. Suspend your confusion for a moment, baby."

I let him lead, sure it didn't matter if I whinged.

He pulled into the carpark behind what people called the "hobby stables". This was where I kept my three horses and where his parents stabled their string of hunting mounts. It was complete with a covered arena and turnout paddock that doubled as a dressage arena, a holdover from Malcolm's eventer grandmother.

"Mal, for once, I am too knackered to do the evening feed."

I often came down to help with evening feeds. I'd say hello to my babies, help bring the broodmares in, and dote on the foals. Malcolm was usually in town or in the city dealing with business that time of day. It was my most energetic point, so I took advantage. It made me visible to the staff and let me get to know them. Malcolm was like a ghost. Niall was too ill to come down as he used to. I learned from my mother and aunt how much face time mattered to staff. This was part of my grand plan.

We stepped into the barn aisle. It was quiet. No one was feeding over here yet. They were bringing in the horses in training and broodmares. Then all three rounds of feeding would begin.

"I wanted to just... take a minute," Malcolm said.

"Okay?" I gestured that he had the floor. "You may proceed."

"I know the timing is odd," he continued. "And might not make sense. And I should have done this ages ago. I only wanted it to be from the heart and totally off the cuff."

"Malcolm, what are you up to?"

"Sabine, I love you," Malcolm said. "With my whole heart. I love your wit, your absolute inability to back down from a problem, your strength, your protectiveness, and your charm. I find you irresistible and have since the day I met you. I don't think I knew I loved you then. I had no clue how much I wanted to just *be* with you. The fact that I now wake up next to you every day feels as it if it always should have been."

I blushed. "You're too kind."

"I am honest. If there is one regret I have, it's that I didn't do this sooner. I regret that I didn't do it back in November before I ever let you leave this place. I suppose we couldn't help it, right? Exams and all that. I'd like to change the timeline, but I regret not telling you I loved you the first time I wanted to back in July. You deserved to know just how much I adored you, needed you."

I began to tear up. "Oh, Malcolm that's... so sweet."

"The future is bleak in some ways. I struggle every day. You know that more than anyone. I tell you everything. I've never had that with anyone, Sab. You're it. I trust you with things I never dreamed I could delegate to anyone. And you assume responsibility without a second thought. You are glad to be busy. I couldn't do life without you. I don't know what I would do."

"You'd survive."

"Survive, but not thrive. And while it is hard and I cannot promise you it will be all roses or easy, I can promise you I will do my best and make it that way when the dust settles. And if that means we move back to London for some time so you can finish your course or do whatever it is, we will manage it. I will pay you back in spades for your loyalty and trust."

I was in tears now.

"Sabine, I would not want to do this with anyone else. It's beyond my imagination. I have no doubt we will be happy. We *want* to be happy, don't we?"

I smiled and nodded, unable to find words.

Malcolm got down on one knee. "I never fucking asked you this question and I should have... but I didn't want it to sound put on or less-than-ideal. Of course, perfection is relative, and I'm doing my best."

"It's better late than never," I said, impressed that this was even still on his mind.

I had given up on a proper proposal.

"Sabine, I promise you I will do everything I can to ensure your happiness and fulfilment. I will support you in every way.

And I will be a partner in everything—that includes family life. It's not going to be easy, but nothing ever has been. The payoff has been worth far more than what I put in."

"Great ROI," I joked through tears.

"Best investment I ever made. You are so wonderful. I would be lost without you. Sabine, would you please marry me and just... be with me?"

I nodded. "Forever and a day, yes."

He stood, sweeping me into a big kiss. I longed for this. Things had been so chaotic, so busy. We'd lost ourselves in it, swept up in everything happening. Suddenly, everything was silent. Completely gone. All we needed in that moment was one another. All we needed was to just *be*. That was all I wanted from him and all I needed.

Malcolm pulled away and wiped tears from my cheeks lovingly. "Was it worth the wait?"

"It was really more of a declaration than a proposal," I said. "But it was so lovely and romantic that I will let it go. I didn't even know you were capable of that."

"I can still surprise you. I've got a lot of time left."

"Please take care of your heart, darling," I pleaded. "This baby needs you around. I don't want to lose yet another person in my life. It is hard enough to imagine losing Niall."

"I know." Malcolm kissed my forehead. "I promise I will take good care of myself—for your sake and mine. And, yes, for this baby. Whatever his or her name is."

"We should work on that," I said. "Really. I think we are at that point. I have an idea if it is a boy, but none for a girl."

"We have a lot of time to discuss it. Let's get through the wedding first before we debate the merits of potential names."

"That is practical."

"Now, I'd like to be impractical and test your patience some more."

"Oh?" I groaned. "Malcolm."

"Give me half an hour and again just go along?"

"Where are we going?"

"The cottage," Malcolm said.

"Why? The cottage is ridiculous. It holds no good memories. It got us into this mess."

"I haven't felt so intertwined with you as I was there. I realise I fucked up. It wasn't intentional, but Sab, I wanted that night to last an eternity."

"You're going to make me cry again."

"Then we should definitely try to cheer you up."

I wanted to tell him food in my belly would be a proper cheer-up, but his excitement was infectious. The cottage was down the lane. I knew what he wanted and, suddenly, I wanted it to.

Malcolm and I flew into the house, not bothering to draw the curtains as we clawed at one another, hungry to be together. Strangely, it was just like the last time. Here he was with me. Here he was—all mine—and desperate to have me near. I realised this was Malcolm's prime coping skill. I was a safe place to land. And when he could put energy into fucking me, he could blow off steam.

Eventually, realising that anyone could wander by and see us in this state of undress, we hightailed into the bedroom. I'd be more comfortable there anyhow. Even now, my poor back and hips were sceptical of anything too wild.

Malcolm pushed me back on the bed, no longer so tender, and ripped off my knickers. I loved when he took control. We were transported to a time when we focused on getting one another off. Or, at least, a time we pretended there was nothing between us but a mutual need for good sex that happened to tick other boxes.

Malcolm dove in between my thighs, his tongue doing all the work. It felt amazing. All the fears I had about the bump I could barely hide and never ignore faded. Here he was, buried in my pussy like a man on a mission. I folded like a house of cards as he sucked my clit and rapidly moved three fingers into me. I was already dripping wet. I grabbed his hair and screamed his name, loud as ever. My legs twitched and I panted, face warm from the absolute pleasure he brought.

Malcolm looked up and said those two words that only made me want more. "Good girl."

Fuck. That was always *so* hot. It was what started this whole thing. It made him even more irresistible.

"You want me to fuck you?" He loomed over me now.

His cock pressed against my pussy, rubbing my folds. It tempted me. He wanted me to beg.

"I shouldn't have to beg." I resisted playfully.

"I am not doing it unless you beg, baby. I need you to beg."

"You owe me this."

"I owe you nothing, Princess."

"Please," I said.

It wasn't enough. He wanted more.

"Please, can I have you?"

"Please can I have you? Have who?"

I toyed with the idea of what to say. I didn't know if it would turn him on or completely off. I suspected it might be just fine, since he loved dirty talk and feeling in charge. Or, at least, he loved it when I made him feel that way.

"Please, daddy, can I have you?"

He kissed me, thrusting inside. I guess it worked? It was certainly not a poor reception. Malcolm's body pressed against mine; my face pressed to his shoulder. I couldn't help but bite it as I came again, collapsing then. He had taken all of me. I was a puddle there, just letting him take me. I watched him as he watched me, lying there satisfied. It was gratifying for him.

As he continued thrusting, harder and faster, I felt him get close. He wanted me to talk to him. I bit my lip, debating if I wanted to selfishly make him make me cum again or just give him a break. He couldn't have been deeper inside me now. He was smashing against my g-spot. I loved the feeling. And I let go. Instead of encouraging him to cum, begging as he wanted me to do, I was selfish.

"I want to cum again, daddy. Please?"

He kissed me again, as if unable to vocalise his approval and willingness. I ramped up, feeling every inch of him inside me. I wrapped tighter and tighter around him and then, like an explosion went off, I came. I squirted for the first time in forever, collapsing again. Malcolm came at the same time, moaning as he fell forward onto me, satiated and exhausted. He kissed my neck, panting, then sucked on my nipples, right then left, and fell to the side.

"That was... amazing," I admitted.

"Do that again," Malcolm said. "Be naughty like that. Always. Don't hold back. I love it."

"I will," I said. "So, you don't want to get all tender just because we're old married people with a baby?"

"Absolutely not. I want you to be my dirty, deviant wife who needs to be spanked and taught to listen. At least here. Otherwise, you're quite capable of putting me in my place."

I looked at him, then at my stomach. He looked at me and did the same, placing his hand on the small bump protruding from my pelvis. It was the only sign things changed. And, I suspected, the first time he'd really examined it up close. Neither of us felt all that connected to this baby in a granular sense.

"We did this. Here," Malcolm said. "It's hard to believe we could make something so perfect."

"The universe had other plans. I worry I'm going to be big as a house and you won't want me."

"That is a silly worry, Sab. I cannot think of a reason I would not want you. It would take a lot. You're the best I've ever had by a longshot. I'm a weak man—especially for you. I won't press you on the matter, but damn if I am not looking forward to you parading around in a bikini for three weeks."

We were headed to a honeymoon in Bora Bora.

"You do realise I will look different by the end of it? That I will be massive, and you'll have to see all the evidence."

"Yes, the result of my unbridled lust and love for you. You'll be just as magnificent. Even more so. Stop worrying about it. Your confidence is sexy as hell. Just be proud of it. You'll be lovely."

I had to trust this wasn't just pillow talk. After all, we'd just had white hot sex. We were stuck together either way. As he said, forever intertwined. I had to trust that my body changing wouldn't spook him.

CHAPTER 42
The Calm before the Storm

MALCOLM

The morning of our wedding began as any good day did. Sabine was in good spirits. She decided to blow me, out of nowhere, and then I fucked her until she pleaded for me to cum. She worried I would exhaust her. Neither of us had given into the nonsense about not seeing the bride the morning of the wedding. We already put the cart far ahead of the horse. What was one naughty morning to add to it?

I changed and headed down to breakfast. Sabine returned to sleep and rest. She needed it for the marathon day. The women set up in a sitting room upstairs. Their dresses, in garment bags, filled the hallway. It looked like I would assume a fashion show did with half a dozen garment racks. Dressers were busy coordinating. Boxes of what I assumed tiaras were employed with a guard on watch. I nodded as I passed, worried he would think I was up to something.

Today, we expected about two hundred guests. This was very small for a royal wedding, even a society wedding, but it was what we could reasonably accommodate on our estate. The ceremony, led by the local vicar, would take place in the ballroom. It would be followed by a reception held in a heated tent outside. We wanted to keep things close to home for father's sake.

I arrived downstairs, surprised that none of Sabine's family was present.

"Where are Simon, the boys, and Gary?" I asked.

"The bride's family was set up in the formal dining room, since they vastly outnumber us," Kiersten said. "I thought it was silly, too."

"We have people here from Scandinavia and everywhere," father said. "It makes sense. The royals want to catch up and I wanted a quiet breakfast. Is the bride getting ready?"

"She's still in bed. Knackered."

I did not disclose why the bride was knackered. I merely smiled to myself. She'd looked beautiful and we'd been up to no good. It was perfection.

"She doesn't need to fuss," Mum said. "It is good for her to rest. The other royal ladies—the VIPs will start hair and makeup first. It's an evening wedding. Sabine isn't expected in hair and makeup until noon. That is if anyone at this table read the schedule."

She glowered. "No one did?"

"I was told when to show up," I insisted. "That is all I need to know. 5:45. I will be there."

"Malcolm, you are so dreadful."

"The wedding is not until seven. I don't even know why I must be there so early."

"Photographers are doing family photos. We still must get a massive photo with all the royal attendees after and you two will take some candid photos. Then, dinner. It will all be fine. Just trust the planners."

I had to. I didn't care what happened apart from marrying Sabine and that my father was here to enjoy the day. Those two things helped me remain excited.

"She's in good spirits?" Papa asked.

"Oh, she was in good spirits last night."

Yes, she blew me, so I would say so.

Mum nodded, approvingly. "Well, she'll make a beautiful bride. The whole day will go splendidly. The only thing I am a bit cross about is that she didn't want to wear the family tiara."

"Mum, it's customary for the bride to wear her own family's tiara," Kiersten asserted.

She defended Sabine now. That was an interesting turn of events. I suspected Sabine's absolutely batshit driving on the way to hospital endeared my wild sister to Sabine. It was odd what made women get on with one another.

"Her aunt bestowed the tiara on her as a wedding gift," I said. "I know nothing more. However, they are very close. I suspect she didn't even think she could turn the offer down. It must have been an expensive gift, too. I wouldn't pry. I can assure you she will have several reasons to wear ours in the coming months. Besides, you have something to look forward to when Kiersten weds."

Kiersten shot me daggers. I snickered. She flicked me off. Our father laughed, but Mum glared disapprovingly.

"I would not turn down a gift from Her Majesty. She is kind to give Sabine such a nice tiara. Her mother and aunt seem keen to spoil the girl."

"Sabine is very loved. Beloved. She's a firecracker. How could you not love her?" I asked.

"You're lovesick. It's dreadful." My sister shook her head. "I didn't think you capable. She makes you mad."

"You like Sabine, Kiersten. You have come around. Be grateful you like your sister-in-law," Papa said. "Could be worse. He could marry someone like that Jessica character."

Kiersten and I snickered. I almost snorted out my tea.

"I think she is trying," Mum said. "You do not like her, Malcolm. That much is clear. And Princess Margaux seems to loathe her."

"She is rude to Sab," I said. "Anyone rude to Sab will catch my ire and Maggie's. She should fear Maggie's ire most. That woman is trifling."

"She's annoying. Thinks she's the centre of the universe. Does she not know how low on the roll she is? Jamie doesn't work. He's notoriously seen as a do-nothing. He's a nice enough bloke. I'll grant him, but she's only making that image worse. He doesn't do anything for the family. She's running him into the ground. I hope he doesn't have children with her. Heaven help him!"

Papa's words were painful, but true.

"I am glad she is not like Jessica," Kiersten said. "And she's grown on me. She's helped us. She loves the horses. That matters. She takes care of everyone. I didn't expect it. She'll make a good Mum."

I was surprised by that admission. My face gave it away.

"Oh, come on, Malcolm! You know it, too. She dotes on you. And she will. I was surprised, given that she's practically a baby, but she's lovely."

"I am... wow. That is... a stunning declaration of support."

"I wish you all the best, brother. And I plan to be a doting aunt, so I suppose I should try to be kinder to Sabine. I've been a bit of a bitch."

I wouldn't agree that she had. Of course, yes, Kiersten had been dreadful to Sabine. Still, it did no good to point it out.

"She will be happy to hear that," Mum said. "You should tell her."

"I agree. I am glad, Kiersten. You two will be friends. She's a lovely person. I am glad you can see that now," I said. "And she will make a good Mum. I'm certain of it."

CHAPTER 43

The Storm

SABINE

I awoke from peaceful slumber around ten, grateful that I could sleep in. Malcolm left me early in the morning. I'd been in a good mood. Still was. Excitement buzzed. I heard people preparing the hall near Carolyn's sitting room. Women chattered. I pulled on shirt and comfortable sweatpants before heading out. I wanted to take a walk and soak up this bit of happiness.

I worried it would feel cheap or less-than only two months before. Now, it felt perfect. I was every bit a bride. My family had been so happy the night before. Malcolm's was on a high. We were coming together. It felt right. I wasn't sure I was completely ready to be a wife or mother but feared I might never feel ready. So, now was as good a time as ever.

I snuck into the room where my dress hung. It was supposed to be for the best guests in the house—my Aunt and Uncle this time—but it had been pulled aside to store my dress. Here is where I would don it, taking the last steps to begin my new life in utter splendour. The dress had to be let out last minute, but my final fitting yesterday produced good results. I looked like a real bride.

I took it in. The beautiful embroidery shone in the morning light. I touched the satin, feeling the delicate embellishments. I sighed. It was perfect. I examined the adjacent veil. I'd elected to wear my mother's wedding veil. We had no time to make a new one and it was gorgeous. It was simple apart from being long—longer than my dress and its short train—and having beautiful lace all around. I'd cried when I'd tried the whole thing on, along with the fringe tiara my aunt gifted me in surprise last minute doting. It was mine to keep, she said. A personal gift, not a loan. She promised me one of those, too. I had time to think about what I wanted.

It was odd to be the first married. I always assumed Margaux would go first. She was sensible and traditional. She loved the idea of being swept up and cared for. I'd not been interested in such things. It would be strange having a new style, some more prestige, fabulous houses, and the ability to tote a tiara to every state dinner and proper occasion. My sister couldn't do that. She wasn't married.

She and Keir were somewhere enjoying one another's company. Since he was back in Scotland on base doing some sort of work, he'd be granted leave for only the weekend. I figured my aunt had something to do with it. Either way, they were deliriously happy together. I was glad. Margaux deserved that much. Keir loosened her up. He made her fun and lively.

I checked myself in the mirror. It was bittersweet. I wondered if my birth mother would have ever dreamed for me to have such a day. I suspected if not for my parents being who they were, I never would have met Malcolm. I worried that if I were just Margaux Bouchard, the average girl, he would not love me. Still, I hoped she would at least be proud of me. I was. I had done a lot in this life. I was strong, resilient, and everything I was told she wanted me to be.

I stared at my changing body. I could hide it still—just barely

— with strategic wardrobe choices. In this shirt, it was obvious. I wasn't trying to shield it from anyone here. The news would come out soon enough. Malcolm and I weren't ashamed of it. I thought we would be, but his love for me and this love we had for this baby made it seem beautiful. It wasn't cheap or silly as it had felt.

I cupped my stomach as I stood in the mirror, trying to imagine what I might looked like in a few weeks after we returned. I suspected I'd be sun kissed and very round. I tried not to worry about it. My dress didn't show any signs of my pregnancy. I wasn't trying to hide it, but I wasn't promoting my pregnancy, either.

"Oh my God. You just confirmed it all."

I heard a voice from the doorway. I looked in the mirror to see Jessica standing there holding a rolled-up mat of some sort. I dropped my hands, pulling straight into princess mode.

"He knocked you up? And that's what this is all about. How you stole everyone's thunder and just went for it!"

"Stole thunder? Last I heard, you weren't engaged until after we were. And he's not marrying me out of obligation. I don't know what you think you saw, but it has nothing to do with today."

I tried storming past her. She stood like a wall, arms crossed. She looked so self-satisfied.

"You cannot be in here," I insisted. "The room is reserved for me and my dress."

"Oh, yes. So no one catches wind of your little surprise? You know, it's not surprising based on how you came to be."

Tears welled.

"Your mother was an addict who drove headlong into another car and almost killed you. She got pregnant and you don't even know who your father is, right? Like, wow. You may have lucked out, but you're still from the same stock as that. Marrying Malcolm won't cover up the fact that you've always been trailer trash. I truly don't understand why your aunt supports this. I suspect she doesn't know."

I sobbed. "She knows. She does because she loves me."

"God, I wish I could crack this case. I thought you had to be born in to be accepted, but you're proof it's just a popularity contest. I'm not sure of what makes you popular, though."

"You can try not being a downright cunt to everyone all the time!" My voice filled the room.

I sobbed. I let her have it. I felt so low, so frightened. She had destroyed every ounce of pride I'd had only moments earlier.

"Doesn't change that I'm from a good family, not an addict, and am old enough to be a mother. I'm not some child bride that landed a man basically by throwing herself at him. Malcolm may be chasing tail and have gotten caught, but all that makes you is a slut."

I sobbed more. "I am not a slut. And I do know my biological father. My birth mother was an addict, but she worked so hard to get clean. She drove me because I wouldn't sleep. She wasn't high. Don't say that about her! She was a good person. A drunk driver killed her!"

"People talk. I think maybe you've been fed a line. God, I cannot *wait* to tell everyone about this!"

"Don't do that!"

"What? If this isn't about the baby and if everyone loves you, no one will care! And I will set up where I want. I'm doing my yoga."

I refused to beg. I flew out of there, frightened. I ran downstairs in a hurry, no make or bra on. I was a mess. I never came down like this. I was trained not to do so. Still, I didn't care. I wanted to find Malcolm. I needed to find him. He sat with his father in his father's little office off the kitchen. They were already partaking in whisky. *God, I wish I could right now!*

Malcolm stared at my panicked face, growing concerned.

I choked, "I need... I need to speak with you."

Malcolm nodded and stood to comfort me. "What is the matter?"

"I..." I pulled him into the butler's pantry. "I cannot do this. I cannot marry you."

"Sabine, what the fuck? What are you talking about?"

"I am not... I will never be good enough. To be your wife... to be anyone's wife. I am not meant to be a Countess or a Duchess and especially not a Princess. People have been kind to me all my life, but no one believes it. I will just dishonour you and—"

"Sabine, I've done plenty in my life to cast dishonour on this house, but you aren't a line in that story. Not a single word. Sabine, I love you. What is causing this? You're every bit worthy. What is going on?"

"I'm the child of an unwed mother repeating itself and... I'm not meant for this."

"Sabine, do you love me?" Malcolm asked.

I nodded. "More than anyone... but... it doesn't matter."

"It does. Because I cannot imagine surviving this day without you. I thought everything was fine. Are you well?"

He checked my forehead for fever. "You're not sick?"

"No. I'm fine. The baby is fine, I think. I just... something happened. Ugly things were said about my birth mum."

"What happened?" His tone changed from concern to white-hot anger. It was like he just *knew* something had happened with an interloper. "Who said something to you? Did something to you?"

"Malcolm calm down!"

"No, I will not. Who is this person? It's not your family..."

"No, Mal. Darling, my family would never."

"Because they are your family! Because you belong to them—and me—and they would never say these things. They are not true. It's wrong to cast your birth mum as something dreadful. She made something so wonderful. Without her, I'd not have you. This amazing, beautiful creature I love so much. And we wouldn't have this baby. Okay? So, never believe anyone who says such things. Who was it?"

He cupped my face in his hands, bringing my chin up so I met his gaze. "Sabine, tell me what happened. I need to know."

"It was Jessica. She said all these awful things. She knows. She could tell and... she swears she will tell everyone. She wants to embarrass us."

"Well, she won't."

"I mean our families."

"She won't. Even if she tells the entire fucking world, neither side will ever say a word to you. If they did, they'd have to fight me. I am enraged!"

He grabbed my hand, and we flew down the corridor. He pulled me into the drawing room where the rest of the party was waiting. I was still a mess. The vein in his neck that rarely made an appearance unless he was defending my honour popped out. He stopped. The entire room stared at us, confused.

"Your Royal Highness... Prince James. I need to speak with you regarding a very pressing matter. Or rather, I guess everyone should just hear what I am about to say."

"Go on," my aunt said.

Uncle Jamie looked on, nervous. He nodded tentatively.

"Jessica is to say *nothing* more to Sabine over the course of this day. If she so much as says a word, I will have her removed from our premises. Let me be clear. This day is about us. Sabine and I will be wed here today. We will go on to have a beautiful life. We will have a child together and there is no shame with that. Anyone who would suggest that my wife is less-than or anything else in the matter is incorrect and unwelcome in our home. I mean this with impunity. Now, I am done with debate. I rest. There is nothing more to discuss."

He sounded like he had just finished his last statement at court. It was ridiculous. It was final. It was undoubtedly the sexiest thing anyone had ever done for me.

"What was said?" Margaux demanded, coming alive. "What did she say to you?"

"I think it is best I discuss this with you and Princess Bethany privately. Sabine is rather shaken up. I will speak with you two, as it is a family matter. Sabine deserves to enjoy her day. We deserve peace, but mostly her. She's doing all the work of carrying the entire event."

I smiled at him. "You're sort of crucial, Mal."

"Nah. They're here for the bride." He kissed me. "I will manage this. Go take care of whatever you need to. Get beautiful or what have you."

"Okay," I agreed.

"Do not worry about anything or anyone, darling," my aunt looked at me and then my uncle.

She shot him daggers.

"I won't. I trust that Malcolm and Maggie have this covered," I said.

CHAPTER 44
The Countess

MALCOLM

When Sabine walked down the aisle, she was beautiful. Her smile radiated happiness as she floated on her father's arm, her visage partially obscured by the ivory veil. I did not turn towards the reverend when she arrived. I wanted to see her entrance. I thought that tradition was stupid. I also longed to give her stupid aunt-to-be a screaming middle finger and put all fears to rest that this was done under duress.

Simon pulled Sabine's veil back, unveiling her lovely, happy face. Her locks, almost crimson in the light, were pulled up high, seated under the fabulous tiara her aunt gifted. She could not have looked more beautiful if she tried. Well, for that moment. I will dispute this claim many years later. She only gets more beautiful to me with age. I thought that was a ridiculous statement until I was living it.

We said our intent, smiling at one another like idiots. She was effervescent. Nothing held her back. I beamed. I didn't care who knew. And, anyway, gone were the days I would have been embarrassed for showing such affection and excitement.

Simon patted my arm and stepped away, leaving us to say our vows. I meant every word I said. Sabine cried as she spoke. Maggie fed her tissues with what could best be described as uncanny, military precision. The mums cried. Hell, as we finished, ready to sign the register, I saw Papa crying. There wasn't a dry eye.

Register signed; we were wed. Sabine was my wife. She was more than I could have hoped for. She was exciting and charming, not at all boring or daft. She was clever beyond measure. She had compassion for days. I was undeserving, as I will say until my dying day. Still, she was mine. I was elated.

We didn't make it to our place in the receiving line before I swept her into a great big kiss—somewhat off her feet. I put her back down. She stared in confusion.

"We're doing that now? We said we would be good?"

"Fuck it!" I chuckled. "I am a weak man."

A cheeky grin crossed her face. She kissed me back, slowly. It was freeing. What was ridiculous was that we could commence God-sanctioned snogging. A piece of paper somehow mattered. I found it ridiculous.

We let people file through the annoying receiving line. Sabine's father, the extrovert talked everyone's ears off. Sabine, too. She insisted on introducing him to Ralph properly. I thought the poor American may never get to leave. Ralph finally stopped.

"You know, it was a beautiful ceremony. Special. Enjoy it. She makes you happy. And you're lucky to have her, buddy."

He patted me on the arm and retreated to the tent where cocktail order was in progress.

"Love that man," Sabine said.

"Ralph knows people."

"So strange he's not married."

"He was like me for years. Still travels a lot. I'd gather he'd settle down for the right girl."

"Could be fun to hook him up."

"Let's focus on us before we fancy ourselves matchmakers," I said. "Given how we felt about matchmaking, I mean…"

"Is there something about being married that makes someone so smug about their capabilities of vetting potential mates for others?" Sabine joked.

"No clue. Never been married before."

"Thoughts so far?"

"Lovely. Everything about it. Just brilliant."

Sabine smiled. I would have kissed her if not for the appearance of my very elderly great-aunt.

We took photos, sitting through the brutal royal photo call. For what was not a royal wedding, it sure felt very royal. Then, the candid photos in which we simply made eyes at one another. I got to kiss Sabine as much as I wanted, which quite suited me. I would have gladly run her upstairs but could sense her hanger. It was unwise. Also, I had no idea how to get the sparkly thing off her head.

"How does that come off?" I asked over dinner.

"Malcolm! Behave!"

"No, no, not your dress. I am experienced at that."

She rolled her eyes.

"The tiara."

"Oh, fuck if I know. I've never worn one before. It's a great big hassle."

Sabine flagged down her mother as she passed the head table to sit.

"Yes, darling?"

"How does one remove a tiara?" Sabine asked. "Never considered I might want to take it off."

Her mother snickered. "Oh, it's quite awful and laborious, same as going on. I will send my dresser to assist. The sooner we get you one up here, the better, huh?"

Sabine nodded. Ah, the lovely expense of marrying a princess. Although, given everything else she did brilliantly, I could extend the offer of a proper staffer without question. Tiaras alone were baffling.

"Tell me when you are thinking about retiring," Beth continued. "You can start the process. Malcolm, it takes time."

Ah, a buzzkill! I suddenly loathed tiaras. Dreadful diadems. Total cockblocks!

Beth retreated to her seat and Sabine laughed. "Oh, poor Malcolm. Don't be so sad. You'll have me all to yourself for three weeks, darling. Don't pout."

"I am not pouting, my love."

"Uh-huh."

I needed to restrain myself just looking at her. She was gorgeous. And the thought of climbing up her dress to eat her out appealed to me. Oh well, that dream was dead if that tiara stayed on her regal head.

Dinner finished, leaving my father to stand before the room to make a speech. He stood with the aid of a cane but insisted on standing. He beamed ear-to-ear. He had been all day.

"I won't yammer on," he said. "I only want to wish them well and welcome you all to our little abode. We like it alright. I know most of you came up here into the cold, so thank you. It means a lot of all of us."

"Malcolm, I think it is fair to say we never thought this day would come. We certainly did not see Sabine coming, but now what would we do without her? Don't know how you managed it."

Laughter filled the room. I looked at Sabine adoringly.

"Malcolm, you're a lucky man. You know that. Sabine, we are blessed to have you. I am blessed to have gotten to know you. You're a delight. Charming, witty, clever, and a carer. This family is forever indebted to the kindness of you and your family."

"When we first heard Malcolm was seeing you, I flat out did not believe it. And then, you just kept it up. You continued seeing him, for some ungodly reason."

Sabine laughed heartily. I shook my head. Honestly, it surprised me, but I didn't mention it.

"Things are a bit mad right now, a bit exhausting, but the two of you will live a full life. I wish you many happy years together, plenty of laughs, good health, and many children."

The place roared with laughter.

"No pressure," he chuckled.

I went over and hugged him. "Thanks, Papa."

"You're alright, son. You'll be good. Glad I got to see it."

I smiled. "Me, too."

It choked me up. The day had been so happy that, barring him being a bit frail, you'd have not known how ill he was. I was grateful for every moment he got with us. I knew he was happy. He was probably relieved. I was finally settled down. I was about to have a child. And, really, that was destiny assured. The man would rest easier. I just wished we weren't losing him. While I knew making it to September was possible, it was unlikely. And he knew it, too.

Teary eyed, I sat next to Sabine. Sensing why I was emotional; she rubbed my back.

"It's a lot. He did beautifully," she said.

"Yep, he did. Took the piss."

Sabine looked over as her father stepped forward.

"Well, I'm not much for public speaking. I usually delegate that to Beth," he chuckled. "But it's pretty easy to be happy for the two of them, right?"

There was a cheer around the room.

"Whirlwind. We got here by the skin of our teeth, but hell. That's the best way to do it," Simon said. "Sabine knows this story, of course. I wanted to share, though. I met her mother when she was studying in Canada—same place where Sabine went on to study. And we fell for each other hard. A year later, I was packing up and moving here without a plan. Just a starving artist missing his girl. I proposed to her in September. We were married in February. In Ottawa, Canada. So, if you all think this is cold, it's not."

They chuckled.

"It was a smaller wedding. Small like this. You know, quite intimate. Only a few hundred people."

That elicited more laughs. The man was on a roll.

"But it happened fast. And I didn't regret it one bit. Now, here we are twenty-three years later with our beautiful, stubborn daughter. How in the hell did it happen? How did it go by so fast? I don't know. What I do know is that Sabine is a lot to manage. She's wild and brave. She's loud and fierce. She's also a great protector, the best confidante to those she loves, and a true team player. Malcolm, you are getting a person in your corner—always. Whether you wanted it or not."

I nodded. Sabine was now tearful. Very tearful. God, the woman cried more in the last twenty-four hours than I knew imaginable.

"Son, I know we are a lot. We've known your parents for ages. I know how they are. I trusted Sabine would easily fit in here and find her feet. I see she is doing that. Or rather, she found the barn and probably doesn't leave it much."

Sabine shrugged.

"But I am glad that you have been brave enough to put up with the rest of us. Especially Maggie."

"Papa! Stop it!" Maggie shouted past her brothers. I snickered.

"Well, it's true. You can scare people. The two of you are a matched pair. It's intimidating. Either way, I think you can handle us, Malcolm. And you can take care of her, love her for all she is, and be a good partner. That's all we ever wanted for Sabine. And I think she has it."

It hit me in the feels. Damn. Simon was madly sentimental. Were all dads so sappy on their kid's wedding day? I didn't know. It hit me that someday, I *would* know. The thought was wild.

I whispered to Sabine, "I want to say something."

"Auntie was going to speak." Sabine nodded as her aunt came to take the mic. "You're going after—"

"The baby. I want to say something."

She looked surprised but not alarmed. "Really?"

"Yes, my love. I want to."

"Do it. Just do it," Sabine laughed. "I'm not afraid. And Jessica is going to run her mouth. Why not?"

I smiled. "Exactly."

"Thank you all for having us up here," the Queen said. "I always love the Scottish borders. And it was a nice escape from the doom and gloom of London. You get snow. It's been nice. I like the cold. My mother was born in Chicago, so I think I inherited her love of it. As did Sabine from her father. She seems to thrive up here. It does you good to have the fresh air, I think."

Sabine nodded.

"Or is it that you now get to have a racing string at your disposal that can compete with ours?" Greta joked.

Sabine giggled.

"I jest," Greta sighed. "Oh, darling, you are so grown. You are so happy. And... this day has hit me hard. I asked to speak because Sabine is my goddaughter. I first held you when you attended your parents' wedding. She was pressed in a little sling against Margaux's chest. Her birth mother adored her but was completely exhausted. We all fought for who got to hold the baby. We all lost repeatedly to Daddy who, to his credit, was the best one to soothe a baby. He did brilliantly with you. But I did finally get to hold you. Our little ginger child. And now, look at you. Fully grown, beautiful, well-spoken, and sharp as a tack. And now *married*. You were always the best surprise. A wonderful gift."

"Now, we get another one in the form of you, Malcolm. You fell for her. Probably faster than you wanted to admit. We all saw it. I was terribly relieved when you two decided to marry. I was glad to give my consent, not that you needed it. But I am a bit cross given that you are stealing her away. Oh well, now I have another place to visit in Scotland."

"Sabine and Malcolm, I wish you good health and a long life together. Be a team. Having a row isn't failure. Conflict is the stuff of life. Talk it out. Trust one another. Remember always that you are the other's greatest champion. I am not a perfect wife or person, but these are the things people told me. And I found them useful. And, if you ever need anything—including someone to hold a baby—I'm just a phone call away."

The idea of ringing the Queen to ask for advice never occurred to me. Meanwhile, Sabine rushed to her aunt crying. She stole my thunder, but I wasn't going to be cross, either. After she settled in her chair, drying her eyes on the tissue Maggie handed her, I began.

"This isn't going to be long. Sabine warned me that this shouldn't be the world's longest opening statement."

The crowd chuckled. "I drone at times, according to my wife. So, I won't beat a dead horse. I am so glad you all could make it and that we could all be here together tonight. It means the world to the two of us that you all took the time and visited. I know it was short notice, but we tend to keep people on their toes."

"Sabine, you are the love of my life. The day I met you, I was drawn to you inexplicably. You are magnetic, clever, terribly charming, and I could spend the rest of my day talking you up. I won't bore the people here with my sappy appreciation for you. You're perfect. I'll hear no argument on it."

She was crying again.

"The point was not to make you cry," I said. "I swear, I didn't mean it."

She gestured that I should ignore her and go on.

"I said I was beyond help and no one would dare put up with me. Then, at some point, I realised the best times I ever had were sitting with Sabine, just talking about everything, at the end of the evening. Things have been chaotic. I thought I needed to pull back and protect her from life's changes and my own stress, but she's not like that. She's made of tough stuff, but she's also the best supporter you could get. Sabine, I love you. I have no idea what I would do without you. I want every day to end with you and every day to begin with you, too."

She was now in full blown tears, once more gesturing for me to go on.

"And while you all joke that we should have many children, I am not sure we have plans to have that many. I don't think we could have ever predicted we had plans to have the first one."

The crowd stared at me. I saw Sabine's aunt gape.

"So, I think that cat is partially out of the bag there, but... in case you didn't know. Most of you don't... Sabine and I are happy to be expecting a baby in the early autumn. And I'm very excited. We wanted to say something since everyone is here. We're not about to make an official announcement yet, but maybe soon."

People clapped. It was a surprise. Yes, we'd shocked them all, but more importantly, we'd just embraced what was happening. The future was ours. It was bright. We would have this baby and build a life together. There was no doubt in my mind that we made the right choice. As I returned to my seat, Sabine leaned over and kissed me.

"I am glad that is over. Now, we can just relax," Sabine said.

"I am too happy to deny it any longer," I admitted.

"Really?"

"Yes. It will be a beautiful life."

Acknowledgments

To Danielle, Sigal, and Elizabeth for loving Sabine and Malcolm as much as I did, thank you!

For my author and publishing friends like Ty, Alby, and Becky who encourage me to get spicier and spicier, your support (and corruption) is much appreciated.

Loved it?

Consider leaving a review on Amazon or Goodreads.

WANT A FREE CHAPTER OF A FUTURE BOOK?

Just scan the code below or click here and join my mailing list. As a thanks, I will give you a sneak peek of *A Right Royal Ruse*, a fake-dating rom-com coming out in March 2024!

About the Author

Maude Winters writes cozy, spicy fiction. She's a horse girl through-and-through and lives in Michigan with her husband, horse girl daughter, and three dogs.

Maude loves to write strong female characters who challenge institutions and find strength in relationships with their sisters in the world as well as heroes who are always there to support the women in their lives.

Maude has lived throughout the world but attributes her interest in writing about the intersection of modern politics, feminism, and royalty with her time spent in the UK as a twenty-something.

Also by Maude Winters

REGENCY AND RIVALRY

The series that started it all! This series focuses on the previous generation of the Lyons family and follows the love stories of Robbie, Duncan, and Beth.

Find it on Amazon

SPARE CHANGE

The Heir Unapparent (Book 4)

Coming soon!

Stranded with Scrooge

A semi-royal Christmas novella

The Planner and the Prince

The start of Sanne and Paul's love story set in small town Michigan.

A Right Royal Ruse

A two-book spinoff which focuses on Princess Kiersten and Crown Prince Olav. Out in March 2024!

RESPLENDENT ROYALS

A new series from Maude Winters which focuses on Alexandra Deschamps, Queen of Neandia and her three royal sisters.

Made in the USA
Columbia, SC
10 July 2024